Stay

Also by Catherine Ryan Hyde

Stay

Catherine Ryan Hyde

A Novel

LAKE UNION
PUBLISHING

Text copyright © 2019 by Catherine Ryan Hyde, Trustee, or Successor Trustee, of the Catherine Ryan Hyde Revocable Trust created under that certain declaration dated September 27, 1999.

Published by Lake Union Publishing, Seattle

www.apub.com

Amazon, the Amazon logo, and Lake Union Publishing are trademarks of Amazon.com, Inc., or its affiliates.

ISBN-13: 9781542042406 (hardcover)
ISBN-10: 1542042402 (hardcover)

ISBN-13: 9781542042383 (paperback)
ISBN-10: 1542042380 (paperback)

Cover design by Shasti O'Leary Soudant

Printed in the United States of America

First edition

Stay

PART ONE: THEN

SUMMER 1969

Chapter One

The Tipping Day

Is it just me, or does everybody have a day in their life like the one I'm about to retell? I'm talking about those days that act like a fulcrum between everything that came before and your brand-new life after.

It feels a little something like this: When I was a kid, I used to like to bust a move on the playground. Boy stuff, I suppose. I'd run up to the teeter-totter and jump on the "down" seat. The one that was resting in the dirt. Then I'd trot up to the middle—the part that sits safely on the bar. And then, when I kept going, I'd hit the spot where my weight would tip the thing. You know it's there, you anticipate it. You slow your step just a little bit, knowing it's soon and you're about to find it. There's a delicious little moment of fear in there, but it's manageable. Next thing you know, you're being dropped safely back to the dirt, but on the other side.

This day was something like that.

It was the summer of 1969. I was fourteen.

—

The day started with a letter from my brother Roy. I was always first to the mailbox, and for just that reason. As soon as I saw that airmail envelope with the APO return address—his name scribbled above it: PFC Leroy Painter—I felt like there was open space in my chest, a lightness for a change. It was always that way.

I carried it into the house.

My parents were fighting again.

Except, really . . . I don't even know why I say "again." It was almost more like a "still." That's not to say they literally fought twenty-four hours a day, seven days a week. My dad went to work on the weekdays, and, let's face it, everybody has to sleep. But it was Saturday morning. They were home, and they were awake, so they were fighting.

I carried the letter upstairs to my room and tried to read it.

It started the way Roy always started his letters to me: "Hey buddy."

He'd called me Luke all my life, ever since I was born. But the previous summer I'd decided I was Lucas. I was going to go by Lucas, always, and I insisted. I guess it was meant to be a signal to the world that I'd grown up and I wanted to be recognized for it. I think it was a hard change for Roy to make. I'm not saying he didn't want to call me what I wanted to be called—he wasn't that kind of brother. I just think it didn't roll off his tongue yet.

So . . . buddy.

Then I tried to read the rest.

I'd gotten letters from him before with censor marks. Or whatever you call them. Standing here now I'd call them redactions, but I didn't know that word at the time. Once or twice I'd gotten letters from him with heavy black bars over a line or two, like somebody had taken a black marker and wiped out a few of my brother's precious words home to me. Well . . . not even "like." That's what had happened.

But this letter took redaction into a whole new universe.

I couldn't make it out. I didn't know what he was trying to say to me, because too much of it was black. Gone.

It started with complaints about the flies and mosquitoes, especially when he was trying to eat. And then it went off in this really serious direction.

"I know this is kind of upsetting," it said, "and I'm sorry if it's too much to put on you." Redaction. "We rolled into . . ." Redaction. "They were our boys. Americans. And their bodies were . . ." Long redaction. ". . . in the trees, upside down . . ."

Pretty much from there down it was a sea of black.

Right up until the last line: "You just can't unsee a thing like that."

My stomach tingled and buzzed, thinking about what might be under those black bars. I tried and tried to piece the narrative together in my brain, but there was just too much missing. The army hadn't left me enough puzzle pieces.

Meanwhile my parents were still fighting downstairs, and it was taking a toll on my mental state. A sudden crash made me jump. Somebody had thrown something breakable. A plate or a vase. Probably my mom. My dad didn't have to throw things. He had the weight advantage. He was stronger.

I stared more intensely at the letter. As though that had been the problem all along: I just wasn't looking hard enough. But there was nothing left to piece together.

It reminded me—kind of suddenly, the way a disjointed thought will hit you out of nowhere—of our late family dog, Weasel. He'd had this cancerous growth on his back leg. The vet had operated twice, but he couldn't get it all. Finally he said he couldn't do a third operation because there wouldn't be enough left to stitch together. Amazingly, Weasel's story had a happy ending. His body got the best of the cancer, and we don't know how. He just flipped and pinned the damn tumor with his immune system, and lived to pass away peacefully of old age.

I wasn't sure enough that my brother Roy would have a happy ending. Not with all those bullets flying around. A couple of months earlier he'd told me one had whizzed by so close to his ear that the air of its passing left a tickle he couldn't seem to shake.

I dropped the letter suddenly, having reached a breaking point with the noise of the fight. It had been there all along. I had pushed it away. It had pushed back in. Over and over. At that moment I lost it. Lost my temper, my cool. All sense of reason. I decided it was the noise that was keeping me from being able to comprehend what Roy was trying to tell me.

It wasn't, of course. But it was damned irritating. It was also the soundtrack to my young life.

I stomped out of my room and over to the railing, where I stood on the landing and shouted down at them with all the voice I could muster.

"Hey!"

Silence.

My mom's face appeared, staring up at me.

"What?" she asked. Irritated. "Your father and I are trying to work something out."

Ha! I thought—and wanted to say. *You never work things out. If screaming ever worked anything out, the two of you would understand each other perfectly by now.*

"I can't . . . ," I began. But the thought stalled along the track to wherever it was going. "I'm trying to . . ."

But in that moment my anger abandoned me. Just all at once like that. I felt deflated. Because it struck me that I could have all the silence in the world and still not know what Roy wanted so badly to share with me.

"What?" she barked, tired of waiting.

"Nothing," I said. "I'm going over to Connor's."

———

Connor's mother answered the door.

Mrs. Barnes was a woman who had been completely abandoned by color. My own mom wore bright red skirts or neon yellow blouses, as if she wanted to shock herself—and maybe everybody else—into remembering she was alive. Connor's mom must've wanted us to forget. Her clothes were some kind of grayish tan, not all that different from her skin tone, which was not all that different from her long hair worn pulled back into a wide ponytail. It reminded me of the old photographs passed down from my great-grandmother, taken in the days of sepia tone. Except I honestly think the sepia was a stronger color.

She never smiled. I don't mean not ever in her life, because how could I know that? But in front of me, never. And she never looked up or met my eyes. She seemed to be speaking to the doormat as she greeted me.

"Lucas."

I honestly wondered how she knew without looking.

She said my name as though it was a good thing that I'd come. But if she was happy to see me, her face didn't know about it.

"Come in," she said. "I'll tell Connor you're here."

I followed her down the front hallway toward the stairs.

A long table lined the hall on my right side, decorated with bowls of pine cones and green fir tree boughs. Just for a second I reached out to run my finger along it, the way I did at home.

Then I remembered there was no dust.

In my house there was always a layer of dust on the furniture, and I was obsessed with leaving my mark in it. Maybe partly as a way of proving I had been there. Maybe as a message to my mom that it wouldn't kill her to pick up a rag or a feather duster now and then. But the Barneses' house was relentlessly clean.

My mind filled with a sudden image. There was something heaped on all those surfaces, but it wasn't dust. It was invisible. And it made dust look good in comparison. It was . . . I couldn't quite get a bead on it at the time, and I'm still not sure I'll choose the right word. Anxiety? Desperation?

I pictured myself picking up some kind of spreading tool, like one of those wide putty knives, and smoothing off the top of the ugly heaps. Or making them thicker in one place or thinner in another. It was just a weird fictional image in my head, but I also think it was some kind of red flag for how real that negative energy felt to me.

I shivered once and shrugged the thoughts away.

Just as we passed the living room, I saw Connor's father. He was sitting in a stuffed wing chair with his head leaned back. He had a folded hand towel over his eyes, and on top of it sat a round, pleated ice bag. All the curtains were closed. Even the light in that house, what there was of it, seemed to be no color at all.

"Does he know you're coming?" Mrs. Barnes asked, knocking me back into the moment.

"Um. No. I just decided."

There probably should have been more to the sentence than that. But there wasn't.

"Connor?" she called as we climbed the stairs, her voice high and shrill.

Connor opened the door to his room and stuck his head out. And I felt this huge relief. As if I'd been down behind enemy lines and he was the first guy I'd seen wearing the right uniform. His face softened when he saw me. He must have been relieved, too. But I wasn't entirely sure why. Or maybe I knew, but I just didn't have the words for it at the time.

———

We sat in chairs by his bedroom window, looking out over the front yard and the street. We had our feet up on the windowsill, but we'd kicked off our sneakers so only our socks touched the paint. Mrs. Barnes would've had a fit if we'd left footprints on the sill.

I watched him read the letter from Roy. Or, anyway, he was staring at it. There wasn't much there to read.

He was holding the paper with one hand, his other hand brushing over the top of his hair. It was buzzed—cut so short that it stuck up on top. He seemed to want to play with the fact that he could touch the blunt tips of all those hairs.

We were both wearing jeans and gray crew socks, but his legs were much smaller and more compact than mine. It made me feel rangy and a little awkward. Though, to be honest, I'd begun admiring my own body by that age. Not in any creepy way—just liking the muscles in my thighs and upper arms, and the way I could see my own ribs, but with a sheet of muscle across them, when I stood in front of the mirror.

I was staring at our legs because I didn't want to stare at the letter, or stare at Connor while he stared at the letter.

"Hmm," he said.

"'Hmm,' what?"

"Sounds like he was trying to tell you he saw something bad."

"Yeah, but what?"

"No idea."

"So I'll just never know?"

"I don't know, Lucas. Maybe you will. Maybe he'll tell you in person."

It was a weird thing to say, and I almost called him out on it. Like, "Right, I'll just happen to be in Hanoi or Da Nang, and I'll bump into Roy on a street corner." He hadn't meant that, of course. He'd probably meant when Roy came home. But even that sent my brain in a lot of bad directions, because I was beginning to worry that Roy might not be coming home. Not everybody's brother was making it back. But there was no way I was going to talk about that out loud.

We didn't say anything for a long minute, and I was bowled over by the silence. Not our silence, the silence in the house in general. I wasn't used to that.

"It's so quiet," I said, my voice a near whisper so as not to ruin it.

"I know," he said. "I hate it."

"How can you hate it? It's wonderful. You've been to my house. This is so much better than my parents and all that yelling."

"At least they're willing to say things out loud to each other."

"Yeah, but *so* loud."

As soon as the words were out of my mouth, I regretted them. It wasn't funny. I could almost laugh at my parents and their battles. Sometimes. But the distance between Connor's parents was the worst thing in his life. It was killing him, and I was beginning to see it. I just had no idea what to do to help.

I took the conversation in a whole different direction.

"You just been sitting here all day like this?"

"Pretty much," he said. His voice sounded weighted, like a person carrying too much heavy stuff all at once.

"What do you do when you sit here? Think?"

"Not really," he said.

"Just sit?"

"Pretty much."

It didn't sound like a good sign. It sounded like something I should save him from. If I was a good friend. Which I hoped I was.

"Let's go somewhere," I said.

"Where?"

"I don't know. Anywhere. Let's go do something."

A pause. As I sat it out, I already knew the answer. And why the answer was what it was.

"Nah. I should stay here."

Connor was afraid to leave his parents alone any more than absolutely necessary. It was something we had never talked about out loud. I doubt it was an actual, logical reason. I don't think he believed any specific real-world thing would happen while he was gone. It was more of a feeling. Like there was so much unhappiness in that house, and it hurt to look at it, but he didn't quite dare look away. Like he had to be right here worrying about it to hold the whole situation together. I'm not sure I would have been able to put it into words at the time, and if I had, it wouldn't have been those words. But I knew it.

"You can go, though," he added. "I understand."

So I did. I left him and saved myself. I feel bad about that, but I did.

—

When Connor's house didn't work—and it generally didn't—I would go out alone into the woods behind my house. Well, behind everybody's house. This whole little town of Ashby is backed up by undeveloped forest land. It's dense and hilly up there, and the ground is uneven. It wasn't someplace where anyone was interested in building a house.

Well . . . with one notable exception. But I hadn't met her yet.

There wasn't much of anything like a trail, I guess because nobody but me was interested in walking back there. But the place was overrun with deer, and they beat down little paths back and forth to the river. Wherever they lived, they still had to drink. So I walked where they walked.

The trees mostly formed a canopy over my head, so whatever sunlight came through was dappled. I liked that. I was really into the dapples. On a windy day, the light came through as moving dapples. If it was *really* windy, I could hear trees creak, and sometimes one would break with a noise like the crack of a rifle, then tumble down. On quiet days I walked as softly as possible to sneak up on the deer. Not because I wanted to hurt one. I just liked being able to get that close. When they finally heard me, they would take off crashing through the brush, sounding like they were fleeing on pogo sticks.

It was a quiet day that day—my tipping day. No wind. Hardly any birds. The leaves on the trees didn't so much as shudder.

The only sound I could hear was the sound I was making by crunching old pine needles and small branches under my feet. So I stopped. And I just listened to all that silence.

It was like Connor's house, except this silence couldn't hurt anybody.

I hadn't realized until that moment why I walked back here. But it was painfully obvious once I stopped to listen.

—

I got lost that day for the first time.

It made me think of my mom, who had told me over and over that I was never to go out into those woods. It was a warning that had started when I was barely in kindergarten.

"You'll get lost," she'd say. "Maybe nobody will ever hear from you again."

It had sounded pretty silly. At the time.

Eventually I crossed the paved River Road and hit the river, which helped me get my bearings.

At first I just stood there and watched it flow. It was wide and muddy, with a current I could see. Not beautiful or inviting in any way. The banks were perpetually slippery. Now and then, when the rainy season got out of hand, it had been known to overflow and flood the town. It hadn't recently—not in more than fourteen years—so I'd never seen that with my own eyes. Still, I knew it had. There was an unmistakable sense that it cared nothing for people at best, and sided against us at worst. I guess all of nature is like that.

I turned back into the woods, more sure now that I knew how to get home. But it was past lunchtime, and I was starving, so I took a shortcut that I knew might only get me into more trouble.

If I hadn't, none of the rest of this would have happened.

I was crossing the metal bar that supported the middle of the teeter-totter, figuratively speaking. The tipping place would be right in front of me, and at any minute I would put my weight on it. Only this time I didn't know.

I looked up and saw the cabin.

It startled me, because I thought it was a given that there was nothing and no one back there. I just stood a moment, staring at it. Then I moved a little closer. Quietly, like I was trying not to tip off a deer.

It was a genuine log cabin, made with rough-hewn logs, cut unevenly at the ends. No big power tools had been involved in its building—that much was obvious. It was unpainted. But it was good work, too. Everything fit together just right. It had what looked like a good, solid roof of blue metal shingles. A plain pipe chimney rose out of it, probably to accommodate a woodstove inside.

I moved around the cabin to try to get a better look at the front.

There was a pickup truck parked near it. Which seemed odd, since there wasn't exactly what you might call a road. But I did see a strip of tire tracks that had worn down the forest floor into what I supposed could double as one. In a pinch.

There was a porch made of wood boards, well crafted and neat. No stairs up to it. You just stepped up once to get onto the porch and one more time at the threshold of the door.

Beside the porch was a small outbuilding that I couldn't quite figure out. It was whitewashed, and too small to be any kind of decent shed. If you stepped into it, you wouldn't even be able to straighten up. It was too small.

I moved a little farther toward the front of the place, still working hard to be silent, and looked at the entrance to the tiny outbuilding. And it struck me, in that moment, what it was. It hit my belly like a fast softball made of ice. The entryway was just an open arch.

It wasn't a small shed. It was a massive doghouse.

I shivered slightly, and I remember thinking, *I never want to meet the dog who lives in that thing.*

I turned to get myself out of there. But in my hurry I forgot to be perfectly quiet. I stepped on a small branch and snapped it.

Just as I was thinking, *Please let the dog be inside the cabin,* I saw him. And then, a second later, it wasn't a him. It was a *them.* Two dogs came spilling out. Pouring out like water. In my shock over the size of them, and even as my blood felt like it was turning to ice, I still observed that about them. They seemed to flow like some kind of thick, smooth liquid. Like the current of that muddy river.

They were huge. Easily a hundred pounds each. Their coats were short and flat, a color like silver. Or maybe more of a gunmetal gray. They stood high on their paws, as though their paw pads were thick and lifted them up—like those wedge inserts men put in their shoes to appear taller. They looked exactly alike—carbon copies of each other— except that one stood a couple of inches higher at the shoulder. I would have found them beautiful if I hadn't been busy fearing for my very existence.

They stopped flowing halfway between the doghouse and me.

They dropped their heads at almost exactly the same time. Synchronized menacing. I could see the outlines of their shoulder blades. Their eyes were a spooky light blue.

For a moment—and I could not have told you how long a moment—we just stood frozen, staring at each other.

I had a flash of a memory.

When I was very little, maybe five, my dad and I were walking along our street at dusk and saw two neighborhood dogs circling to fight. They looked into each other's eyes and never broke off that direct gaze. My father told me that the first dog who looked away would be attacked by the other. It was a sign of submission to look away. Plus it gave the enemy an opening.

For another eternity that might have been only a second, I held their terrifying gazes.

Then I turned and ran like my life depended on it. Because I figured it probably did. It was the wrong move and I knew it, but I couldn't stop myself. It had been utterly instinctive.

Now my gut was filled with the sickening realization that I could not possibly outrun them. They would catch me, and . . . I had no firm idea, and I couldn't bring myself to imagine. But of course I did know the kinds of things dogs tended to do.

I put on a burst of speed.

I could hear them right behind me. Not even a full step behind me. Once, I saw one of the heads in my peripheral vision as a dog drew even with me. Why he hadn't taken the opportunity to bite, I didn't know. I didn't know anything in that moment. The panic had flipped a switch in my brain to off.

I just kept running.

My only hope was that they would be satisfied when I got far enough away from their property, and would turn for home.

Still I heard their paws crashing in the brush just a step behind me, no matter how far and fast I ran. My chest began to catch fire. I developed a stitch in my side, but I didn't dare stop running.

I have no idea how long I ran that way. At least half a mile. It might even have been more. Time played tricks on my brain.

Then the whole thing came to a crashing halt.

I caught the toe of my sneaker on a root.

I flew forward, still trying to rebalance myself. But the root was still holding my toe back behind me, so there was no way to recover. I slammed onto my belly on a bed of old leaves and pine needles, scratching the heels of my hands as I tried to brace my fall.

It was over. I felt lifted outside my body by the fear. Disconnected from myself. I honestly thought it might be the end for me. I covered my head with my arms and waited for them to do their worst.

And waited.

And waited.

Finally I peered out from under my arms. I had to know.

I saw one dog clearly. His mouth was open, long tongue curled out and dripping. It bounced as he panted. It looked almost as though he was smiling.

I sat up and looked at both dogs, one after the other. Each returned a faint tail wag.

"What the hell?" I asked out loud.

I dropped onto my back. Stared up through the trees for a moment at a perfect cloudless blue sky, absorbing the new reality that I was not about to die.

Then I sat up and looked at the dogs again.

The larger one made a move that I could only interpret as an invitation. He bounded two steps, bouncing much higher than necessary, then stopped and looked over his shoulder at me with that same lolling-tongued grin.

The message was strikingly clear: *I'll run more if you will.*

I took a few minutes, just sitting on the ground like that, to get over feeling incredibly stupid. To adjust my reality completely from my assumption that they were dangerous dogs to the simple truth that they had never meant any harm to anyone—that being huge didn't automatically make them killers.

I got to my feet and ran again, back toward their home. But it was different this time. It was exhilarating.

I paced myself, but I was still fast. Frankly, I was amazed how fast. I honestly hadn't known I could run like that. Now suddenly I couldn't imagine how the talent could have escaped me, lived so dormant in me for so long. I'd also had no idea how much of the turmoil inside me running could solve.

I put on bursts of speed, then smoothed out, then put on the gas again. I placed my feet as if I were running through a giant game of chess, always strategizing three or four moves ahead. The dogs ran one behind me, one in front where I could see him. Now and then he turned his head and glanced over his shoulder at me, his light blue eyes gleaming. He was having so much fun that he had to check and make sure I was, too.

And, oh, I was having fun!

I felt free for the first time in as long as I could remember. Everything that had weighed me down every day of my life seemed to have been put behind me. I had left it all in the dirt. I was too fast for my troubles. The crap of my life was eating my dust for the first time ever. I felt light, as though running could turn into flying. Then I felt as though I *was* flying, despite the fact that my feet never stopped hitting down.

When the cabin came into view again, I forced myself to halt. I leaned forward onto my own knees and panted. I felt as though somebody had hosed out the inside of me, leaving everything empty and clean.

The dogs went home. Reluctantly.

So did I. Also reluctantly.

It might sound trite to say I knew something important had changed in that moment. Also, it's not entirely true. I knew something *felt* changed. What I did not yet know is that I had placed the first domino in a stack of events that would literally alter the world as I'd known it.

—

That night before bed I wrote a letter back to Roy.

I told him the truth. That the army censors had gone so hard at his letter that I still had no idea what it was he'd seen. And that if he tried to tell me again, they'd likely do the same again. But that he'd come home, given time, and that we'd go off somewhere private and I could hear about it straight from the horse's mouth.

As I wrote those words, "You'll come home . . . ," I knew I was reaching. Sure, Roy might come home. He also might not. I was stating something as a given, even as I knew in my heart it was anything but.

I wondered if he'd have the same thought as he read it.

Probably. If anybody could grasp the big picture of the danger Roy was in, it was Roy.

Chapter Two

Also a Day of Big Changes

It was about two weeks later when things began to shift further.

It was the second-to-last day of school. I was about to get my life back for the summer. And the last day was a half day anyway, so I was nearly free.

I got up an hour early, as I'd done every weekday since I met the dogs, so I'd have time to run with them before school.

I had a pattern, which I followed to the letter that morning. I'd set off at a light jog down my street. Pick up a faint deer trail into the woods. It took me up to the cabin from a different direction, so that when I finally saw it, I'd be coming over a rise. Just as I crested it, I would see the back of the cabin, and that's when I would step on the gas.

I kept to a slow pace on the street, to save my energy for the big sprint. But I was already starting to feel it—that tingly, delicious sense of anticipation you get when your brain and your gut know you're about to do something good. Something that can actually change the crappy way you feel.

When I finally saw the rise in front of me, I could barely contain myself. The feeling ricocheted around in my stomach like a case of the shivers. I crested the rise and floored it, barreling past the cabin as fast as my legs could carry me. Of course the dogs came spilling out.

They never barked. They never whimpered in their excitement, though they were clearly excited to hear and then see me. They were always mute. Absolutely silent.

I loved that about them.

We ran.

We ran around in a big arc, so we wouldn't have to stop at the edge of the woods. So we wouldn't have to face the prospect of civilization. We ran past the cabin again, but on a path too far away or too heavily wooded to see it flash by.

We ran all the way across the River Road and stopped at the bank of the river. I squatted on my haunches, panting, and pulled a sandwich out of my pocket. I'd had breakfast, but I always needed more after all that running, and a sandwich was the only thing I knew to make on my own that I could put in a plastic bag and stick in my pocket.

Nobody noticed the missing food. Nobody noticed me getting up earlier. Nobody asked why I was leaving the house more than an hour too early for school. I was like a ghost in that house. Unless I was interrupting their warfare, I might as well not have existed at all.

The dogs crowded close, whacking me with their swinging tails, and I fed them each a bite of sandwich and watched the pull of the muddy water.

Then I got nervous.

They were not my dogs. I had no idea whose dogs they were. I wasn't really supposed to have them away from their home with me. What if one of them stepped too close to the river and slid down the muddy, slippery bank? What if they darted back into the road? Cars didn't come along it often, but when they did, their drivers almost always took the straightaway much too fast because there was no one around to notice.

"Come on," I said to them, and they lifted their ears and turned them to face me to show they were listening. "Let's go back."

I looked both ways at the road. From that spot you could see just about forever in each direction. There was nobody coming, so I took a chance. I wanted to try an experiment.

I ran with them down the dirt shoulder of the road for a tenth of a mile or so. I wanted to see how much faster I could go without having to play chess with the trees. But the experiment was a bust. Maybe I went faster. Who knows? But it wasn't fun. There was nothing *to* it. It was just slapping my feet down.

I missed the constant dodging. The blur of tree trunks racing past in my peripheral vision. More to the point, my brain was so disengaged that I started thinking, though after all these years I don't claim to remember what about. I needed the absolute concentration of the on-the-fly route finding, but I hadn't known it. It required every ounce of my concentration. It left me unable to entertain any thoughts.

"Come on," I said to the dogs. "We're turning around."

I'm sure they had no idea what that meant. But I stopped and turned, and that they understood.

Just then something caught my eye.

I was jogging along past the graveyard. I'd run by it once, but I must've been looking away. What made me look, made me stop my feet, was a spray of bright yellow flowers. What kind of flowers, I don't know. I wasn't good with that, and I'm still not. But they were the kind that bloomed in long stalks.

Now, at face value, there was nothing so strange about it. Just two things made me wonder, and drew me in closer.

One, nobody had died in this town for a really long time. Maybe six or seven years, with the exception of old Mr. Walker, whose body was shipped back to Michigan to be buried with his family. Granted, you can still miss a family member six or seven years later. You can still be thinking of them and want to go visit their grave. But then there was the other odd thing. Those same flowers had been laid on two graves. And the graves were much too far apart to be members of the same family.

I walked through the gate, the dogs wagging behind me. Up to the first grave.

The stone read, "Wanda Jean Paulston, November 10, 1945–December 18, 1952."

Only seven years old. That must have been a heartbreak for the family. Part of me wondered why I hadn't heard about it. But people don't like to tell their kids about stuff like that. Besides, it all happened before I was born.

I walked to the second grave. It said, "Frederick Peter Smith, April 11, 1946–December 18, 1952."

I stood a minute processing it in my brain. Both died young. Both died on the same day. Somebody missed them both.

But it seemed like a mystery that I didn't have the clues to solve, and not a very pressing one at that. So they had a mutual friend. So what?

Besides, I'd been in a hurry to get the dogs home.

"Come on," I said to them. "We're going."

And they both gave me this look like it was about time.

We sprinted back to the approximate spot where we'd burst out of the woods, and we burst back in. I ran them home. For every second of those few glorious minutes, I thought about nothing at all.

———

I was in the hallway opening my locker when Connor came up behind me and said what he said.

"You're trying out for track, right?"

I turned around and shot him what I'm sure was a confused look.

"School lets out *tomorrow*."

"Right. That's why I was thinking you shouldn't wait."

He was trying to be helpful. I know that now, and I might even have known it at the time. But he wasn't making any sense.

"But . . . what's the point? I'll just try out in the fall."

I wouldn't. I already knew I didn't want to. I wanted to run in the woods, not on a flat track. I wanted to run with those dogs, not guys my age, most of whom I didn't much like or trust.

"Oh," Connor said. He sounded disappointed. "Coach Haskell might ask you to try out before fall."

"Why would he do that? How would he even know I'm interested in running these days?"

"You told me you loved running," he said. "I was talking to Coach. I didn't think you'd mind."

"I don't," I said. But it was a lie. I lied to keep from hurting his feelings. It was dawning on me that I was likely to try out for the team to keep from hurting his feelings as well.

I opened my mouth to say something more, but I was saved from a reply by Libby Weller. She walked by in a huge plaid A-line skirt that swung well below her knees. A short-sleeved sweater. She purposely caught my eye and paused.

"Lucas," she said. "Heard anything from your brother?"

I was always nervous around Libby. Always had been. "Um . . . no."

She nodded vaguely and walked on. Then I was forced to look up into Connor's questioning face.

"If I'd told her I heard from him," I said, "the next question she'd've asked is 'How is he?' I just didn't want to get into that whole thing."

He nodded his understanding. I pulled my math book out of my locker and slammed it shut, and we walked down the hall together. In silence at first.

Then Connor said, "I really think she likes you."

He'd said it before. On many occasions. I hadn't bought it any of the previous times, and I still wasn't buying it. Thing is, Libby was a very pretty girl. As in, out-of-my-league pretty. And if I believed Connor, it would be a long way down if he was wrong. And I figured he was wrong.

"I don't think so," I said, as I always did. Then I added something that had been true all along but had not yet been spoken. "I think it's just the thing with her brother."

Libby's brother Darren had come home from the war a few weeks earlier missing his right leg from the calf down. I mean, did Connor really not notice that Libby always asked how Roy was and never asked anything about me? It wasn't hard to put two and two together.

I opened my mouth to say more, but never got there. Instead I looked up to see my path down the hallway blocked by the enormous Coach Haskell. He was about six five with shoulders like a mountain, standing spraddle-legged in sweatpants and a school T-shirt. He had his arms crossed over the whistle hanging around his neck. He was trying to catch my eye and I was trying to prevent it.

I made a move to duck around him. But of course it was not to be.

"Painter," he bellowed.

I stopped.

"Yes, sir?"

"Tomorrow at eleven. You're trying out for track."

"Wouldn't it be better if I just tried out in the fall?"

"I need to know who I can count on next semester. So be there and don't let me down."

Connor offered me an apologetic glance and slunk away.

—

I woke up the following morning before my alarm. *Long* before my alarm.

I had set it for the normal time. I mean, the old normal time—just early enough to get to school. Because it was a half day, like I said. I figured I'd go run with the dogs afterward. It would be a celebration of sorts.

But I was wide awake, and it was not only earlier than I needed to wake up to get to school on time, it was earlier than I'd been getting up to run.

And it's funny, looking back. I think about it from time to time. A thing happens, and it's a thing big enough to save a life, and you don't know why it happened. And you sure didn't know it was such a big deal at the time. But, looking back, you wonder why things work out the way they do.

I tossed and turned for a couple of minutes, then gave up.

I dressed quickly in sweats and trotted downstairs. Everybody else was asleep. The kitchen was dark and quiet, and I poured a bowl of cereal without turning on any lights. While I wolfed it down, the sky began to lighten outside the window.

I set my bowl in the sink and slipped out the door. Jogged toward the entry point where I always picked up a trail into the woods. Right away I could feel my lack of sleep dragging on me. It felt like something was missing inside my gut. But I kept going.

It was just light enough to make my way over the dropped branches, around the trees.

When I came over the rise and saw the cabin, the dogs were already outside. They were not in their doghouse. Which was unusual. They were on the porch of the cabin. Fretting. That's the word that came into my head when I saw them, and I still think it's the best one.

The bigger dog, the boy, was pacing on the porch. Literally pacing. Padding three long strides to cover the length of the boards, then spinning on his haunches and repeating the strides in the other direction. The smaller one, who I now knew was female, was scratching at the door. And I do mean scratching. Not the way a dog scratches to tell you he needs to go out. Not a little downward swipe with one paw. I mean the way a dog scratches when her goal is to dig straight through solid oak. And as I walked closer I could see she had done some fair damage.

They both looked up when they saw me trotting down the hill. But they didn't come to me. They just looked away again and kept doing what they were doing. That's when I got that sick feeling in my gut, knowing something was deeply wrong.

Normally I tried to stay as far away from the cabin as possible, out of respect to whoever owned it. That morning I walked up onto the porch boards for the first time. I had to duck out of the way to keep the pacing male dog from bowling me over. He didn't even slow his step or change direction for me.

I took a deep breath, gathered all my courage, and rapped hard on the door.

Nothing. No answer.

"Hello?" I called. "Everything okay in there?"

Silence.

I heard the birds singing in the trees, excitedly. Probably they had no idea of any trouble below them. The sun was coming up, and they were likely reacting to that welcome daily occurrence. The light, lovely sound of them was punctuated—and made ugly somehow—by the obsessive scratching.

I rapped again. Harder.

"Hello? Anybody there?"

Nothing.

There was no window in the front of the cabin, so I moved around to the side. My feet crunched through pine needles as I walked up to the window. I took another deep breath and looked inside.

A woman was lying in the bed, eyes closed. On her back, as if sleeping peacefully, a patchwork quilt pulled up under her armpits. She was an older woman. Not ancient-old like my great-grandmother, but old compared to me. Mid-fifties, maybe. Her long, straight gray hair fell around her face and shoulders. It would have been a peaceful enough scene if not for the reaction of the dogs. I would have just figured she was a heavy sleeper.

I knocked on the window, braced for her to open her eyes and scream at the sight of a guy staring through her window.

She did not open her eyes.

I banged harder.

"Ma'am?" I shouted. "Are you okay? Is everything okay in there?"

No reaction.

That was when the panic of the thing really set up shop in my gut. Because I had banged *hard*. I'd yelled *loudly*. Nobody was that sound a sleeper. It struck me with a shiver that I might be shouting at a corpse.

"Ma'am!" I screamed, my volume powered by the fear rushing out of me. "Ma'am, are you okay?"

Then I stopped yelling, leaned on the windowsill, and pulled a couple of deep breaths.

She was not okay.

I took off running.

"I'll get help!" I shouted as I ran by the pacing, scratching dogs on the porch.

They paid me no mind at all.

—

My parents were still asleep when I burst back through the kitchen door.

I ran straight to the phone. On the side of the refrigerator my mom had a sheet of emergency numbers held up with a magnet. She'd ripped it out of the county phone book.

I dialed the sheriff's office with trembling hands.

"Taylor County Sheriff," a high female voice said.

"I need to report a . . ." But I stalled there for a second or two. What exactly did I need to report? Two uneasy dogs and a woman who would not wake up? ". . . somebody who might be in trouble."

A longish silence on the line, which I took to be this woman rolling her eyes at my stupidity. But it turned out she was transferring me. After a click on the line I heard a bored-sounding male voice.

"Deputy Warren," the voice said. "Who do I have on the phone?"

"Lucas Painter. From over on Deerskill Lane."

"And what kinda trouble we talkin' here, son?"

"I don't know," I said. "There's this lady. She's by herself in the middle of nowhere. And she's in bed like she's asleep, but nothing wakes her up. Nothing."

"Maybe she's just a heavy sleeper," Warren said, still apparently bored.

"I banged on her window like crazy. Nobody could sleep through the noise I was making. And her dogs are all upset. One of them is trying to dig through the door to get in to her."

A silence on the line. Then I heard him sigh. Maybe because we had just crossed the border into his believing he might need to get up and do something.

"Okay, gimme her address. I'll go look in on her. Check her welfare."

"I don't have an address."

"That doesn't help our situation, son."

"Sorry. I don't think there is one. She lives out in the middle of the woods. There's no street. So how can there be an address?"

"Middle of the woods, you say?"

"Yes, sir."

"Log cabin? Tin roof?"

"Yes, sir."

"Right. I know it. That's Zoe Dinsmore's place. I figured it must be. If we have more than one lady living all by herself out in the middle of those woods, it's news to me. Okay, son. I'll go see what's what with her."

And he hung up the phone.

I looked up to see my mother leaning in the kitchen doorway, watching me with sleepy eyes.

"Everything okay?" she asked. But not like she really wanted to get too deeply into things.

"Yeah. Fine. I was just on my way to school."

"In sweats?" she asked, looking down at the lower parts of me.

"Oh. No. I was going to go change first."

I ran upstairs and did that.

———

When I got out onto the track for my 11:00 a.m. tryout, there were two other guys there. Juniors, I think. So, older. I didn't really know them. I mean, I'd seen them. But why would juniors want to be anywhere near a mere freshman like me?

We took our places with one of them on either side of me, which felt vaguely intimidating. There were starting blocks in place, and I'd never used them before. They looked simple enough, but a guy isn't born knowing how to brace his body to push off against a thing like that. Looking back, I know I should have asked. But I was too embarrassed.

One of the guys, the one on my left, was staring straight ahead down the track, perfectly focused. All serious intensity. The other guy was watching me struggle with the blocks and my starting position, snickering.

The coach made short work of that. He stepped up from behind us and whacked Snicker Boy on the back of the head with the flat of his open hand.

"Ow!" the guy said, and rubbed the spot where he'd been struck.

"Stop acting like you're better than everybody else, and show him how to use the blocks."

So I took a quick lesson while the coach loomed over us to be sure there would be no more trouble. I could actually see the great shadow of him falling over us the whole time. My mind kept straying back to the lady in the cabin, as it had all morning, but I had to push the image away just long enough to do my run and do it right.

We lined up, ready to go, but then the coach came around and adjusted my position some.

He stepped back and raised his starter's pistol. Fired it.

The guys on either side of me launched down the track.

I stumbled badly.

I was a good twenty feet behind them, but I knew I could find more inside myself. It was just a matter of wanting it, I think, for me. I had to want it so badly that I just did it, whether I was really able to do it or not. Sounds weird, but that's how it felt. And I wanted it that day. Enough. Not because I liked the way I felt running on a track. Not because I wanted a place on the team. Because the guys who were beating me would still be snickering when they beat me, if they beat me, but just on the inside where Coach couldn't see or hear it. Which meant nobody could stop them.

As I came around the bend I pulled close enough to reach my hand out to where I needed to be. I mean, I could've. I'm not saying I did.

I barely made up the distance coming down the final stretch, running almost completely on heart.

I could see the tape coming up, and my chest was not the closest to it, so I put on an extra surge. I passed Focus Guy, who had lost a step, pulled an inch or two ahead of Snicker Boy, and hit the tape.

Then I slowed and stopped, and leaned on my knees, panting.

"Okay, Painter," Coach Haskell said. He had crossed the infield and was standing beside us at the finish line, staring at his stopwatch. "You're on the team."

I straightened up and looked him right in the face. "I don't *want* to be on the team," I said. I was surprised to hear myself say it out loud. I tended to bow to authority at that age. But Connor was nowhere around to hurt. And I think it had not yet dawned on me that my tryout would be anything but a blessed flop.

"Too bad," he said. "Because you already are."

I shook my head and said no more about it. I knew it wouldn't do any good. At least I had the whole summer to figure a way to wriggle out.

"How long you been training?" Coach added.

"Training? I'm not sure I really train. I just go out and run."

This time both boys sneered at me. They were standing behind the coach's back, breathing hard. They laughed at me as though I had just said the stupidest thing imaginable. But they were smart enough to do it silently.

"How in the Sam Hill do you think a runner trains," Coach bellowed, "if it's not by going out and running?"

"Oh," I said. "Okay. About two weeks, then."

Three mouths dropped open. The two boys shook their heads and turned away from me, shuffling off toward the locker room. Focus Guy shot me a dirty look over his shoulder.

Coach and I just stood a moment, staring at each other.

"Did those other guys not make the team?" I asked, hoping to understand what I had done to offend them.

"Those other guys have been on the team for more than a year," he said. "You just beat my two best guys. On a couple of weeks of training."

"Oh," I said.

My dream of wriggling out of the commitment more or less abandoned me in that moment.

———

I ran back to the cabin the minute school let out, my stomach jangling from my track experience and lack of sleep, but more from the general awfulness of my morning. And the not knowing. The not knowing *how* awful things might have turned out to be while I was gone.

The dogs were lying on the porch, listless. They tapped their tails on the boards when they saw me but didn't bother getting up.

The door was ajar. I could see about a three-inch gap, through which I could look in at the unmade bed on the other side of the single room.

I stepped up and knocked, just to be sure there was nobody there. Nothing.

"Hello?"

Nothing.

I looked at the dogs and they looked back. Their eyes told me that my morning had been a damned picnic compared to theirs.

I wondered if they had eaten.

I walked around the property for a few minutes. Taking stock. There was an old-fashioned well that worked on a hand pump. A tiny building that I realized with a shudder must be an outhouse. A shed that I was hoping might contain dog food, but which—when I cautiously opened the door—only contained tools and such. There was an aluminum water bucket against the side of the doghouse, its handle secured on a hook so the dogs couldn't upend it. It was less than half full. They each had a plastic food dish in front, but both bowls were dead empty.

I carried the bucket over to the well and hung the handle on the pump nozzle, and cranked until it filled up with water. It wasn't easy. I was out of breath by the time I was done. I figured that middle-aged lady must have arms like a wrestler and the stamina of a mule.

I secured the bucket back into place and decided the dog food must be inside the cabin.

I rapped on the door again, just to be safe, then pushed the door partway open and peered in. It wasn't much for a person to call home. A woodstove right in the middle for heat. An ancient cookstove, a porcelain sink standing free. Nothing much in the way of counters. A little half refrigerator like the kind people put in their travel trailers or fallout shelters.

There was a floor-to-ceiling cupboard that looked like a pantry, so I walked to it and opened the door. I found canned soup, and rice, and spaghetti, and tins of pork and beans. And a fifty-pound sack of dog kibble.

The dog food had a saucepan inside to be used as a scoop, so I figured that was more or less what each dog was supposed to eat. I filled the pan. Carried it out and poured it into a bowl. Repeated.

The dogs paid no attention to the food, and very little attention to me. They were caught up in full-on mourning. It was written all over their faces.

As I left, I tried to shut the door behind me. But its lock had been broken, and part of the doorframe molding that held it had been torn away. It gave me a little shiver, because I realized the sheriff's guys had literally broken down the door to get the lady out of here.

I found a dish towel hanging over the oven handle of the cookstove. I folded it up and used it to wedge the door shut.

I looked at the dogs and their full bowls of food and realized I'd have to come back before sundown to see if they'd eaten. If not, I'd have to take up the food overnight. Otherwise it would attract raccoons and heaven only knows what other variety of wildlife, and the last thing I wanted was the dogs fighting it out with raccoons. They could be vicious little beggars.

The dogs looked back at me with eyes that said, "Can you believe how bad this is? Have you ever seen a day this awful in your life?"

"I'll come back," I said. "You won't go hungry."

They turned their eyes away and set their chins down on their paws, and I couldn't shake the feeling that they were disappointed in me. Because they couldn't seem to make me grasp that food was not the problem.

I walked home. I did not run.

—

When I got home, my mom was not there. She'd left a note on the table that said, "Gone grocery shopping. Eat cookies."

Under the note was a small dessert plate with six chocolate chip cookies covered in plastic wrap. I shoved one into my mouth whole and dialed the sheriff's office again while I chewed and swallowed.

"Taylor County Sheriff," the same high voice said.

"Hi. It's Lucas Painter. Can I please talk to Deputy Warren again?"

"Hold please," she chirped in a singsong voice.

Then Warren was on the line. Just like that. With hardly any pause.

"What can I do for ya, son?"

"I just wondered how she was. Is she okay?"

"Not so okay," he said. "No."

"What happened to her?"

"Overdose. Prescription meds."

"You mean, like . . . accidentally?"

"Son, I have no idea," he said, in a voice sharp enough to close off that area of questioning. "But I *will* tell you this. You did a damn good thing to call it in. She'd gone over into a coma, and if you hadn't found her, I can't say I'd like her chances much. You probably saved her life. Or . . . well, what I mean is, if she survives, it's because of you. So tell me something. How exactly did you happen to be out there in the middle of nowhere to notice?"

"Oh," I said. "I was going there to see those dogs. I really like those dogs."

"Folks won't get you a dog of your own?"

"No, sir."

"Well, if you like 'em so much, you might want to go by and see they got food and water."

"I already did."

A long silence on the line. Then I asked the obvious question. Even though I already knew he didn't have my answer.

"Is she gonna be okay?"

"Son, I may be many things, but one thing I'm not is a doctor. You'll have to call over to the County General Hospital for information like that."

"I forgot her name already."

"Zoe Dinsmore is who *she* is."

It was a strange sentence, and he said it in a strange way. As though being Zoe Dinsmore were truly noteworthy in some way, and the way did not sound good. There was subtext. But I could not imagine how to dive into it. There seemed to be no entry point.

I thanked him and hung up the phone. Then I got the number for County General, and called, and got exactly nowhere. They wouldn't tell me a thing about her condition because I wasn't family to Zoe Dinsmore.

I wondered if anybody was.

———

I had to run back out there at sunset, lock up the uneaten dog food in the shed, then go back to my life not knowing.

I had to go to bed that night not knowing.

I thought it would be a wonderful thing to have saved somebody's life. Something I could feel good about. Something even most grown-ups couldn't say.

But I didn't know if I had saved a life or not. For that, the person you tried to save has to survive.

Chapter Three

Any Family

I was out at the cabin again at dawn, putting down kibble that I knew the dogs wouldn't eat.

They were lying on the porch, heads down but eyes open, as if they had no choice but to feel every terrible thing. I guess they *didn't* have a choice. They were dogs.

I was a human boy with a variety of methods to avoid the emotions I didn't care to feel. Yet those options seemed to fail me in that moment.

I found myself lying on the porch beside them, sharing their sense of despair. I wondered what would happen to them if the lady never came back.

I would have taken them home with me in a heartbeat if my parents would've allowed it, but I knew they never would. Maybe they could keep living out here in their doghouse, and I could come out and feed them and care for them and run with them. But I couldn't shake the sense that I would come out one day and find that someone had swept them away. Animal control, or some member of the lady's family. Which made me wonder again if the lady had any family.

I picked up my head and looked the female dog in the eye. She tilted her head slightly without lifting her chin off the porch boards, her signal that she didn't understand what I wanted.

I pushed to my feet against the boards and took off running. Just four or five long strides. Then I stopped and looked back over my shoulder at her. She allowed me to catch her eye, then carefully averted her gaze.

I walked back and sat on the edge of the porch and stroked her silky ears.

"Worth a try, I guess," I said.

I patted the boy dog on the head and he sighed.

I wanted to tell them something encouraging. That she'd come home. That they'd be okay. But I couldn't bring myself to lie to them. So I had nothing.

———

My mom was in the kitchen when I got home. Doing up a few dishes. Probably the ones from the breakfast she undoubtedly would have made for my father before sending him off to work. I was surprised that any dishes had survived that much time around my parents. Or, anyway, that was the dark joke I told myself in my head.

"Where've you been?" she asked me, sounding only half-interested.

She was wearing a faded flower-print apron. Her hair had been pinned up but was now trailing down in a number of places.

"I like to go out and run in the morning."

"Since when?"

"Couple weeks now."

"Why haven't I noticed?"

Good question, I thought. *Why haven't you?*

"Probably because I went right off to school afterward."

"Oh. Right. Have you had breakfast?"

"I could eat," I said, to avoid telling her that I had scarfed down a ton of cereal but I still wanted more food.

"Sit down," she said. "I'll make you some eggs."

—

She was pushing scrambled eggs around in a too-big cast-iron skillet when the phone rang. She turned the gas flame to low and jumped to answer it.

"No, he's at work," I heard her say into the phone. Then she fixed me with a strange and disturbing look. I can only call it withering. "Oh, *Lucas*," she said. "Yes, *Lucas* is here." She covered the mouthpiece of the phone receiver with her palm. "Why is the sheriff's office calling for you, Lucas? What have you done?"

"I didn't do anything."

"Then why is some deputy sheriff calling? Your father will have a fit if you've brought some kind of trouble down on this house."

Right, I thought. *Heaven forbid this house should see any trouble. We're all really content as it is, with you guys fighting your own personal war and Roy overseas with bullets whizzing by his head in a real one. Be a shame if anybody spoiled all that happiness.*

"I just reported something is all," I said. I kept the rest of those thoughts to myself.

"Like somebody else committing a crime?"

"No. No crimes. I just reported somebody who needed help."

I was starting to worry about the poor deputy sheriff waiting on the line, so I reached for the phone. She frowned at me, but she handed it over and hurried back to the stove. I wondered how badly my eggs had been burned. I knew I'd be expected to eat them regardless.

"Hello," I said.

"Morning, son," Deputy Warren said. "Hope I didn't get you out of bed."

"No, sir. I've been up a couple hours. Already been for my morning run."

My stomach had begun to churn uncomfortably because it was occurring to me—for the first time, oddly—that he was calling to tell me the lady died.

"Well, I just wanted to let you know she pulled through," he said, and I breathed out a long exhale I hadn't known I was holding. "I mean, not that we know absolutely, but that first twenty-four hours is critical. The fact that she got through it bodes well for her chances. Nurse at the hospital told me somebody called looking into her welfare yesterday, but they couldn't give out any info because he wasn't her family. I figured that was you."

"But *you're* not her family," I said, and then immediately felt stupid.

"But I'm law enforcement."

"Right. Duh. So . . . does she *have* any family?"

I heard a big sigh on the line. "Yeah. More or less. She has an ex-husband, but I can't decide if that counts or not. Probably not. And she has two grown daughters, but they both got married before they moved away from here, and I don't know their married names off the top of my head. But I'm doing some research on it."

"I'm thinking they'd want to hear about this," I said, and then felt stupid again.

"I'm thinking the same, son. I'll do what I can."

"Thanks for letting me know."

Then we said our goodbyes and he hurried off the phone.

I sat back down at the table, and my mom set a plate of scrambled eggs and toast in front of me. I poked the eggs with my fork. They weren't exactly burned, but they were awfully dry.

"We got any ketchup?"

She sighed theatrically and flounced over to the refrigerator. I was waiting for her to ask me about my conversation with the deputy. You know, take some interest in my life. But she seemed lost in her own head.

"I saved a lady's life," I said.

She set the bottle of ketchup down in front of my plate.

"That's nice, dear." She said it the way a person says "That's nice" when you're talking to them while they're trying to read the newspaper. "I'm very proud of you."

I got in touch, suddenly, with how nice it would feel if she actually was. Proud of me, that is. And maybe she was. Looking back, it's hard to say what somebody else is feeling. But the moment felt unconvincing.

—

I don't think it was the next day when I ran out to the cabin and ran into some of the lady's family, almost literally. I think it was the day after that.

I had taken the water bucket off the hook on the doghouse, and I was carrying it near the front of the cabin, headed toward the pump. All of a sudden someone came around the corner and we nearly slammed into each other. We both let out a yelp of surprise.

"Oh," I said. "Sorry."

Then we just stood a moment, neither one of us seeming to know what to say.

She was a woman in her early to midtwenties, with short, curly hair. Small and compact. She wore a frown that seemed to have permanently creased itself into her face. She was holding a narrow strip of wood, which I recognized as part of the framing of the door—the part that had been broken when the deputies crashed through it. Apparently she had pried it off somehow.

"I was just getting some water for the dogs," I said.

"Okay."

I kept expecting her to ask me who I was. But she didn't seem particularly curious.

"I'm Lucas Painter," I said. "I'm—"

But she cut me off in midsentence. "I know who you are."

"You do?"

I wanted to ask how, but I was getting lost in awkwardness.

"You're that kid who's been coming to see the dogs. Taking them running with you."

"How did you know that?"

"My mom told me."

"How did *she* know that? I didn't even think she saw me."

"Oh, she saw you."

Then the conversation stalled again. I could feel myself sink into the embarrassment of what she had just told me.

I looked down at the strip of wood trim in her hand. "Fixing the door?" I asked.

The bucket was getting heavy. The dogs hadn't drunk much.

"Trying. She'll be home in a day or two, and she has to have a door that closes. So I took off the lock. Figured I could take it to the hardware store and get a new one. But I also have to replace this." She held up the strip of wood. "But I have nothing to measure with. And also, I have no idea what I'm doing. I know nothing about home repair."

I shifted uneasily from one foot to the other.

"Maybe I could help," I said.

"You know anything about home repair?"

"Not really. But I know where the hardware store is. And the lumberyard."

She looked into my face as though I might be stupid, but she was still trying to decide. "So do I. I grew up around here."

"Oh. Sorry."

I wasn't sure why I needed to be sorry. But it was something of a default position for me at that age.

"But none of it does any good if I can't find a tape measure," she said. "And I can't."

"What about some string or twine?"

"I don't know about that. But she's a knitter. So I have yarn."

"That'll do," I said. "Go get some of that."

She turned to walk back into the house, and I set down the bucket and followed her. It was a relief to be behind her, out of that intense, frowning gaze. I hadn't realized how uncomfortable I'd been, squirming under her stare, until it was over.

I waited on the porch.

The dogs wove themselves around me, softly wagging their tails. It seemed to have improved their moods to see their owner's daughter. It struck me that I didn't even know this woman's name. She hadn't bothered to tell me.

I reached down and patted their heads as they brushed by.

I looked up to see her bring out a skein of yarn, which I took from her. I tied a knot in the free end and reached up and held the knot at the very top corner of the doorframe.

"Here, hold this," I said, tossing my head upward. In the direction of the knot.

She made no move to do as I had asked. Just snorted a bitter laugh. I realized that she couldn't reach nearly so high. She was a small woman. I placed the knot in the lower corner instead.

She set the broken strip of wood on the floor and then knelt down and held the knotted end of the yarn, and I ran yarn up to the top of the frame and marked my place with the tip of my thumb.

She brought me a scissors and I cut it there.

I picked up the broken trim.

"Okay," I said. "I'll take this to the lumberyard, and you take the lock to the hardware store, and I'll meet you back here and we'll get this done."

She only nodded. She didn't thank me. I wasn't sure if that felt okay or not. But it was clearly all I was going to get.

—

I stood inside the little cabin with her, holding the strip of molding in place while she hammered in the nails. I knew it would probably look like hell when we were done, and I was too cowardly to take responsibility for messing up her place with our bad workmanship.

We stepped back and viewed our work. I frowned. She frowned. But then, she was always frowning, so it was hard to tell.

"I guess it won't look right till it's painted," I said.

The other sides of the doorframe were painted an off-white color.

"I don't know that it'll ever look quite right," she said.

"But it'll keep the door closed."

"We don't know that. We haven't tried it."

I walked up to the door cautiously. As if it might be a spider or a snake.

I saw the dogs on the porch through the partly open doorway. They tapped their tails at me.

I pulled the door closed and tried the new lock. It was a dead bolt that locked with a simple turn from the inside, a key from the outside. I gave it a turn, but it hung up quickly. We hadn't positioned the new lock quite right. The dead bolt pin wouldn't go all the way in. But it wedged in enough to keep the door closed.

I turned to find her right beside me, looking over my shoulder. Well, around my shoulder. She wasn't tall enough to look over it.

"It'll do," she said. "When she's feeling better, she'll tinker with it. That's a given. She'll get it perfect. Story of her life—everything has to be perfect. No matter what we do with it today, she'll tinker. Meanwhile it holds the door closed, so it's good enough for now."

She gathered up the tools she'd used and carried them out to the shed.

I walked out onto the porch and sat on the low edge with the dogs. The male dog put his head on my thigh.

I was thinking I should go home. But there was so much more I wanted to know. Still, even if I stayed, I wasn't sure I could bring myself to ask her all my questions.

She brushed by me again on her way into the cabin.

I looked down into the boy dog's face. "I should go now," I said.

He seemed to know what that meant. He laid his ears back along his neck and his eyes took on a sorrowful expression. Or . . . *even more* sorrowful, I guess I should say.

A second or two later the woman—the daughter, whose name I still hadn't asked—came out and sat next to me on the edge of the porch, her jeaned legs stretching out next to mine.

"Fortunately I know where my mom keeps the tequila," she said, and plunked down a bottle and two short glasses.

I said nothing. I stumbled over what I even had up my sleeve to say. Not much, so I was hoping she'd figure it out on her own.

A second later, she got there. "Oh. What am I saying? You're just a kid. What're you, like, fifteen, sixteen years old?"

"Fourteen," I said.

She poured herself what looked to me like a very large serving of tequila. Then she poured just a splash into the other glass. My glass, I supposed. A couple of tablespoons.

"Go ahead," she said. "That little bit won't kill you."

I just stared at it. I was still petting the boy dog's head.

"Ever had a drink?" she asked me.

"I had half a beer once at a party."

"This is nothing like that. This stuff'll blow the back of your head off."

I watched her down the whole drink as if it were a shot, then slam the empty glass onto the boards of the porch.

I was thinking I liked the fact that my head had a back to it. You know. Intact and all. But she looked over at me expectantly, so I sipped at it. It felt like drinking liquid fire.

"That's not how you do it," she said. "You toss it down all at once."

I did as she said—I think because I generally did what grown-ups said. I hadn't yet learned that I had a right to refuse. Or not fully, anyway. I guess I knew I could, but it was so desperately uncomfortable that I usually didn't.

It made me cough violently, and my eyes watered. I couldn't stop blinking and coughing.

She poured herself another glass. I thought it was strange how we weren't talking about her mother.

I sat quietly for a minute while she downed her second tequila— just stared off into the woods and watched the breeze move the dappled sunlight around. For that minute, everything felt nearly normal again.

Next thing I knew she was grabbing me by two big handfuls of my shirt. Suddenly. Almost violently. I was seized by panic, but I didn't try to get away, except in my head. My fight-or-flight reflex got stuck in the middle on "freeze."

"You have to do something for me," she said, her voice intense and full of distress. "Promise me. Promise me you'll do it!"

The alcohol had obviously gone quickly to her head. Mine had kicked in a little bit, too. My arm and leg muscles felt tingly, my belly hot. Then again, it was hard to know how much of that was fear.

"I don't even know what it is yet," I said.

Which was brave under the circumstances. Even faced with that kind of pressure, I was not about to promise to do something until I knew what I was promising. I took promises seriously, even then. All these years later, even more so. That seemed to override my tendency to do as adults commanded.

"Tell her you won't take the dogs."

"*Take the dogs?* I was never going to take the dogs. Did she think I was trying to steal her dogs?"

"No," she said. "No, no, no." Her words had begun to slur. "You're not getting what I'm saying. You're not getting it right at all. Tell her that if anything happens to her, you won't take them. Or take care of them."

"Um . . . ," I said. And then, because I was extremely uncomfortable, "Could you please let go of my shirt?"

"Oh. Sorry."

She unclenched her fists and let go. Smoothed out the places she had wrinkled. Or tried to, anyway.

I breathed for what felt like the first time in ages.

"I couldn't take the dogs if I wanted to. My parents wouldn't let me have them."

"Good! Tell her that. Promise me you'll tell her that."

"Why?"

"If you use your head, you'll know."

I stared off into the woods for a minute, but nothing came to me. Maybe because I was still shaken.

"Sorry," I said. "I have no idea."

"The dogs need her. They would have no one else to take care of them. If *you* wouldn't, I mean. So that's her reason to stay. Get it?"

"Yeah," I said. "I get it."

"You sound like you don't."

She was probably right about that. I probably sounded like I didn't get it. Because my head was still so full of the parts of the thing I didn't understand. I was wondering if the lady, her mom, had almost left the planet accidentally or purposely, and, if purposely, why the dogs hadn't held her here. And also I was wondering why she didn't have more reasons to stay than just that.

"I just think it's too bad," I said.

"Damn straight. Nearly everything *is*."

She was slurring badly now. But she still poured herself a third full glass. She poured a little more in my glass, but I pretended not to notice.

"Wait," she said, staring at the side of my face. I could see it in my peripheral vision. "Which part?"

"The part about how the dogs are her only reason."

She didn't answer straight away. Just sighed noisily.

We sat quietly for a minute or two. I was wanting to make a break for it and go home. But for the moment I was rooted to the spot.

"I don't know why she stayed in this damn town," she said. Wistfully, as though staring at a pitiful situation I couldn't see. "Nobody knows why. Everybody thought it made sense to go far away. Well . . . everybody except her, I guess. She could have started over where nobody knew her. What was keeping her in this town, I don't know. Instead she had to live like *this*."

She swung one wild arm back toward the cabin.

"What's wrong with this town?" I asked. A bit defensively. After all, this was my town.

"People are crap, that's what's wrong with it. They don't let her forget. They say exactly the wrong thing. They ask these rude, stupid, intrusive questions without stopping to consider how they make her feel, how they bring it all crashing back. And that she's heard them a thousand times before. They whisper behind her back, and I mean to this very day."

I allowed a silence to fall. In case there was more. There didn't seem to be more.

"I feel like I'm missing something," I said.

She stared at the side of my face again. I didn't dare look over, but I could tell.

"Oh," she said, drawing the word out long. "You don't know."

"Don't know what?"

"That's right. Of course you don't. You're fourteen. You weren't even born yet. Well, that'll be nice. You can come see her when she gets home, and you'll be the only person in her life who doesn't know who she is. She'll like that."

I took that to mean she wasn't going to tell me.

"I should go," I said.

I moved the boy dog's head off my leg and stood. Stared down at the daughter for a moment. The drunken daughter.

"You're not going to try to drive back to the hospital, are you?" I asked.

No reply.

I looked around for a car—which was silly, because if there had been one, I would have seen it long before that—but I saw only the pickup truck that was always there. That had been there since I'd stumbled on the place.

"Are you even driving?" I asked at last. Because so far she wasn't answering.

"Yeah," she said, the word muddy with effects of tequila. "I got a rental car parked out on the River Road. But don't worry. I'll sleep it off in the cabin before I go anywhere."

And with that, she disappeared inside.

I didn't run home, because that little bit of alcohol had made me feel shaky. But I definitely got myself home. I think I can honestly say that a big part of me was still unable to process what had just happened.

Chapter Four

The Lady

When I got out to the cabin the following morning, everything had changed. And I knew it immediately.

The dogs were no longer moping on the porch. They had been in their doghouse, but they heard me coming as I trotted down the hill, and they came spilling out. Pouring out, I guess I should say. Just like the old days.

I put on the gas and they ran with me.

Somewhere in the back of my head I knew that must mean the lady was home. But I put it out of my mind again because I had missed this so much. I had needed this so much. I think the dogs had missed it, too. They ran with their mouths open and their tongues lolling out. It looked for all the world like they were grinning widely.

Then I started to worry about what the daughter had said: that her mother had seen me running off with the dogs. I wondered if she had seen me that morning. Probably not, I figured, because she was likely still confined to bed. But the thought continued to nag at me. And, as I think I've said before, I couldn't run through those woods and think any real thoughts at the same time. That was the whole point of doing the thing.

I slowed to a jog and then stopped.

When the dogs noticed, they came back and bounded around me in circles, hoping I'd go on.

"We better go back," I said.

They were clearly disappointed. But they did as I asked.

———

I could feel their tails hitting the backs of my thighs as I knocked on the door.

"Mrs. Dinsmore?" I called.

I pressed my face close to the edge of the door. The edge that would have opened in if she could have gotten up and opened it. As if it would increase my chances of being heard through solid oak. Then I raised my volume a few notches, realizing that would be more helpful.

"You don't have to get up, Mrs. Dinsmore. Don't get up for me, okay? Because I know you're still probably feeling pretty bad. It's just me, Lucas Painter. You know, the guy who was coming to see the dogs? I just wanted you to know I was feeding them while you were gone. They weren't eating, actually, but I made sure they had it there if they wanted it. And I made sure they had water. They did drink a little water. And I came back at sundown and locked the food up in the shed so it wouldn't draw raccoons or coyotes or whatever. I didn't want the dogs getting into it with the wildlife. Anyway . . . I just wanted to say I'm glad you're—"

I got no further than that.

The door swung open.

In front of me stood the lady whose life I had saved. Zoe Dinsmore. She was not tall, but built big and solid—a little overweight but not huge. Just built like a tank. Her face was creased and set hard. Maybe against me, or maybe it had been that way before I was even born.

Her expression made her daughter look like a happy, friendly elf in comparison.

I took a step back.

She just stood there in the open doorway, taking me in. Sizing me up, from the look of it. She was wearing a blue checkered nightgown that came up high around her neck in a ruffle. It didn't seem to suit her at all. She was not a frilly woman, to put it mildly.

After a second or two of staring at me in silence she nodded a couple of times. Not approvingly. More as though she had resigned herself to taking me as I came, disappointing though she seemed to find me.

Or maybe I was reading too much in. Maybe it was life in general that kept falling short of her expectations, and maybe I was only getting the brunt of her disapproval because I happened to be standing in her line of vision.

She opened her mouth and spoke, and I heard her voice for the first time. It was gravelly and deep, as though something had happened to her throat. Or maybe it was the voice of a woman who'd been drinking hard for years. It was impossible for me to know.

"Would you take the dogs if anything happened to me?"

My head spun with her words, and I remembered the promise I'd made to her daughter. How could I forget it?

"I can't," I said. "I couldn't if I wanted to. My parents would never let me have even one small dog."

"Maybe you could come here and take care of them."

"No," I said. And I was surprised by the firmness I heard in my own voice. "No, they would hate that. It would kill them to have to live out here all alone. You should've seen them while you were in the hospital. It would've broken your heart. They were miserable. They wouldn't eat. They would hardly even pick up their own heads. You can't do that to them. They need you."

I paused, and braved a look at her face to see how my very direct words were settling in.

For what seemed like a long time she said nothing.

Then she croaked a simple statement into my face.

"You're not as helpful as I'd hoped you'd be."

She opened the door wider and invited the dogs inside with a sweep of her arm, and they happily accepted the invitation.

She started to swing the door closed, but I stopped it. And her. Stepped forward and stopped the door with my hand, and stopped her from slamming it with my words. It was unlike me. But she had dug down and found what anger I had.

"Wait a minute!" I said. "I don't understand how you can say a thing like that to me. I saved your life."

She leaned in closer, through the half-open doorway. Leaned in until her nose was only three or four inches from mine. I thought I smelled tequila on her breath.

"I didn't. Want it. Saved." Her deep voice came out eerily calm, with tiny groups of words forming their own weighted sentences.

Then she slammed the door and set the poorly aligned dead bolt.

I walked home. What else could I do?

That was my first meeting with the infamous Zoe Dinsmore. It was also the day my curiosity tipped, and I couldn't stop wondering how she had gotten so infamous.

—

I broke Connor loose from his house the best way I knew how. Really the *only* way I knew how by then. I offered to buy him an ice cream.

There was this place on Main Street. That's actually what it was called—the Place. It was about seven blocks from his house. They made a treat he couldn't resist. It was a sugar cone with that swirly soft-serve vanilla, spiraled up all pretty and then dipped in a vat of melted chocolate that hardened immediately into a candy shell. And you had to start eating it right away to keep it from melting, so he couldn't even ask to sit in his room while I brought it to him.

We stepped out of his house, and I saw him squint up into the sun. Maybe I was exaggerating the situation in my head, but he reminded me of a vampire. I wondered when he'd last gone outdoors. I think school had been out for four days.

While we walked to the Place I told him about my experiences of the past twenty-four hours. Both with the lady and her daughter.

He didn't say much. Once he made a little noise in his throat and then said, "That's weird."

We turned the corner onto Main Street, and I saw the ice cream place at the end of the block. I was surprised we'd gotten there so fast. I guess I'd told the story in more detail than I'd realized.

"So . . . ," I said, ". . . you don't know anything about what happened. Do you?"

"Tell me the lady's name again?"

"Zoe Dinsmore."

"No. Can't say that rings a bell."

That was honestly the way Connor talked. At age fourteen. I guess that helps explain why we had no real friends except each other.

"But her daughter said people bring it up to her *to this day*. Like everybody knows about it, whatever it is. So if everybody knows about it . . . why don't we know about it?"

He answered with no hesitation at all. As though the answer had been fully formed in him all along and just waiting to burst out.

"We're kids. People keep stuff from kids. They think we're supposed to stay all pure or something until we grow up, and nothing should upset us. So they whisper about bad stuff behind our backs so we don't get upset. But it's so totally useless, because then at the same time they're always doing stuff that's really upsetting."

"Wow," I said. Surprised by how much he knew and how well he could put it into words. "That's so . . . true."

We stepped into the shop together.

"What're you getting?" he asked. He seemed happy enough to change the subject. He was staring up at the menu board behind the counter, but I had no idea why, because he always got the same thing. "I know you know what *I'm* getting."

"I'm getting the chocolate ice cream with the chocolate coating."

"That's a lot of chocolate," he said.

"You don't say that like it's a good thing."

We waited in a short line.

When we had been handed our cones and I'd paid for them, he did something that disappointed me.

He headed for the door.

"I thought we were going to sit here and eat them," I said.

He shook his head and looked down at the black and white squares of linoleum. The way his mother would have, if she'd been there.

"I should get back."

So I resigned myself to our eating them on the way home. I knew I'd have to spit out what I wanted to say fast, because I only had seven blocks to get it all covered.

"So, how do you find out a thing like that?" I asked as we walked away from the shop.

"I'm not sure." He took a bite of his ice cream as if it helped him think. Then he added, "You could ask your parents."

"Nah."

"Why not?"

"I was three when we moved here, remember? And this happened before I was born."

"They still might've heard about it."

"Maybe. But there's another thing. I don't want my mom to know I've been out in those woods. She'd be really mad."

"What does she have against the woods?"

"She thinks I'll get lost in there."

"Oh. Did you ever?"

"Once. For a little bit. But then I came out on the River Road, and then I knew where I was again."

We walked in silence for half a block. I ate my chocolate ice cream, wondering why anyone would get vanilla when they could get chocolate. I thought he was out of suggestions, which was disappointing. I wasn't sure which way to go with this thing. I needed somebody's help, and Connor was pretty much my whole set of options.

"I could ask my mom," he said. "She's lived here all her life."

"Yeah. That would be good. Would you?"

"Yeah. Sure. Why not? And if she doesn't know, well . . . if I were you, I'd go talk to Mrs. Flint."

"How could *she* help?"

"She's a reference librarian."

"Well, I know, but . . ."

"They know everything."

"But whatever happened, it's not like somebody wrote a book about it or something. Or even if they did, I wouldn't know the title or the author."

"She knows about more than just books. They keep the newspapers there. And when they get too old and there are too many of them, they put them on microfilm. So if something happened around here, and it was in the paper, she could probably find it for you."

"Oh. That's actually a pretty good idea. Thanks."

"But let me ask my mom first. Save you the walk down to the library if she knows."

———

He handed me what was left of his ice cream cone in that long, dark front hallway of his house.

"Don't let it drip on the rug," he said.

There was a runner of Persian carpet nearly the full length of the hall. I happened to know it was passed down through Connor's family on his mother's side. Might've cost more than everything in my house put together. It made me nervous to be charged with protecting it.

"Tell me the lady's name one more time," he said.

"Zoe Dinsmore."

"Right. Right."

With that he walked down the hall and into the kitchen.

The kitchen had big windows that let in a spill of sun. It was the only fairly light room in the Barneses' house. I could see the shadows of Connor and his mother stretching out halfway into the hall, enveloped in that wide beam of light, as he said hi to her and she said hi back to him.

Connor's ice cream was already starting to drip. It didn't seem right to lick it, so I let it drip onto my hand and then licked it off my hand before it could drip onto the rug.

"So, hey, Mom," I heard him say. Timidly, I thought. "You know anything about something that happened a long time ago with a lady named Zoe Dinsmore?"

Silence. I moved down the hall a few steps in case she was speaking but too quietly for me to hear.

"You're not saying anything," Connor added after a time. "Why aren't you saying anything? Was that something I shouldn't have asked?"

"Oh, honey," she said, and paused. Her voice sounded as though the question had rattled her. Or just weighted her down too heavily. I couldn't tell which. I just knew she didn't like it and was trying to wiggle past it and squirt out the other side. "I *do* wish you wouldn't ask me about those kinds of things. You know I don't like to talk about things that are so sad like that. Life is sad enough without dredging up the worst of the past. Those poor families probably never got over it. The whole town never really got over it. But it was before you were born, so can't you just grow up and be happy?"

If Connor answered, I couldn't hear him. But it struck me while I was waiting—and licking—that it was a ridiculous question. Of course Connor couldn't be happy. He hadn't been happy a day that I'd known him. And I'd known him since we were three.

I looked up suddenly to see him walk out of the kitchen and down the hall to where I stood.

I reached out to hand him back his cone.

"You didn't lick it," he said. "Did you?"

"No. I didn't lick it. That would be gross."

"Okay. Thanks. You'll have to go to the library, I guess."

"Thanks anyway," I said. "You know. For trying."

———

Mrs. Flint was an interesting character, I thought. She seemed to have studied books and old movies and absorbed every possible stereotype about small-town librarians—and then imitated them to the letter.

She had mousy brown hair, pulled back into a bun. Oversized tortoiseshell reading glasses. She wore gray or brown skirt suits over starched white shirts with button-down collars. She looked like the fictional librarian in just about every film or television show ever made.

I stepped up to her desk, and she whispered to me. Because you whisper in the library.

"Lucas," she said. "I don't see you in here very often. Can I help you with something?"

"I need some information," I whispered back.

All of a sudden I felt deeply in touch with how uneasy it made me to ask about this situation. Whatever it was.

"That would be my department, yes."

"I need to know about something that happened in town before I was born."

"Okay. Do you have the date?"

"Um. No. I just know it was before I was born."

"If we're looking in the microfilm of the county newspaper, we'll need a date."

"I know the name of the person it happened to. Or . . . I don't know. Because of. Or something."

She made a discouraging little noise in her throat and shook her head.

"It's not like we can scan every paper for years' worth of articles just looking for one name. Although . . . if it's important enough to you, I can leave you in there and you can hunt around as long as you like. What's the name? Maybe I already know something about it."

"Zoe Dinsmore," I said.

The silence that followed was a stunning thing. It seemed to zoom around the room. Bounce off the walls. I watched her face get a little whiter and her lips set into a long, tight line.

"December 18th, 1952," she whispered.

"You know the *date*?" I might've said it too loud.

"Hard to forget *that* date. It was exactly one week before Christmas. It was the last school day before the children went out on their holiday vacation."

I opened my mouth to ask her to tell me about it. But she got up from her desk.

"I'll be right back," she said. And walked away.

I waited.

And waited.

And waited.

I felt my heart bang around in my chest, but I wasn't even sure why. I mean, this whole thing had nothing to do with me. Did it? I hadn't even been born yet in 1952. Still I couldn't shake the feeling that I was in it chest deep now, whatever it turned out to be. Whether I liked it or not.

I looked up to see Mrs. Flint motioning me into the back room.

I stepped inside and sat down in a hard chair in front of the micro-film machine. It was a big white box that projected one page of the newspaper onto a vertical screen in front of my face. It had a crank on either side to move the film from one reel to the other, a page at a time.

The headline of the article caught my eye immediately, along with the photo. It was the front page of the morning paper, the *Taylor County Gazette*. December 19, 1952. The day after the incident.

The photo was black and white and printed large. It was a school bus, partially submerged in the river. Upside down. It made me queasy to look at it.

I remembered a handful of nonredacted words from my brother Roy's letter: ". . . in the trees, upside down . . ."

The font of the headline was huge and bold. "Tragic School Bus Accident Claims the Lives of Two Local Children."

"This should be everything you need," Mrs. Flint said, her eyes averted. From the news, and from me. Both. "I'll just leave you alone with it."

She walked out, closing the door behind her. Leaving me in a dark-ened room lit only by the glow of the screen against my face. Leaving me to learn what I had been so sure I wanted to know.

To say I was no longer sure would be an understatement.

I began to read. How could I not?

> Yesterday tragedy struck the town of Ashby as a bus serving the Unified School District veered off River Road and rolled down an embankment, land-ing upside down in the river. The driver, Mrs. Zoe Dinsmore, suffered only minor injuries, and managed to pull most of the children to safety, diving back in again and again and wading to shore with them two at a time. But two children did not survive the crash.

They are: Wanda Jean Paulston, 7, of Ashby and Frederick Peter "Freddie" Smith, 6, also of Ashby.

One child whose name has been withheld is hospitalized in stable condition and seven others were treated and released with injuries ranging from minor to moderate.

Mrs. Dinsmore has been driving a school bus route in Taylor County for well over twenty years. "Everybody loves her," said Charlene Billings, the superintendent of schools, when reached for comment. "Students and parents alike, everybody looked forward to saying good morning to Mrs. Dinsmore. And she had a spotless driving record. Not even so much as a parking ticket."

Mrs. Dinsmore was held at the Taylor County Sheriff's Office for several hours, where she was subjected to questioning, as well as tests to assure that her blood showed no signs of alcohol use or other impairment. No such impairment was found, according to Deputy Leo Brooks.

Mrs. Dinsmore told sheriff's deputies that her two young girls, Katie, 4, and Delia, 5, had influenza, and she'd been up most of the night caring for them. She said she thinks she fell asleep behind the wheel of the bus for less than ten seconds, and that it was the shrieking of the children that woke her. But by then the bus had begun to roll down the river's embankment, and there was nothing she could do to bring it back under control.

The *Gazette* attempted to reach Mrs. Dinsmore for comment, but was told she had gone into seclusion and was speaking to no one.

The crash has been officially ruled an accident, and no charges will be filed.

The *Gazette* will announce the dates and times of the funerals and/or memorials for Wanda Jean Paulston and Freddie Smith when such information becomes available.

I read it completely through a second time. I really couldn't say why. Then I sat back and turned off the machine. The room went completely dark. There were no windows in the microfilm room, and the darkness all around me was a good match for my insides.

In that moment the whole world felt dark.

Chapter Five

You Know Now. That's Too Bad.

When I returned the dogs to the cabin the following morning, I got into quite a back-and-forth with myself over whether I should knock.

I had run with them at least a mile each way up and down the River Road, and I was pretty convinced that Zoe Dinsmore's daughter had gone home again. Because there had been no parked rental cars anywhere to be seen.

I was worried about the lady. You know, whether she had everything she needed. Whether she was feeling well enough to *get* everything she needed. That sort of thing.

I stepped up onto the porch. Walked boldly to the door. In that moment I was the very picture of decisiveness. I was actually proud of my courage. Noticeably proud.

Briefly.

I raised a hand to knock, then lost my nerve and turned away. Strode two steps to the edge of the porch. Stopped myself and turned back. Walked to the door. Raised a hand again. Spun away again.

I turned back to the door one more time, and this time I planned to force myself all the way through the thing. But I never got that far.

A sudden voice from behind made me jump out of my figurative skin.

"Make up your mind. You want to knock on my door or don't you?"

I knew it was Zoe Dinsmore because no other voice sounded like that one.

I spun around to face the voice and saw, to my embarrassment, that she was just leaving the outhouse. She was wearing an old pair of men's green plaid pajamas. Her hair was pulled back into a gray braid.

"Yeah," I said, making my voice sound stronger than I felt. "Yeah, I was going to knock. Just to . . . you know . . ."

While I was stalling, she walked right up to me and stared directly into my face. It made me nervous, which made me lose my train of thought.

"No, I *don't* know," she said in that deep signature voice. "I barely know my own mind, kid. I wouldn't even pretend to know somebody else's."

She looked even more deeply into my face for a moment, as if running after something she thought she'd seen there, and I averted my gaze to the point of stressing my neck muscles. As if I could run away from her without ever moving my feet.

"Oh," she said. And she was disappointed in me. I only needed that one word from her to know it. "You know now. My daughter said you didn't know. But now you do. That's too bad."

"I don't know why you say that."

"Because it's true."

"But I mean . . . how do you *know* that?" I realized, the minute the words were out of my mouth, that I had just admitted she was correct. I stood there with my neck craned away and felt my face burn.

"You think after seventeen years I don't know the look on somebody's face when they know? I wish I didn't, kid, but I know it better than I know the inside of my own eyelids. And when I close my eyes, most times I don't even see the inside of my eyelids, I see those looks. Well, if you came here to ask me about it, or offer your opinion on it, you're out of luck. I've been there and done that, and I'm not going there again for anybody. It may be news to you, kid, but to me it's anything but. I don't exist to help you get things settled in your own head."

When I was sure she was done, I adjusted my neck into a more normal position, nearly facing her, and defended myself with the truth.

"I didn't come for that. Not at all. I was only about to knock on your door because it looked like your daughter had left again, and I was just going to ask if you were okay or if you needed anything."

I waited, but she didn't speak. I didn't dare look at her face to try to get a bead on what she was thinking or feeling.

So I added, "*Did* she go back?"

"Yeah. She's gone. Not that I blame her. She's got an eighteen-month-old son. Babysitting *me* hardly fit in with her plans. So, okay, I'm not the best at apologies. Not my strong suit. But anyway, sorry I didn't give you credit for trying to be helpful. Hope you can see your way clear to let that go by."

"Yes, ma'am." I felt all the tension leave my body, and I was stunned by how much tension it had been. I felt like I could float away after it lifted out. "So . . . *do* you need anything?"

I braved a glance at her face. Fortunately, she was looking away. Off toward the cabin, as though it helped her think.

"Milk was sour when I got home," she said. "It was a little close to the line when I left, but if I'd been home, I could've finished it. And if I was feeling better, I could've gone out for more."

"I could bring you back a quart of milk."

She looked right at me, and for a split second I looked right back. And in that second, something was established. Some wall was broken through. We were no longer two wild animals who would spook and flee at the sight of each other, or try to claw each other apart for our own safety. We had made the initial connection on the assembly line of trusting each other.

"Thank you," she said. "I'll go inside and get you a dollar."

—

When I got back with the milk and her change, she took it from me, but didn't say much. I mean . . . she did say thank you. But not much more. She carried it inside. To put away in the fridge, I guess.

I waited on the porch with the dogs, but I wasn't sure why. And I wasn't sure if she'd meant for me to. I had asked her what she needed. She'd told me. I'd brought it to her. That should have been the end of it.

It wasn't.

I sat down on the edge of the porch, poking around inside myself for the reasons I didn't feel like I could leave. It was a sort of generalized paranoia. Something bad would happen to the lady if I left. And then for the rest of my life I'd have that thought in the back of my head. Or maybe it would be a ball of feelings in my gut. *What if I'd played that day differently? What if I hadn't left her alone?*

For the first time I truly understood how Connor felt.

Also it might've been a look through the window into what the lady had been going through for seventeen years. *What if I'd called in sick that day? Had that extra cup of coffee? What if I'd pulled the bus over, even though that would've made the kids late for school?*

I heard her footsteps on the porch boards behind me, and I glanced over my shoulder. The dogs jumped to their feet and wagged at her in greeting.

"I can't help noticing you're not gone," I heard her say in that deep, rumbly bass voice.

"No, ma'am. I guess I'm not."

She sighed deeply. It sounded like she was playacting some irritation she didn't entirely feel.

She sat beside me on the edge of the porch, and the dogs settled around us. One in between, one on the other side of her. For a few minutes we all stared out into the woods and didn't say a word.

She'd gotten dressed while I was running to the store, thankfully, and was now wearing denim overalls over a red plaid flannel shirt. Heavy work boots that laced up at the ankle.

"I keep forgetting to ask you their names," I said after a time.

I felt alarm rise in her, even though I'm not sure how a person can feel a thing like that. But I did feel it. I'm just not sure by what means.

"Whose names?"

"The dogs. I still don't know their names."

The fear seemed to settle out of her. Drain away. I wondered if she had thought I was asking about Wanda Jean and Freddie.

"The boy is Rembrandt and the girl is Vermeer."

"Rembrandt like the painter?"

"Actually they're both painters."

"Oh," I said. "Like me."

"You paint?"

"No," I said. "No, I didn't mean that. Just . . . Lucas Painter. That's me."

She said nothing, so after a few seconds I glanced over at the side of her face. She did not seem impressed by my small note of coincidence with the dogs. I think she would have liked it better if I had been an artist. But I wasn't. And I'm still not. And that's just the way it is.

"Look," she said. "I know why you're not leaving."

"You do?"

"I think I do. I think you think if you leave me alone, I'll do something stupid."

"Um . . . ," I began. And did not finish. Probably wisely.

"I'm not making you any promises about the rest of my life, kid. But if you go home today . . . I'll still be here when you get here tomorrow for your run."

"How do I know that for a fact?"

"Because, for all my faults—and if you ask around, you'll hear they're legion—I never look somebody in the face and tell them a damn lie. And besides, I already took every pill I had in the house."

My eyes went immediately to her pickup. Her old blue truck. She must've seen them go.

"You think any local doctor's going to write me a prescription or any local pharmacist's going to fill it? After what just happened?"

I wasn't sure, so I continued to sit.

"Look," she said. "Kid. Believe me or don't. It's up to you. But there's a better reason why you can't sit here on my porch for the rest of your life. Because you can't control other people. You can't be responsible for somebody else. Not if it's a fully grown adult human, you can't. Sooner or later you have to go home, and you know it."

I sighed. Pulled to my feet.

I stood facing her and the dogs. She cut her gaze away from me, and it struck me that she was ashamed. She hadn't meant for anyone to know as much about what she'd just done as I knew. She hadn't meant to let anybody in so close, to make so many observations.

"Well," I said. "Goodbye, Vermeer. Goodbye, Rembrandt. Goodbye, Mrs. Dinsmore."

She gave me a little wave, her eyes still angled away.

"Here's a question," I said, while I continued not to leave. "Your daughter said you saw me running off with the dogs every morning. All along."

"I did," she said. Quietly.

"Why didn't you stop me? Why didn't you say, 'Hey kid, those are *my* dogs—leave 'em alone!' That's what most people would've done."

"It was nice for them to have somebody to run with. They're young dogs. They need that."

"But you trusted me to bring them back?"

"I trusted *them* to *come* back. They know where they live."

"Right," I said. "Got it. Well . . . bye."

I couldn't think of any more reasons to stall, so I turned to walk away. I got about ten steps, then was seized with a thought. A weirdly disturbing thought.

I stopped. Turned back. The three of them had not moved.

"Wait a minute," I said, walking closer.

"Now what?"

"You saw me out the window. With the dogs. For a couple of weeks."

"What about it?"

"And you figured out that I liked them."

"Yeah. What of it?"

"You figured I would take care of them if you couldn't."

This time, no answer from her.

"So here I am thinking I saved your life, but I'm the reason you tried to take it in the first place. If I'd just stayed away, none of the rest of this would have happened."

We stood there in silence for a painful length of time. Well, I stood. She sat. The dogs lay.

"Listen, kid," she said at last. "Here's a lesson for you in the fact that you're not the center of the universe. You don't run the world. I make my own choices. You can't keep me here, and you can't make me leave. You don't control as much as you think you do. I'm not trying to be cruel. Just the opposite. You'll have a much happier life if you get a strong bead on what's your responsibility and what isn't. Now go home and have a good summer and stop worrying about me."

"Yes, ma'am."

I went home.

But I did not stop worrying about Zoe Dinsmore.

———

"I actually do think I heard about that," Connor said. "Now that you tell me all those details."

Then he passed me the basketball.

We were playing a game of H-O-R-S-E in his backyard. In the driveway, right where the concrete went wide in front of the two-car garage. His dad had mounted a hoop over the garage doors. Years earlier. Connor couldn't have cared less about it. He never wanted to use it. I'd had to practically drag him out here.

"Why didn't you tell me?" I asked, and then began to dribble.

He tried to block my drive to the hoop, but I turned my back to him and did a spin move and left him in the dust. My spin moves always left him in the dust. For a compact little guy, he was surprisingly heavy on his feet.

I leapt into the air and dunked the ball with both hands.

"*R,*" I said.

Connor had no part of the word *HORSE*. Only I had three letters of it. Only I had any letters at all.

Maybe this was why Connor never wanted to shoot hoops with me. Odd that the thought hadn't occurred to me sooner.

"Time," he said. He made the time-out gesture, the T, with his two hands.

I dribbled in place while he leaned on his knees and panted.

"So why didn't you tell me?" I asked again.

"I didn't know," he said.

"You just said you heard about it."

"Now that you tell me all the details, yeah. I've heard a couple of the details before. But nobody ever said 'Zoe Dinsmore' in front of me, so how was I to even possibly know it had anything to do with *your* thing?"

"It's not *my* thing," I said, and dribbled over closer to him.

At least, I really wanted it not to be my thing. But I was pushing back against a strong—and growing—sense that it was.

"It's the thing you were trying to find out about."

"Right," I said. "That's true. So what did you hear?"

He leaned back against his garage door. Looked up and squinted into the strong afternoon sun, then looked down at his feet to give his eyes a break.

"A few years ago I remember a lady saying something to my mom about two kids who died. She didn't say how they died, but it sounded like they were on their way to school. She just said something like, 'Sure, Pauline, we all want to think our kids are safe. But what about those two poor little souls who never showed up to school that day?' Those weren't the exact words, of course. It was a long time ago. But you get the idea."

"Yeah," I said. And just stood for a minute. Maybe longer. "So, come on. Let's finish the game."

"I forfeit this game," he said.

He walked across his yard and sat under the big oak tree, leaning his back against the trunk. Right where we'd found that bird's nest back when we were six or seven. With three tiny blue eggs that had tumbled out of it when it fell. It was just a thing that came flooding back into my brain as he sat.

I put the ball down and joined him under the tree.

I should have considered the fact that he would tire out faster than I would if I pushed him to play basketball. I had been out in the woods running lately. He had been up in his room worrying.

"So you think that's why she tried to kill herself?" he asked.

It was such a blunt statement. So much more direct than anything I had ever said about it, even in my head. It felt like a knife, just hanging there in the air between us, warning me to be careful not to cut myself on it.

"I don't know," I said. "I have no idea why somebody would do a thing like that. I mean, it was seventeen years ago, the bus thing. Kind of a weirdly delayed reaction, don't you think?"

"I don't think you really get over a thing like that, though."

"Maybe not. But still."

"Maybe she got tired of the fact that it wasn't going away."

"I don't know," I said again. And then I really thought about it. About making a decision like that. And I was just bowled over by how much I couldn't imagine it. "I can't even . . . I mean . . . how can a person even *do* a thing like that? I mean, you're in bed. And you're alive. And you have this handful of pills, and suddenly you make this decision that now you're not going to be alive anymore? I can't even stretch my brain around it."

"You don't know if it was sudden," he said.

"It doesn't matter how fast or slow it was. It was *her life*. I mean, a person's *life*. It's all you've got. It's everything. Without it, you're . . . well, you're *not*. You're literally not anything. You're not even . . . I just can't understand a thing like that at all."

"Well . . . ," he began. And I could tell an opposing viewpoint was coming, though I couldn't imagine where he would find one. "We all *think* about it."

"Well, but . . ." Then it hit me. Kind of belatedly like that. "Wait, what?" I whipped my head sideways to look at him. Possibly for the first time that day. I usually didn't look too directly at Connor. It seemed to make him nervous. So I had learned to use a series of near misses. "You think about it?"

"No," he said.

"You just said you did."

"No. I said everybody does."

"But *I* don't. And you're part of everybody."

"I'm going in," he said.

He pushed to his feet, and I followed him.

I followed him into the house. Through the back door. Into the mudroom, where we wiped our feet carefully on a scratchy mat before stepping onto the Persian runner carpet in the dimly lit hallway. Past the kitchen and up the stairs to his bedroom.

"But—" I began.

He whipped his head around and stopped me with a finger to his lips.

I followed him into his room, and closed the door behind us.

"So, seriously, Connor. Anything you want to tell me?"

"No. It was nothing. I was just talking. I wish you'd drop it."

"How can I drop it? You're my best friend, and you just said you think about it."

"Not seriously, though. Not . . . I just think weird thoughts sometimes. Don't you ever think about weird things like that?"

"I think about weird things," I said. "But not like *that*."

Then neither one of us knew what to say.

I knew he was done with our visit and wanted to be alone. But I wasn't leaving yet. I didn't even feel close.

He flopped onto his back on the bed and I just stood there, feeling clumsy and awkward. And thinking about what Zoe Dinsmore had said. About how I'm not the center of the universe and I don't control things as much as I think I do.

"So . . . ," I said. Kind of testing the water. "Just one question. And then I promise I'll go home and get out of your hair."

"Yeah," he said. "That would be good."

It was the closest he'd ever come to saying he didn't want me around, and it made my face burn. But I talked right through it.

"Are you okay?"

He sat up and looked directly into my face. Which was weirdly rare, to put it mildly. Then he looked down at his bedspread.

"How would I even know that, Lucas? I have no idea if how I feel is what other people would call okay. I'm just the way I've always been."

It was such a blazingly honest—unguardedly honest—answer. It was so direct and so true that even though it didn't put my mind at ease, I really had no choice but to thank him for it and go home alone.

Now I had two people I was worried about. But it was even worse than that. When I was worried about Zoe Dinsmore, I could go talk to Connor. But when I was worried about Connor, where could I go?

I pondered the question all the way home, and got exactly nowhere.

Well. I got home. But I got no closer to an answer regarding what was weighing on my mind.

Chapter Six

Asking for a Friend

When I got out to the cabin the following morning, the lady was out-side, hanging up her wash on a clothesline. And the dogs wouldn't go running with me. They would only come along when she was inside the cabin. They weren't about to give up the chance to be close to her.

She glanced halfway over her shoulder as I walked up behind her.

"Oh," she said. "You again."

She didn't really make it sound as bad as those words could have been.

"Yeah," I said. "Me."

"Well, make yourself useful. Grab the other end of that bedsheet."

The wet laundry was piled in a basket, which was sitting on the dirt at her feet. I wondered if she had a washing machine. I didn't think she did. I had been all over the property and hadn't seen any such thing. I figured I would know if she had one. Then I wondered how hard it must be to wash a bedsheet by hand.

She lifted it out of the basket and began to unfurl it, and I took it by one corner and stepped away until it was pretty well stretched out.

"Give it a good shake with me," she said.

So we did that.

The dogs were wagging all around us, weaving in and out. Brushing under the wet sheet, which I figured was probably not ideal for something that was freshly clean. They seemed over-the-moon ecstatic to have both of us out and moving around at the same time. Some kind of doggie jackpot.

"Fold about four inches of that corner over the line," she said, and handed me a clothespin. "So it won't come down again."

We pinned it up, and I stepped back to see if it would hold. When it did, I really had no idea what to do next. So I just stood there and watched her work. Watched her hang socks one at a time. Then, when it came to her unmentionables, I had to avert my eyes.

"What would you do if you had a friend . . . ," I began. I waited to see if she was listening. She seemed to be. "Who you thought maybe wanted to . . ." But it was hard to go on.

"To *what*?" she spat after a time. "Just say what you're thinking, kid."

"Go," I said.

"Go where?"

"Like . . . die. But not accidentally or anything."

Her hands stopped moving and she shot me a scorching look. I mean, I honestly felt burned.

"You're not supposed to do that 'asking for a friend' thing *to* the friend in question."

"I'm not talking about you," I said.

She hung up the last item in the basket. The overalls. Pinned them by their straps.

"Oh," she said. "A 'friend.'"

"Right."

"Got it." She let out a big, deep sigh. As if preparing to run a marathon she really didn't want to start. "Okay. Go ahead and tell me what's so terrible about your life."

We began to walk back toward the cabin together, the dogs wagging all around and between us.

"*My* life?"

"Yeah."

"Oh. Okay."

I wasn't sure I understood. But I didn't have it in me to disobey her.

We reached the porch, and I sat on the edge of it. The girl dog, Vermeer, took advantage of the lack of height difference and kissed me right on the face with her long tongue. Neither dog had ever licked me before. I was ridiculously flattered.

The lady sat next to me and picked up something she had clearly been working on before the laundry project. It was some kind of whittling. A curved knife and a thick stick of wood that was beginning to take a shape, but I had no idea yet what it was trying to be.

"Well," I began. "My parents fight like cats and dogs. And I don't just mean they argue. They scream. They throw things. My dad'll try to get me to side with him just to spite my mom. Once he crashed his fist right through the living room drywall."

"Better that than right through your mom."

"Yeah, I guess," I said. "But then there's my brother. He got drafted. And I think he's having a really hard time over there."

"Who wouldn't?" Then she waited a couple of seconds. I guess to see if I was done.

I wasn't done.

"And the thing is . . . I just . . . *love* him." I said it as though it was some kind of revelation. Something that had never crossed my mind before.

"Don't sound so surprised," she said. "He's your brother."

"But I never really thought enough about it until he was gone. So now I'm worried because I think maybe I didn't tell him."

"You have an address to write to him, don't you?"

"Yeah. Sure."

"So tell him."

I just sat a minute, letting that sink in. I never answered her.

"So, listen. Kid. Not to dismiss what's bothering you, but . . . these are temporary problems. Your brother'll come home. Your parents might not stop fighting, but you'll grow up and move away where you don't have to hear it."

"But what if he doesn't come home?"

Her knife held still for a beat or two. No curls of blond wood fell onto her porch boards.

"Well, that's a whole other ball game, kid. But there's a good chance he will. So you have to hang around and find out, don't you? You're talking about using a permanent fix on temporary problems."

I just stared at her for a moment, and she stared back. I wasn't understanding her. And then, a second or two later, I got it.

"Not *me*," I said. "You thought I meant *me*?"

"Oh. An *actual* friend?"

"Didn't you hear me say it was my friend?"

"Yeah. But I didn't believe you." More whittling. Then, "What's your friend's story?"

"I don't know," I said. "Well. I sort of know. But I don't know that it's any one great big deal, like . . ." But then I didn't want to say like what. I didn't want to make any reference to her situation. *Her* great big deal. "He's just always been sort of sad. His parents don't say a word to each other, and it's just really heavy and dark and strained in that house, and it's getting to him. I think. Maybe there's more, but if so, I don't know it."

"So what makes you think he's thinking about it?"

"Because he said he thinks about it."

"Oh. That's pretty damn clear."

For a minute or two I watched the curls of wood, and the shape they were leaving behind as they fell. It was beginning to look like a monkey. I could see its long tail curved around the inside core of the stick.

"Is that possible?" I asked. But then I didn't know how to be any clearer than that. I wasn't sure how to put into words what I thought I meant. "Like . . . even if nothing huge happened?"

"Anything's possible. Sure, a person can just be depressed. Maybe his parents grew up hard and they haven't even begun to heal the insides of themselves. And then yeah, sure. He can grow up hard, too. I don't know because I don't know him. But it's not always about big stuff happening to us. Not as much as people think, anyway. Could just be his brain chemistry or a bunch of little things adding up big."

I sat quiet a minute.

Then I said, "So what do I do?"

She looked at me like I was crazy. Stone crazy. Like I'd just told her I see flying monkeys or some weird vision like that.

"What?" I asked, feeling defensive.

"Well, first of all . . . you obviously weren't listening yesterday. I told you. You can't make somebody leave and you can't make them stay."

"You said I couldn't with *you*."

She sighed. "With *anybody*. And another thing. You're looking for advice on keeping a friend alive. So you go to a person who tried suicide a few days ago and might try it again tomorrow. Does that sound like good sense to you?"

I stood.

My face was burning as I stared down at her. Partly because she was chastising me for not making good sense. Partly because she'd just told me she might try it again tomorrow.

"Okay," I said. "Got it. I'll go now."

But I was only two or three steps into leaving when she stopped me with a single word.

"Kid."

I turned back. Waited.

"Just be a good friend to him. Might work. Might not. But it's really the only shot available to you."

I didn't say thank you. I didn't say anything. Because I wasn't sure if I wanted to talk to her anymore. It felt like such a minefield, everything that happened when the lady was around. Or even sometimes when she wasn't around, like that moment with her daughter. When Zoe Dinsmore was involved, things got explosive.

I just nodded.

Then I ran home.

—

I managed to drag Connor out to the park, but it was a mistake. I knew I should have left well enough alone as soon as we got there and those two guys were there. The ones I beat by a step or two at the track tryout. They were on the other side, on this hilly part of the grass, but it was a small neighborhood park, so they were closer than I would've liked. They were playing tackle football with two other guys I had seen but didn't really know.

And they were aware of my presence. That much was uncomfortably clear.

I had my bat along, and a couple of softballs. In case Connor hit one of them out of the park and we never found it. Connor wasn't what you might call a star athlete, but he did have his moments as a surprisingly good hitter. He swung hard and missed plenty. He was just as likely to strike out as connect with the ball. But when he connected . . . man. His swing was unreal. Home run nearly every time.

I thought it might be good for him to play at something he was good at for a change. I didn't think till later that his massive hits might have had something to do with anger boiling up.

I also hadn't factored in the guys who were sneering at me.

"Come on," I said to Connor. Ignoring them. I handed him the bat. "You're up first. I'll pitch you some."

I paced off the distance I thought should represent home base to mound.

When I turned around to face Connor, I was face to face with those two guys. They had abandoned their game and walked over, following me across the grass.

"Hey, Speedy Gonzales," one of them said. The one who'd snickered at me for not knowing how to use starting blocks.

"What?" I said, already not liking the feel of this. Already with a bad sense of where this was headed.

"See that guy?"

"What guy?"

He pointed over to one of the boys in his four-person football game. He had wandered closer, too, and was standing maybe ten steps away. I didn't know where the fourth guy was. I didn't see him anymore.

The guy in question raised his hand and waved at me. Not in a friendly way. More like, "Yeah. Me."

"What about him?" I asked, noticing that my throat was feeling tight.

"His name is Arnie."

"That's nice," I said, trying to sound casual. I don't think it was working.

"He used to have a spot on the track team. But now he doesn't. Guess why not?"

I knew why not. It was pretty obvious. The coach had given me a spot and then dropped his slowest guy. It wasn't my fault that Arnie was his slowest guy. It didn't make me feel guilty or like I'd done something I shouldn't have. But that was on the inside. On the outside, I figured I'd better come out with something better than "Who cares?" or "Not my problem."

"Look," I said. "I don't even want to be on the damn team. It wasn't my idea to try out. Coach made me. I'm not even going to take the spot come fall. I'm going to get out of it somehow."

While I talked, he moved closer to me. Menacingly, like he was trying to intimidate me into backing up.

Over his shoulder I saw Connor making wild pointing gestures. And I knew what he was trying to tell me. Maybe it was just really good pointing, or maybe it was because I'd known Connor for so long, but I read him loud and clear. There was something behind me.

My guess was that one of them was crouching down back there, and as Snicker Boy forced me to back up, I'd fall backward over him.

So I didn't back up.

I stood my ground as he got closer and closer. Until his nose was nearly touching mine. I could feel every muscle in my body tight like a drawn bow, but I wasn't in a complete state of panic. Because I really didn't think he was going to hurt me. Trip me, make me fall down, laugh at me. Yeah. But there were cars going by. Lots of them. Lots of drivers who lived in this small town. Nobody was going to get seriously hurt.

"Says you," he said.

He seemed to be losing patience with my unwillingness to play the game.

He took one step back, reached out with the palms of both hands, and pushed me hard in the chest. I flew backward. And, sure enough, his idiot friend was crouched back there. I just kept falling until I was on my back in the grass, staring up at the sky.

By the time I'd scrambled to my feet, Connor was flying across the grass. And I do mean flying.

He hit Snicker Boy with his full weight and brought him down, probably more with the element of surprise than anything else. Connor fell with him, fell on top of him. Then he raised himself to his knees and started swinging. Snicker Boy was so caught off guard that all he could really do was try to cover his head with his hands.

Then one of the other boys pulled Connor off the kid.

But Connor wasn't done. Not even close.

He turned around and started punching the boy in the head. Lefts and rights, both. Over and over.

Now, I'm not defending those guys. They were idiots. But all they'd wanted to do was cause me to fall on my ass, laugh at me, and then walk away. Nobody—with the exception of Connor—had meant to escalate the thing to this level. But, let's face facts. You can only punch a guy in the head just so many times before he swings back.

The guy swung back.

He connected with Connor's jaw so hard that I heard it from ten steps away. Connor flew backward and landed in the grass, holding his jaw.

All four guys laughed at him.

Then they turned their backs on us and walked off laughing. And that should have been the end of that whole disaster.

It wasn't.

Connor rolled over, launched to his feet, and picked up my bat. And he went after the guys with it.

It's times like that it pays to be really fast.

I caught him with an arm around his waist, and spun him around, and brought him down to the grass again. Brought us both down.

As I did, I looked around for possible assistance. Just my luck. In that moment, there was no one going by.

I managed to wrestle the bat away from him.

I looked up to see the boys looking down on us. They had walked part of the way back to stare. And get off one parting shot.

"Your friend is a freak," Snicker Boy said. "What the hell's wrong with him? You oughta keep that freak on a leash."

Then they turned and walked away.

—

"Is it swollen?" he asked on the walk home, turning his jaw toward me to give me a better view. And leaning in, as if I were half-blind. It was the third time he had asked. "Is it starting to look bruised?"

"It's a little swollen," I said.

The first two times I had said no. But now it was beginning to swell, and no amount of positive thinking could convince me I was only imagining it. And I wasn't going to outright lie to him.

"I just don't know what I'm supposed to tell my mom," he said.

"Maybe she won't notice. It's kind of dark in your house."

"She's pretty good at noticing stuff."

We walked in silence for a time. I could see his jaw working as he ground his molars together. Maybe he was testing it to see how much it hurt. Maybe he was just grinding his teeth with stress.

"For me, I don't even really care," he said. "But my mom worries about me. She can't handle it when she thinks I'm not safe."

"Can I do anything to help you with telling her?"

"No!" he said. Shouted, actually. "No, you should go home. It's better if I talk to her alone."

"Tell her it was an accident. We were playing touch football, and you tripped and landed on a rock."

"That's good!" I watched his eyes change. Soften. To something slightly less fierce than a suddenly uncaged jungle animal. "She'll tell me a billion times to be more careful, but it won't break her heart like if she thinks somebody hit me. Yeah. Thanks. That's good."

We were almost back at his house, and he stopped dead in the middle of the sidewalk. And I knew he didn't want me to walk any closer with him. I have no idea how I knew. But I knew. Sometimes, when you're really good friends with somebody, you just know, and they don't have to say much out loud.

I opened my mouth to ask him why he'd gone after those guys the way he did.

Then I closed it again.

First of all, he'd done it for *me*. I hated to sound ungrateful. And, also, though I could not have formed it into coherent words at the time, the truth was painfully clear. Something had popped the cork on a bigger bottle of anger than the situation warranted.

"Good luck," I said.

He looked into my face for a weird length of time. It was starting to feel spooky.

"Please don't make me go out anymore," he said. It was as sincere a plea as I had heard in my young life to that date. "Please?"

"I won't. I promise."

He walked into his house to face the music, and I walked home to mine. To face the fighting.

———

My parents were indeed fighting when I got home, so I locked myself in my room. And I wrote a letter to Roy. Even though I hadn't heard back from him since my last letter.

> Dear Roy,
> I think this is kind of a weird thing to say to your big brother. And I think, if we were both home and I said this to you, you'd probably laugh at me or hang me up on the coatrack by my shirt or something. But you're not home. That's the problem.
> I love you.
> I'm sorry. I just had to say that, because I've been thinking about it but I can't remember if I ever did. Tell you, I mean.
> Be careful, and please come home.
> Your brother,
> Lucas

Chapter Seven

I'm Alive

When I got out there the following morning, Mrs. Dinsmore was nowhere to be found. And the dogs were gone. It was a jolt I felt right down through my gut and below.

I thought maybe she had put the dogs somewhere and . . . I don't know. Taken them to the pound, maybe. Or done something to herself and then one of her daughters had . . . Well, it's hard to recount what I was thinking. It was just a lot of thoughts flying in a lot of directions. All terrible.

I panicked.

I started running through the woods, yelling for the dogs. Yelling both of their names. But I had no idea of a direction, so I was more or less running in circles, flipping the hell out. If there was ever a better example of a human imitating a beheaded chicken, I haven't seen it to this day.

After a minute or two of that insanity Vermeer appeared out of nowhere and gave me a strange look, with her head tilted. As if to say, "What on earth are you so upset about?"

Then she turned back into the woods, stopping once to look over her shoulder at me. To see if I was going to follow. I followed, my heart still banging around in my chest.

She led me back to Rembrandt and Mrs. Dinsmore. The lady was sitting on a little folding chair, on a high hillock of ground that looked down through hundreds of trees at a snippet of the river. She had an artist's easel in front of her, and she was painting the forest.

She was a good painter.

I sat down on the ground next to her, still trying to settle my heart and breathing. She knew I was there. I could tell. But she didn't look directly at me or say anything. She just painted.

I liked the way she handled the light.

The sun was just barely showing behind a sea of leaves. And she had painted that, though the sun was higher in real life than on her canvas. She must've been out there working for a long time. The rays extended in a circle, clearer in a few places where gaps in the leaves let them through. It wasn't perfectly realistic, the way she had painted it. Not exactly like a photograph. It was . . . *more* somehow. A little *more* than the real sun. A little bit stylized. But she had certainly captured it.

"I like the way you do light," I said.

At first she only grunted.

Then she said, "Thanks. What were you yelling about back there?"

"Oh. I didn't know where you were. Or where the dogs had gone."

"What did you think?"

"I don't want to talk about what I thought."

I watched her work in silence for a minute, Rembrandt's big head in my lap.

"I wrote to my brother," I said. A minute or two later. "Said what I needed to say."

"Good."

"I mean, he hasn't seen it yet. I only just dropped it in the mailbox this morning. It takes forever for mail to get back and forth."

"Government work," she said.

"I'm not sure what that means."

"It means government never works very well."

"Oh."

Another long silence. I watched her work for more than a minute on one leaf. Just the way the light touched that one leaf out of hundreds. The part of the painting that should have been river was still blank white canvas. I wondered if she didn't want to paint that part. I wondered if she'd be happier if I went away and left her to work in peace.

"And I tried to be a good friend to my friend," I said. "But I didn't do a very good job of it."

"But you tried," she said.

I wasn't sure if I had her full attention or not. It was hard to tell.

"But the problem was, I tried to get him to do things that would be the right things for me to do. But I don't think they were the right things for him. I was trying to help him the way *I* thought he should be helped, but he's not me."

She let her brush hand fall to her side and looked over at me. For the first time that morning. Really studied my face.

"What?" I said. "Did I say something wrong?"

"No. Not at all. You just said something very intelligent. Something that puts you ahead of most of the adults I know."

"Oh." I hadn't expected anything like a compliment from her, and it caught me off guard. "Why do I do that?"

"Do what?"

"Try to take responsibility for everything and fix everybody."

"What makes you think *I* know?"

"Not sure. You just seem to know things."

She sighed. Scratched her nose with the back of her hand, probably to avoid getting paint on her face. "Sometimes when a kid's got nobody really running things in his life, he'll decide to take over and take charge of everything. Otherwise the world just seems to be spinning out of control. That seem to hit a note in you?"

I didn't want to say how much it did, so I just said, "You know, I could go away and leave you alone if you'd rather just paint in peace."

She sighed, and began to pack up her paints into a tote bag by her feet.

"No, that's okay. That's enough for one day anyway. I've been out here for hours. Enough is enough."

I helped her pack up, and I carried her folding chair. She slung the straps of the tote bag over one shoulder and carried the wet canvas carefully. And we walked back to the cabin together.

"What will you do with it when you're done painting it?" I asked.

"No idea," she said.

"I didn't see any paintings hanging up in the cabin."

"I don't hang them up."

"Do you sell them?"

"Not really. My daughters have a few. There are some out in the shed."

I looked up to see that we were almost back at the cabin. And I knew suddenly that I wanted to say something to her. And that it was important. And that I didn't have very much time. With Mrs. Dinsmore, you never wanted to assume you could tell her tomorrow.

"I think you should stay," I said.

She stopped walking. Shot me an odd look without really turning her head.

"Stay where?"

"You know. Not . . . go."

"Oh. That kind of stay."

"Yeah. That kind of stay."

We walked again. Up to the cabin.

She stepped up onto the porch and turned to face me. I just stood, looking down at the dirt, one hand on each of the dogs' heads.

"And why do you think that?"

"Because you help me."

"Can't really stay just for somebody else," she said.

"No, I didn't mean that. I didn't mean stay just for me."

"Well, what did you mean, then?"

"I meant . . . you have things about you . . . I just think . . . I don't know how to say what I think. I guess I think people can learn things from you. You know. So I hate to think about going back to . . . without you."

"You might be the minority opinion on that," she said. "But I'll take your thoughts under consideration."

The old me would have retreated. Not questioned her. But I was having to learn to step up. Being around Zoe Dinsmore was forcing me to be a slightly new Lucas. To be *more* somehow, like the sun in her painting.

"What exactly does that mean?" I asked, still petting the dogs' heads.

"It means I'll give your opinion the weight it deserves."

"In other words, you think it deserves nothing."

"No. I didn't say that. What *I* think I should do is more important to me than what *you* think I should do. But that doesn't mean your opinion has no value to me at all. Now, I'm going in. You should go running with the dogs. You've been missing a lot of mornings, and I think it would do all three of you good."

And with that she was gone.

The dogs and I ran. Probably six miles or more.

It did all three of us good.

———

I was jogging down Main Street by myself, doing what I more or less thought of as a cooldown, when I heard a female voice call my name.

I stopped. Turned all the way around.

At first I saw no one.

Then a second later Libby Weller stepped out of the doorway of the ice cream place, and waved at me.

I waved back, all ready to run on. But she motioned me over.

I went, because I couldn't figure a way to ignore a direct order like that one. But I really didn't want to talk about Roy.

"Hi," I said.

She was wearing short-shorts. Her legs were long and tan, and it was all I could do not to stare at them. Her hair was pulled back into a light brown ponytail. She was every bit as tall as I was, maybe even half an inch taller. And I was pretty tall. She was a year older than me, which always made it feel weird to talk to her.

"Hi," she said back.

A little shyly, I thought. What she had to be shy about . . . well, I had no idea.

"I was just going in for an ice cream soda. Want to join me?"

"Oh. I can't. I'm in training."

I would've killed for an ice cream soda, and training had nothing to do with it. If anything, another pound or two would have done me good. The problem was, I had no money in my pocket. None. And you didn't ask a girl to buy you an ice cream soda. That would be totally humiliating.

"At least come sit with me while I drink mine."

"Okay," I said.

But I really just wanted to run home.

—

"So how's Darren doing?" I asked after a minute of watching her nearly turning her cheeks inside out trying to get a plug of ice cream up and out of her straw.

She took her mouth off the straw. Frowned. I wondered if I shouldn't have asked.

"Not so good," she said. "He's depressed, I think. Nobody'll say it but me, but it's so obvious. And he's getting really frustrated. He's supposed to get a prosthetic. You know. A false foot he can strap on. But now the stump is infected, and it's much too painful. He'd rather die than put any weight on it. So it's going to be another couple of months at least. And he hates the crutches, because when he uses them, it pulls on these muscles in his chest where he took some shrapnel. So he mostly just stays in bed."

"Oh," I said, wishing I had never brought it up. "That's too bad."

"I just hope when Roy comes home, he comes home in one piece. You know. All of him."

"I just hope he comes home," I said.

She shot me a funny look, and I realized I was setting my hopes weirdly low. So I added, "Yeah, but . . . of course. Uninjured would be great."

For a good minute or more we lived out an awkward silence.

"Does he have anybody he can talk to?" I asked.

"Well. Me."

"Yeah. Right. Of course. But I guess I meant . . ."

"Somebody who knows about war stuff."

"Right."

"He has a counselor at the VA. But it's the government, so I don't know how good the guy is."

I thought about Zoe Dinsmore and what she'd said about government work. How it never works very well.

Then Libby spoke again, knocking me out of those thoughts. What she said knocked me out of everything, actually. My whole life up to that moment.

"How come you never ask me anywhere?"

Honestly. That's what she said.

"Ask you anywhere?"

"Yeah."

"Where, for example?"

"You know . . . out. For example."

Then I felt like a complete idiot. Because Connor had been right all along. And I'd been too stupid to see it. Even a second before she said it, I hadn't seen, though we'd been sitting together for several minutes and she hadn't talked about my brother much. Not even when I brought up hers. My first thought was that I wanted to tell Connor about this. Tell him he'd been right. Because that's always a good-feeling thing when somebody lets you know you were right. Then my second thought was that I shouldn't tell Connor, because it was bad enough he was stuck in his house and feeling all desperate and angry and depressed. Hearing that I was not only out and about but making a date with a pretty girl would have to be something like rubbing salt in his wounds.

"Well . . . ," I began. "I guess I just didn't know you wanted me to."

"I talk to you every chance I get."

"I thought it was just because of my brother being drafted, like yours."

"I didn't know what else to talk to you about," she said.

And with that we fell deeply into that humiliated silence. The one where you have no idea what else to talk about.

"I could ask you somewhere," I said. Anything to break the stillness. "A movie, maybe."

"That would be nice. Tonight?"

"I was thinking Saturday."

I got my allowance on Fridays. But I didn't want to say that, because it made me sound too young and too broke and too utterly ridiculous.

"Okay," she said. "I accept."

"What do you want to see?"

"I don't care. You choose."

"Okay," I said. But it was not okay. It was a huge burden, and I felt in no way up to the task. What if I chose something she hated? "I'm going to finish my run now. But I'll call you."

"You better."

I smiled without meaning to.

Then I got up and left the shop. Picked up a run before the door had even swung closed behind me. As I ran by the window she waved at me, and I waved back. I felt my face redden to a humiliating degree. Fortunately, that takes a minute to play out. And it only took a couple of seconds to run by the window. So I don't think she saw.

So that's how fast the world changes, I thought as I ran home. *I'm minding my own business, thinking it'll be a day just like any other. And then all of a sudden I realize I might be about to have a girlfriend for the first time ever.*

And I hadn't even seen it coming. But maybe you never do.

—

When the dogs met me outside the cabin the following morning, Mrs. Dinsmore was nowhere to be seen. I figured she was just inside. At first I didn't think anything about it. I was all ready to go running without giving the lady another thought.

Then I started worrying, and I didn't want that on my mind the whole run. It was hard enough trying not to think about Libby Weller. Add a worry onto that and I figured I'd probably crash into a tree or something.

I stepped up onto her porch and rapped on the door.

"Mrs. Dinsmore?" I called.

"I'm alive, Lucas," she called back.

"That's good to hear, ma'am."

"It's what you wanted to know, isn't it?"

"Pretty much, ma'am. Yeah."

"Then go run."

I made eye contact with the dogs and launched myself from the porch, and then we were off.

We hadn't gotten more than an eighth of a mile before it started to mist rain. That was unusual for June, to put it mildly. First I slowed, thinking we might have to go back. Then I thought, *What the hell?* It wasn't cold—in fact, it was clammy and warm. So if I got wet . . . so what?

I ran faster, and the dogs kept pace with me, and then the rain came down harder. Bigger drops. It made all three of us blink and squint our eyes against it, but we didn't stop.

We ran all the way to the cemetery. Because I'd been thinking about it. And I wanted to see it again. I wanted to stand in front of those two grave markers again, now that I knew who those two young people were, and how they intersected with my life. I wanted to see what I would feel.

The old yellow flowers had been taken away. They had not been left there to wither. In their place were two similar stalks, but blooming with purple flowers. They looked like they must have come from the same garden or shop as the last ones. Only the color had changed. They looked fresh.

I read the names of the children again, but I can't really say what I felt. I didn't know them, so I didn't know what to feel. But I did feel bad for the people who *had* known them. It was just obvious that I hadn't gotten to be one of them. Part of me regretted that. Painful as it must have been, I felt as though I'd missed something important.

Then we shortened our run by jogging straight home from there. Not because I was soaked to the skin, although I was, but because the leaves and pine needles under my feet were getting too slippery. As I did, I let the tragedy of the past fall away, and the excitement of my first date come back in to replace it. Part of me felt bad about that. But it happened all the same.

I came back at a light jog for the sake of safety, the dogs trotting beside me. Halfway back to the cabin the rain stopped, and the sun came out. Just like that. The sky was blue everywhere except to the east, where the clouds had gone.

Mrs. Dinsmore was outside the cabin when we got there. She was around the side of the place, standing on a short stepladder cleaning the windows with a rag. The same windows I'd looked through when I'd seen her that first time. When I thought I might be looking at a corpse. And I wasn't far enough from wrong, either.

She turned partway when she saw me.

"I hate dirty windows," she called to me. "Especially water-spotted ones. What's the point of living out in the middle of nature if you can't even have a good look at it out your windows?"

I didn't answer. Just moved closer and watched her work for a minute.

Then I said, "Can I get your advice about something?"

"I suppose."

"If you're going to take a person to a movie, and this person says it's up to you to pick which movie, how do you pick? I mean, how do you know how to pick so you don't end up with something this person'll hate?"

She wrapped up her work on the window right about then. Stuffed the rag into her overalls pocket. As she backed down off the stepladder, she looked right into my face.

"So *that's* why you're grinning like a damn fool," she said. "You have yourself a date with a girl."

I hadn't known I was grinning. But when she said that, I checked my own face. You know, from behind. And I do think I might have had some of that "nervous cheeks" thing going on. I wondered if that was why my mother had been staring at me over dinner the night before. It had been just the two of us. My father had been late coming home from work, and my mother didn't like him nearly enough anymore to hold dinner.

"I do have a date," I said. "And I just thought you might be able to help me with the picking problem. Because I'm not a girl. And you are. Or you were. Or, anyway . . . you're female, is what I mean to say." I felt my words get stumbly and my face hot. "I guess I really stepped in something with that, didn't I?"

"Your good intentions will excuse it this time. Did you look in the paper or call the theater to see what's playing over in Blaine?"

Blaine had the closest theater. Three screens. Ashby was too small to have a theater. Not even a one-screener.

"I did, yeah."

"So what are your choices?"

"There's that western with John Wayne. And then there's a scary one. I forget the title, but it's supposed to be really bloody. And then the one about the little VW Beetle car that talks. Or maybe it doesn't talk. Maybe it just flies or something. I saw a trailer for it, but I don't remember much about it now."

"Interesting," she said. She folded up the stepladder. Tucked it under her arm. "An interesting set of options."

"Interesting how?"

I walked with her to the shed to put the stepladder away. That seemed to be the only way I was going to get my advice.

"Because each choice says a lot about you as a date. Let's say you choose the western. I can't say for a fact that this gal doesn't like westerns. Some girls might. But she's less likely to enjoy them than you are. And even if she does, choosing the boy movie might be seen as a way of saying, 'Well, you let me have my choice, so I just chose what *I* wanted.' Might come off a little selfish. Now, a lot of boys'll pick the horror flick for a date. Even though that runs the risk of putting her in a terrible mood and making her have an upsetting time. Know why they might pick that one anyway?"

I stopped outside the shed and waited for her.

"No, ma'am. I don't think I do."

"Because they're hoping for the girl to snuggle in close when she gets scared. But here's the thing you need to know about girls: We're not stupid. We know about how boys do that on purpose. We can figure stuff out. So you run the risk of her thinking you're only after one thing."

"I'm not," I said, disturbed by my motives being questioned even in casual conversation.

"I didn't think so," she said. "But you don't want her to get the wrong impression."

"So, the *Love Bug* one."

"Sounds like a safe choice. It's a comedy, right?"

"Yeah."

"Well, that's good, I think. A comedy. That sends the message that you want her to have a nice time. That you're trying to make a fun date for her."

We started back toward the cabin together.

I felt layers of stress dropping away with every step. It was so easy. Just take her to see the *Love Bug* movie. I couldn't believe I'd wasted half the night tossing and turning over something that had proved to be so simple.

"Thanks," I said. "That's good advice."

"Worth it to have somebody call me a girl again," she said. "It's been a while."

Chapter Eight

The Key

I knocked on Libby's door promptly at six. And by promptly I mean I'd walked around the block for ten minutes, glancing obsessively at my watch. Then I'd stood on her welcome mat watching the second hand tick around to the top of the hour. It was all downright silly, looking back.

I was wearing clean khaki pants that I'd pressed myself, and a short-sleeved white shirt. And a necktie. Probably overkill, but that was me at fourteen. Overkill Boy.

Besides, I knew I was going to have to meet her parents first. She'd told me.

Libby answered the door, and the way she smiled at me made my knees wobbly. I had to pay attention to standing steady.

She was wearing her hair long and straight, falling around her shoulders, and a peachy-colored, off-the-shoulders light dress, like a sundress. It had high short sleeves and a short skirt, and once again I had to work hard not to stare at the wrong places.

"Sorry about this," she said, tossing her head back over her shoulder to indicate something in the house behind her. I knew what she meant.

She was embarrassed that her parents insisted on meeting me. "They're kind of old-fashioned that way."

"It's not a problem," I said.

She stepped back and I walked in.

It was true and it wasn't true, what I'd said. I understood her parents wanting to meet me. She was their only daughter. And who was I, after all? It was a small town, of course, so I wasn't a literal stranger to them. They probably could have picked me out of a crowd and told you my name and who my parents were, along with what my father did for a living. But we had never sat down and talked, so I guess they weren't sure enough of who I had grown up to be. So I got where they were coming from. But it *was* a problem—to me, anyway. It made me so nervous that, if I made the mistake of stopping to think about it, I felt like my seams were unraveling all down the inside of me.

I took a deep breath and followed her into the living room. And I forcefully put all the fear and insecurity stuff aside. Just locked it out for the time being.

Her parents stood to greet me, and I stepped up to each one of them, starting with her mom, and shook their hands with pretend confidence.

"Mrs. Weller," I said. "Pleased to meet you."

I was careful that my grip was firm when shaking her father's hand. Not aggressive or challenging. Just firm.

"Mr. Weller. Pleased to meet you."

They motioned for me to sit.

I perched on the edge of the couch, trying to look less nervous than I felt, and Libby sat close to my left hip.

"So you're Bart and Ellie Painter's boy," her father said. He was smoking a filterless cigarette, high up in the crook between his first and second fingers, and it was burning dangerously low.

"Yes, sir."

"How *are* your parents?"

"Very good, sir. Thank you for asking."

They weren't very good. They were never very good. But that's not what you say when a grown-up asks.

"And you're their older boy?"

Libby's mother answered for me. She was sitting in a stuffed wing chair with wild paisley upholstery, smoothing her skirt with her hands as though she just realized she'd forgotten to iron it.

"No, honey, their older boy is Leroy and he's overseas. Remember?"

"Oh, that's right. Sorry, son. I have trouble keeping the local boys straight. You know our Darren just got home from overseas."

"Yes, sir," I said. "I did know about that."

"I guess word gets around," he said. Then he let an awkward pause fall. "Well, enough pleasantries. Let's get right down to it. What will you two young people be doing when you walk out our door tonight?"

"Well, sir. We're going to walk down to the bus stop on the corner. Catch the thirty-three line into Blaine and get off at the Triplex Theater. See a movie. Afterwards we can get a soda or an ice cream if Libby wants one. And then I'll bring her right home. Shouldn't be later than nine thirty or ten, even with the soda."

"And what are you planning to see?" Mrs. Weller asked.

"I was thinking we'd see that Herbie the Love Bug movie. About the car that . . ." I still didn't remember exactly what the car did that was so different. But it was no ordinary car. ". . . kind of has a mind of its own."

Mrs. Weller sat back in her chair in a gesture that I can only describe as satisfied. She had been leaning slightly forward, as if grilling me. And the grilling had just ended.

I had passed the test.

"Well, I think that's a very good choice," she said. "I've heard it's funny. And it's a very wholesome film. I think it speaks well of you to choose it. I was afraid you were going to say you intended to see that awful slasher movie."

"Oh, no, ma'am. I don't like all the blood and gore."

"You two have a good time, then," Mr. Weller said. Which meant I had passed his test as well.

A silence fell, but it wasn't awkward. It was peaceful and encouraging. As if nothing more needed to be said.

In that moment I was filled with a feeling. I doubt I had words for it at the time, but even then I could've told you it had something to do with Zoe Dinsmore.

I have words for it now. Zoe Dinsmore had solved the riddle of the movie for me. And now, having won Libby's parents' approval with that choice, I felt as though Mrs. Dinsmore had pressed a key into my hand, and that key had just opened up some secret part of the universe that had always been a mystery to me. Sounds like an exaggeration, but I guess you'd have to know how utterly baffled I'd been by life up until then.

A movement caught my eye, and I looked up to see Darren leaning in the doorway to the living room. The movement had been his final hop.

He had no crutches with him, and he was wearing only white boxer shorts and a short-sleeved white undershirt. My eyes went straight down to his missing leg. I couldn't help it. It was bandaged, and it looked too narrow at the end to be a full-size calf like the one on the other side. It was weirdly tapered. But the shocking thing to me was not what was above the line of amputation, but what was below it.

Nothing.

Funny how we get so adjusted to exactly what we should see on every human body we encounter. And then when it's missing, it's just . . . well, I already said "shocking," but it's really the only word that fits the bill.

He also had a lot of scarring on the exposed parts of his legs. Places that you could see had recently held stitches.

I forced my eyes up to his face again.

Everybody stood—Libby and both of her parents—so I stood, too. It seemed to be in response to Darren's presence, but I wasn't sure why. It was something like the way men stand when a lady walks into the room, but it had a different feel to it. A darker feel.

"Darren, honey," Mrs. Weller said, "we have company, and you're not dressed."

"Come 'ere," Darren said. But not to his mother. He was ignoring her entirely. He was staring straight at me.

I didn't move at first. I was feeling frozen.

He said it again.

"No, really. Come 'ere. Don't make me go over there. It's too hard."

I walked to where he stood leaning in the doorway, steadying himself on the frame. I was afraid, but I didn't know why. Afraid of him, afraid of what he might be about to say. Afraid of what he knew about what my brother was going through. I couldn't even sort it all out in my head.

I stopped and stood in front of him, feeling like I owed it to him to let him say or do whatever he had on his mind. I just opened myself up to that moment.

When he spoke, his voice was soft and low. Nothing like before.

"How's Roy doing?"

"I think . . . ," I began. Then I realized I wasn't going to lie to him. Or even smooth down the truth. He knew too much. And he deserved more. "I think he's having a really rough time."

"Well, yeah. He's normal. And it's Nam. Of course he's having a rough time. Who wouldn't? But he's not, like . . . injured or anything?"

"No. He's not injured."

"Good. Let's hope it stays that way."

"Did you . . ." But then I got stuck in the middle of the thought.

"Did I what?"

"Did you know him? Over there?"

"No, not over *there*. I knew 'im. But I never saw 'im in Nam. It's a big country, and we're all over it. I just knew Roy from growing up in town. Had a drink with him the night before he shipped out. Right before I found out I was going, too. Never saw a guy that scared in my whole life. I mean, until I got over there. But I haven't seen 'im since."

"Right," I said. "Got it."

I guess I'd been hoping he had some kind of inside information about Roy. Maybe he'd been hoping the same about me. I let that expectation go again. It hurt a little on its way out.

"Next time you write to 'im, tell 'im I said hi."

"I will."

And with that he turned and hopped his way back down the hallway, sliding his hand along the wall for support.

I turned around to see Libby standing right behind me.

"We should go," I said. "We don't want to miss our bus."

———

Halfway to the end of the block she slipped her hand into mine. I got that funny feeling in my knees again, and a strange sensation in my low belly. Buzzy, like electricity. But I liked it.

"You didn't tell me your brother was having a rough time," she said, breaking a long silence.

I could've told her that I'd only learned about it from his last letter. And, since I'd told her I hadn't heard from him last time she asked, that would make it sound as though I'd heard about his troubles more recently. It would have been a half truth, if I had gone that route.

Or I could've quoted her brother.

"Well, yeah. He's normal. And it's Nam. Of course he's having a rough time. Who wouldn't?"

I didn't.

I decided that if somebody is your girlfriend, or might be about to become your girlfriend, you probably owe her a different level of the truth. I figured, for somebody like that, you can just damn well do better.

"I know," I said. "And I'm sorry about that. It was a thing I was having trouble talking about."

She gave my hand a squeeze.

We walked the rest of the way to the bus stop in silence.

———

"So what did you think of the movie?" I asked her as we walked out into the dusky night.

I was so on edge waiting to know that I'd stuck my hands in my pockets so she wouldn't see them shaking. Or reach for one and feel it shaking.

"I liked it," she said.

I breathed for what felt like the first time in months. Why was I so tied up in knots inside when I was young? I swear I have no idea.

"Didn't *you* like it?" she asked when she realized I was not about to answer.

It was a complicated question. I'd been of two minds about it all through the film, and trying to guess which way her mind was going. I felt like . . . if I could only know her opinion, I'd know which view was "right." It was possible to stand outside the movie and think it was silly, or to stop judging and go with it and think it was funny. But all I could do was shift back and forth, wondering what my date was thinking.

"Sure," I said. "It was funny."

We walked right past the soda shop, and she said nothing about stopping. I breathed a great sigh of relief, as quietly as possible.

Libby had wanted popcorn, a soda, and a giant candy bar during the film. So I guessed she was too full for an ice cream soda now. But

I'd been a little scared about that, because I now had just enough money for the bus home for both of us, with only about fifteen cents change. I would've had to tell her out loud that I couldn't afford it, which would have been humiliating.

I took my hands out of my pocket, because now they were holding still. I reached one out in her direction, and she reached back and took hold of it. And we walked toward the bus stop that way.

A grown-up lady with a bag of groceries passed us on the sidewalk, coming toward us, and she smiled approvingly at our faces. And then at our linked hands. I took it to mean that we looked like a nice young couple. It made me think maybe we were, which opened up my thinking about the world quite a bit in that moment.

And then, of course, I got too honest.

"I'm glad you liked the movie," I said, "because I was really worried about that."

She stopped dead on the sidewalk, and her hand tugged at mine until I stopped, too.

"Why would you worry about a thing like that?" she asked.

And I thought, *Oh great. I've gone and done it now. I let her look at the inside of something about me, and now it turns out it's completely weird in there.*

"I just wanted you to have a good time," I said.

"That's nice. But it's not like you made the movie yourself or anything."

"But I picked it out. I didn't want you to think I had terrible taste in movies."

"But you hadn't seen it. If you'd seen it nine times and really wanted me to see it the tenth time with you, and I hated it, I might think you had bad taste in movies. Which isn't the most terrible thing in the world, by the way. But you were just guessing. Anybody can guess wrong."

"Hmm," I said.

We started to walk again.

"I guess I worry too much," I said.

"Well, at least you worry about nice things, like whether I'll have a good time."

Just for a minute I was filled with a great feeling. Like she wasn't judging me and it really was okay to be myself around her. I think the only reason the feeling didn't last longer is because we saw the bus coming. And we had to run.

———

I walked her up onto her front porch, and to her door. By then it was mostly dark out, but the porch light was on. It was glaring, and I found myself blinking because of it. Blinking too much.

"Well . . . ," I said.

And she said, "Well . . . ," in return.

She wasn't going to let me off the hook on this. I was the one who had to find the perfect words to wrap this up.

"I sure had a nice time with you tonight," I said.

"Me too," she said.

She was standing close, and she had her face turned up toward mine in a way I could only think of as . . . well, I hated to think it was expectant, because then it would be on me to know what she was expecting. I'm not trying to suggest I had no idea at all. I wasn't a total child, and I hadn't just crawled out from under a rock. I knew what tended to happen at the end of dates. I just wasn't sure *enough* that I was right about what she wanted.

It hit me that all through the date I'd let her make the first moves. She was the one who'd reached out and taken my hand. On the way out. On the bus. In the movie. Even on the way home, when I reached a hand out to her, I just reached it out. And waited.

There was just no getting around that for me. It was the only way I knew how to be. I had to be sure of what she wanted. I couldn't be one of those boys who just took what he wanted from a girl. That was utterly foreign to me.

"I'd like to call you," I said.

"You better."

"And see you again."

"I should hope so."

"Well okay, then."

"Well okay," she said.

The moment was getting more awkward. It felt like she was driving me toward a kiss by steering the conversation down a dead-end street. But I still wasn't sure enough.

To make matters worse, I had never kissed a girl before. And now that you know how much I worried about whether she'd like the film, you can imagine my horror over her possibly not liking the kiss.

"Well," I said. "Good night."

I turned to walk away.

Yes, I was really going to chicken out. It seemed the only way to get out of the situation and off her porch in one emotional piece.

"Hey!" she said.

I stopped. Turned back.

"Aren't you even going to kiss me good night?"

So that took care of the first part of the equation. I was now sure of what she wanted.

I stepped in close, and she turned her face up in that expectant way. She had her eyes closed, so I closed mine. And I leaned in. And I just did it. Right or wrong, I had to try.

I pressed my lips lightly against hers and held them there. Maybe for the count of two.

Then I went to pull away.

But I didn't get away.

She put her hand on the back of my head, and *she* kissed *me*. More deeply this time.

It wasn't hard to know what to do, even though I was a total novice, because all I had to do was respond. Accept her lips with mine and do the same in return. I wondered how many boys she had kissed before. She seemed to know what she was doing.

Then I started liking the kissing. Really liking it, and not worrying about doing it wrong, because nothing that wonderful could be wrong. And then it was me kissing her again, but more firmly. Less hesitantly.

And then the porch light started flashing.

Off. On. Off. On.

We stepped apart.

"I think I'm wanted inside," she said.

"Yeah. Seems that way." I sounded like I was out of breath. Because I was.

"Good night."

"Good night," I said.

I waited until I saw she was safely inside, then stepped down off her porch and started the long walk home. Not two seconds later I broke into a full-on sprint. I needed a way to vent all that energy.

I had this wonderful feeling inside as I ran. Like I'd gotten a sneak peek into love, and it was okay in there. It wasn't a terrible place where I'd be torn limb from limb. I could go there like everybody else.

I was flying along the sidewalk, hardly noticing my feet touching down, and I was thinking, *I can go to this love place and I can be okay.*

And, as the old saying goes . . . that's what I get for thinking.

Chapter Nine

The Belonging

When I got out to the cabin the following morning, the front door was yawning wide open. Mrs. Dinsmore was standing in the doorway, a toolbox at her feet, tinkering with the lock her daughter and I had so poorly installed.

"You're alive," I said, the dogs whipping the backs of my thighs with their strong tails.

I thought it was a subject I could half kid her about. It felt like it had become something of a dark private joke between us. But the minute it was out of my mouth, I doubted my words, and my nerve in saying them.

If she was offended, she never let on.

"Seems that way," she said. Then her hands stopped moving, and she looked right into my face. "I was going to ask you how your date went. But now that I've looked at your goofy grinning face, there's really no need."

"She liked the movie," I said.

She didn't answer, so I just sat down on the edge of the porch and watched her work for a minute or two. Rembrandt plunked his big butt down on my left foot, and Vermeer kept licking the air about an inch from my face.

"Why do I worry so much what people think of me?" I asked the lady.

It surprised me. A lot. I'd had no idea I'd been about to ask that.

"Because you're human?" She asked it like a question. Like maybe she wasn't sure either.

"So you're saying everybody's like that?"

"Some more than others, I suppose. Being young doesn't help. Younger you are, the more you're not sure what's the right way to be in the world. The more you think you might be getting it wrong, the more sensitive you'll be about it. As you get older, like me, you stop caring so much what people think." She tinkered in silence for a second or two, working with a screw that didn't seem to want to go in straight. Then she added, "Not sure anybody ever stops caring completely, though."

"Can I ask your advice about another thing?"

I could hear her sigh from a good four paces away.

"Have I got a choice?"

It stung me a little. I won't lie.

"Never mind," I said. "It's okay."

She sighed again, and set down her screwdriver. Came and sat with me on the edge of the porch.

"Sorry," she said. "I was just being snarky. Sometimes I think it's expected of me. Go ahead and ask."

"Thanks." I think I was more relieved than I cared to let on. "I want to take her out for another date. The sooner the better. But now I'm totally broke. I've got fifteen cents to my name. And after I get my next allowance again, well . . . I want to take her out to eat. Maybe lunch, maybe dinner. I guess lunch is cheaper, but dinner is fancier. But even if I've just gotten my allowance, I don't think I can afford that. Unless I just take her to the Burger Barn. But even at the Burger Barn . . . I can't tell her what to order. What if she gets the most expensive thing on the menu? And then I have to just get water. But she'd see right through that and know I was out of money. Besides, who takes a date to the Burger Barn? It's a date. It's supposed to be someplace nice. Why is it so expensive to take a girl out on a date?"

I stopped. Breathed.

The air around the four of us seemed to throb with all those words.

"Whew," she said. "It really *is* a tough place inside that brain of yours, isn't it?"

I didn't answer, because I didn't know what to say. I wanted to ask if it was too weird in there. If she thought there was something abnormal about me. But if I'd asked, she might've answered.

"Okay," she said. "Here's what you do. You get yourself a nice big basket."

That was definitely not the direction I'd expected the conversation to go.

"*Basket?* What kind of basket?"

"Just some nice big basket with a handle, like maybe a gardening basket. I've probably got something if you don't."

"My mom has a basket she used to use when we'd go out and get produce from the farm stands. Back when we used to take Sunday drives. You know. The whole family."

Back when my brother wasn't off fighting a war and my parents could stand to be in the same car together, but I didn't say that. I still had no idea what a basket had to do with taking a girl out for a meal.

"That's perfect. So you take the basket. Make sure it's nice and clean. Wash it under the hose and then dry it out in the sun if you have to. Then you go into the fridge and make some sandwiches. You know how to make sandwiches, right?"

"Yeah. Sure."

"Now, I don't know what kind of food and stuff your mom tends to keep around the house. Maybe you'll find everything you need right in the fridge, and it'll be free. Or maybe you'll have to get a few things at the store. Either way, it'll be cheaper than the Burger Barn. You'll need a couple of sandwiches for each of you. Don't want to run out of food in case she's hungry. Maybe some fresh fruit. Bananas or apples. Or both. And a couple sodas. If your mom has cloth napkins, bring two of those. They're nicer. If not, paper napkins'll have to do. Maybe something sweet for dessert. You pack all this stuff up in the basket. And then you get a nice tablecloth. I'm sure your mom will have something around. Don't use a white one—it'll get dirty and she'll shoot you if all the stains don't come out. Iron it if you have to. Fold it up all nice and neat and put it on top of the food in the basket. Like a cover. Then you take it over to this girl's house and you say, 'I decided a picnic would be more romantic.' Take her to some nice quiet spot out in these woods with a pretty view. Looking back down over the town, or overlooking the river. Most people think the river is a nice view. I don't, but she probably will."

I sat a minute, letting the sheer brilliance of her plan sink in.

"A picnic," I said when I could find my words again. "Ooh. That's *good*."

"Wait. There's one more thing. You got any kind of flowers growing in your yard at home?"

"My mom has rosebushes all along the back fence."

"That'll do it. Go out and pick the nicest, most perfect rose you've got. Just one. Make sure you cut the stem real nice and long. And break the thorns off it so she doesn't stick herself on them when you hand it to her. Put it on top of the food, right under the tablecloth. And when you uncover everything, take the rose out and hand it to her and tell her, 'Here. This is for you.' Then go about setting up your picnic just so. She'll like that."

We sat for another silent moment.

Then I got up off the porch and fell to my knees in front of her. Literally. Fell to my knees. And there had been no forethought about it.

"Please don't go," I said. "You help me so much. Nobody else tells me these things. Please?"

She sighed and turned her face away.

"We've been through this before," she said.

"No we haven't. I told you I thought you should stay. Thought it. Just words in my head. Now I'm telling you how I really feel about it. You know things I don't know, that no other grown-up I know seems to know. Or at least that they're willing to tell me. What would I do if I couldn't come ask you these things?"

I was hoping I'd broken through to a new place between us. But when she answered, I knew I had only hit a wall that would prevent me from getting there.

"You'd figure it out on your own, trial and error, like everybody else. Now get up off your knees, boy."

I did as I'd been told.

"Okay," I said. "Sorry. I'm going to go running with the dogs now. I didn't mean to upset you."

"Whatever," she said. "Yeah. Go run."

But before I could get a step away, she stopped me with a kinder thought.

"You let me know how that picnic idea turns out."

"Yes, ma'am," I said. "I will."

It was always a give-and-take with Zoe Dinsmore. But then I couldn't let myself get too confused about it, or think too hard. Because the dogs and I were running. And I didn't want to smack into a tree.

—

I had been avoiding going over to Connor's house for a few days, and not really talking to myself about why. But I knew I couldn't go on that way much longer.

I jogged by his house on the way home. Didn't even bother to go home and clean up and change out of my running clothes first. I thought if I waited too long, I might talk myself out of going.

To my surprise, Connor was outside.

He was in the backyard, in just a pair of long khaki shorts, sunning himself on one of those cheap folding lawn-chair-type lounges. The kind with the plastic webbing. I could see the vague shape of him through the fence when I was still halfway down the block.

I walked up his driveway and sat down in the grass beside him. The skin of his chest was pasty white, and I worried about Connor getting a vicious sunburn. I could see every one of his ribs, but without any appearance of sinewy muscle stretched over them. Just skin and ribs. He looked like a guy who'd been sick for a long time.

First he said nothing at all.

Then he made a face and said, "Phew! Mind sitting downwind of me?"

"Sorry," I said.

I moved to the other side of his lounge.

Under different circumstances I might have gotten a little ticky about a comment like that. But he was mad at me for not coming by, and I knew it. And he was going to lash out at me, and I should've seen it coming. And I deserved it.

"I guess it's bound to happen," he said. Then a long pause. Then, "Running in all this heat."

"What're you doing outside in the sun? Seems unlike you."

"It was my mom's idea. She thinks I'm getting too pale."

"Oh," I said. What else could I say?

I sat there with him in silence for a minute, cross-legged on the grass. Then I noticed the garage door was open. And there was only one car in it. His mother's car. And it was Saturday.

"Where's your dad's car?" I asked, not realizing it was a big question. Mistakenly thinking it was harmless small talk.

"With my dad, I guess."

"Where's your dad?"

"No idea."

"You didn't ask your mom?"

"I asked. She has no idea."

I just sat a minute. Wondering if I should say more or not. I was beginning to get a sense of the weight of that whole thing.

"How long's he been gone?" I asked after a time.

"Three days."

He didn't go on to say, "If you'd come by to see me, you'd've known that already." Then again, he didn't need to. It went without saying.

My mind was spinning around in circles, wondering what that meant. Wondering whether I should ask.

But Connor stopped my mind in its tracks.

"When were you planning on telling me?" he asked. His voice sounded stiff. Rehearsed, almost. And like we didn't really know each other very well. Like the voice you use with a stranger you sit next to on a bus bench.

"Tell you what?"

"That you're dating Libby Weller now."

"Oh. That. It's pretty new. How did you even know about it?"

"I watched the two of you walk by my house holding hands yesterday. You must know I have nothing better to do than sit up in my room and stare out the window."

I was stunned. Not so much by the fact that he'd seen it. And said it. More by the fact that it had never crossed my mind. I'd been so busy holding Libby's hand that it never occurred to me that the walk to the bus stop took us right by Connor's house. How could I not have thought of that? How did a girl's hand have that kind of power over me? When you stepped out of the thing and looked at it from a distance, it didn't make much sense at all.

"It was our first date," I said. "I was going to tell you."

"Well, I figured. When I saw you were here just now, I waited. I waited for a few minutes. You know. For you to say something like, 'Hey. Big news!' I mean, it *is* big news. It's sort of huge. And I'm your best friend."

"You are," I said. I couldn't think what else to say.

"Did you figure I was so miserable and my life was such a mess that it would break me into a million pieces to hear that something good happened to you for a change?"

Now, I like to tell the truth. More and more as I've gotten older. But I was pretty attached to the truth even back then, if only because it stressed me out to have to juggle chunks of fiction and keep track of what I'd said. So much easier to stick with the facts. But this was one of those situations where the truth simply would not do. Because the truth was, yeah, that's exactly what I'd figured. And that would've been a pretty cruel thing to go and say.

"No," I said. "It's not that at all. I just . . . I just wanted to wait and see if we even liked each other. If there was even going to be a second date. I think I just didn't want to tell anybody I was getting my hopes all up. Because then if it came to nothing, I'd have to tell them. And they'd see how disappointed I was. And then they'd be all disappointed *for* me. And that's worse than anything."

I paused, in case he had thoughts he wanted to voice. While I waited, it bothered me just a little that it was so easy for me to make up such an intricate lie. But then I thought back over what I'd just said, and there might have been a grain of truth to it.

He wasn't saying anything. So I added, "You know what I mean about that, don't you?"

"Yeah," he said. "Sure."

He didn't sound all that sure.

We sat in silence for a weird length of time. Quite a few minutes. I was getting tired of baking in the sun. I wanted to go home and take a shower. Make plans for a romantic picnic.

I looked over at Connor, and saw that his chest was broken out in beads of sweat.

"Don't stay out too long," I said. "You'll burn to a crisp."

"Oh," he said. A little surprised, as if I'd wakened him. "You going?"

"I think so, yeah."

"Okay."

"But I'll come by again. Sooner. I mean, I won't let so much time go by this time. That's what I mean."

"Okay."

I pulled to my feet. Stared down at him for a minute. His eyes were squeezed closed.

"Think your dad's coming back?"

I hated to ask. The last thing I wanted to do was upset him. But how weird would it be to act like it wasn't a big deal, or like I didn't even care?

"No idea," he said. "And don't say ask my mom, because she has no idea either."

"Oh. Sorry. I hope he does. I mean, I hope he does if you hope he does. Do you hope he does?"

I was making a mess of things and I knew it.

"Yeah. I hope he does. I don't know what my mom's going to do without him. She's pretty broken up about it."

"Sorry," I said.

"Not your fault."

"Still sorry."

Then I didn't know what else to say. So I just said goodbye and jogged home, thinking. Well, actually, I was trying *not* to think. But that didn't go my way at all.

—

My mom was in the kitchen when I got home. And I wanted her not to be. I wanted to look around and see what we had in the way of picnic ingredients. But you don't just ask your own mother to leave her own kitchen.

She was leaning her back against the fridge, reading some kind of women's magazine. Holding it with one hand, its pages folded back. In her other hand was a half-eaten apple that she seemed to be ignoring.

She looked up and blinked at me. As though she'd expected to look up and see some entirely different scene.

"Lucas," she said.

I wondered where my father was. It was Saturday, and the house was quiet, so he must've been far, far away. Golfing, maybe. Or now, in retrospect, I think he might even have been having an affair. I was getting used to his unexplained absences, which had been accelerating.

"Who else would it be?" But it wasn't really as grumpy as I make it sound. Just a tossed-off comment, meant to be halfway funny.

"I didn't see you last night. Your father was out late, and I think I might've fallen asleep on the couch before you got in. How was your date?"

"It was good. Actually."

"Don't sound so surprised. I always thought she seemed nice, that Weller girl. Are you going to see her again?"

"Yeah," I said. "Looks that way." Then I took a big, deep breath and faced a new path through the world: I decided to take a chance on letting my mother know my plans. Not the easiest thing for a fourteen-year-old guy to do. "I was thinking I'd invite her out on a picnic. So I was wondering if we have stuff around. For a picnic. Like sandwich stuff and fruit and some kind of dessert. Drinks. Because I spent my whole allowance last night, so if we don't have what I need, I won't be able to ask her out again until after I get my allowance Friday. Which seems like a really long wait."

She smiled in a way that struck me as a bit sarcastic. Looking back, anyway. At the time I probably just felt like she was making fun of me.

"Ah, to be fourteen again. Where a week feels like a lifetime."

She set her magazine down on the drainboard of the sink, which I could see was wet. I wondered why she hadn't noticed that. She threw her half-eaten apple into the trash bin under the sink.

She opened the fridge and began to root around in there.

"A picnic," she said. Like it was just such an amazing word that she had to say it out loud. Savor it. "What a nice idea. You really are growing up to be a thoughtful young man. You know that?"

"Thank you," I said. But I felt bad. Because I never would have thought of such an idea. Not if you'd given me a hundred years to think.

"Where are you going to go for your picnic?"

See? This is why I tended not to share stuff with my mother, who would be horrified to hear I had ever stepped foot into those dark, dangerous woods.

"The park, I guess."

No answer for a time. Just the sound of her rooting in the fridge. I was thinking that was a lot of cold escaping.

"Well, I think we're in good shape," she said, pulling her head out and swinging the door closed. "We have sliced turkey. Ham. Then in the cupboard we have some canned things—tuna fish and deviled ham. Bananas and oranges. You know I don't like you to have sodas, but if you insist in this case, you can buy your own. But we have bottled apple juice and orange juice if that'll do. And those cookies you like."

"Do we have cloth napkins?"

Then I had to look away because of the expression that came over her face.

"Cloth napkins? My, my! Aren't we the fancy guy? This girl must be very special."

"Jeez, Mom. Can you just answer a question the normal way for a change?"

"Yes, you can use two of the good napkins. But bring them back! And we have a couple of print tablecloths I wouldn't mind you using on the grass. I can always bleach them."

"So I'm set," I said, eyeing her rosebushes through the kitchen window.

"Looks that way. Is it time for us to have the talk?"

For a minute, I didn't know what talk she meant. Then I looked away from the roses and into her face, and then I did. Horrifyingly did.

"Oh my God, Mom! Please. No! We're just going to eat sandwiches. How could you even bring a thing like that up?"

"You're growing up," she said. "Much as I hate to admit it."

"I'm going up to my room."

Before I could even get out of the kitchen, I could feel my face going beet red. I remember thinking, *Right. That's why I never talk to my mom about real stuff. How could I have forgotten?*

———

I was lying on my back, reading a comic book. Or so it would have seemed to anybody who walked into my room. In reality I had been staring at the same page for probably half an hour.

I was obsessed with the details of making food for a picnic. *Obsessed.* I couldn't stop thinking about whether she would like sweet-pickle relish in the tuna, along with the mayonnaise. And how much mustard to put on the turkey. And whether to bring some kind of trash bag for the orange and banana peels, so they wouldn't just sit around on the tablecloth and look nasty.

I knew it was stupid, and a waste of my time. But the details wouldn't let me go. So I just lay there, wishing I could think about something else.

Then, a minute later, I got my wish.

Be careful what you wish for.

My mom rapped on the door to my room.

"Someone here to see you, Lucas," she said through the door.

I flew off the bed. I swear I don't even know how I made that move, and I never could've made it again. It was something like levitating.

I threw the door open. It seemed to startle her.

"Is it Libby?" I asked, my voice sounding out of breath.

"No, it's Mrs. Barnes."

"Mrs. Barnes?"

"Yeah. You know. Connor's mom?"

I know who Mrs. Barnes is, I thought.

I just had no idea why she would be here to see me.

Then, as I was flying down the stairs, I started to be able to think of some possible reasons. And, oh, they were not good.

It was all my fault. I had that in my head already. Something had happened to Connor. He had done something terrible. And it was all because I hadn't been a good enough friend to him. Mrs. Dinsmore had tried to tell me to be a good friend to him. And I'd gone and fallen down on the job.

I should've gone to see him the minute I found out I had a date with Libby Weller. Told him the big news. I should have gone straight to his house this morning to tell him all the details of how it had gone.

And now I could never change it. And I would have to live with it all my life.

Now I was about to find out how it felt to be Zoe Dinsmore.

I stepped into the living room and looked at Connor's mom, and she looked back at me. She seemed concerned. Her lips were drawn into a tight line. But she was not crying. She didn't look as though her whole world had come to an end.

"Is Connor okay?" I asked, wondering why it was so hard for me to manage my own breath all of a sudden.

"Why, yes," she said. "He's fine."

I just stood a minute, letting all the awful thoughts rush out of me. When they had gone, I was left with just one new thought.

I have another chance and I'm not going to blow it this time.

My mom stepped into the room behind me and invited Mrs. Barnes to sit down. I sat on the couch, and Connor's mom perched next to me, holding her purse tightly in her lap.

"I want to ask you a question," Mrs. Barnes said. "And it's very important that you give me an honest answer."

So already I was in a minefield. Because you never want to be in a position to have to give truthful answers to your best friend's mom. There are sacred trusts involved.

"What is it, ma'am? What do you need to know?"

She sighed. Leaned back ever so slightly. I could hear my mom in the kitchen putting a kettle of water on the stove. Probably so she could offer our guest a cup of tea.

"I think you probably know by now that Connor's father has left our house."

"Yes, ma'am," I said, staring carefully at the carpet.

"This morning he came by to get the rest of his things. But one of his belongings is missing. Do you know the belonging I'm referring to?"

"No, ma'am. I have no idea."

"It's the kind of belonging you wouldn't want falling into the hands of young boys."

I was beginning to get a deeply sinking feeling in my gut. I thought the "belonging" in question might have something to do with relations between married people, though I couldn't imagine what kind of "belonging" that would be. I thought "belonging" was a strange word to use when you could just say "thing."

I wasn't answering. So she went on.

"I can definitely see how it would hold a fascination. But maybe you boys don't know how terribly dangerous an item like that can be.

One of you could be hurt playing with a thing like that. Or even killed. Or a total stranger, a passerby, could be wounded. And I just know you wouldn't want to have something like that on your conscience."

Speaking of fascinations, I had grown fascinated with a tiny spot on the Persian carpet, where one bit of nap seemed to have been forced in the wrong direction, altering the pattern. I couldn't have looked at Mrs. Barnes if you'd paid me good money to do it.

"With all due respect, ma'am," I said, "I haven't got the slightest idea what you're asking me about."

"Then why won't you look at me?"

Oddly, I felt a little flash of anger at her. Mrs. Barnes, of all people? Acting like she didn't know why it was hard to look somebody in the eye?

"I think because you're scaring me with this. Can't you just tell me what this thing is that you think we took?"

A long silence. I could feel how much she didn't want to say.

I looked up to see my mom leaning in the doorway. Listening to all that silence.

"Connor's father . . . ," Mrs. Barnes began, and it startled me, ". . . kept a firearm in the house. For the purpose of home protection. I'm sure you understand."

I didn't. I looked up at her. Just like she'd been wanting me to. I think I was blinking too much.

"A firearm?"

"A gun," my mother said.

"Oh. A gun." I'd known what a firearm was. It just took time to absorb.

"Did you and Connor take the gun, Lucas?" Mrs. Barnes asked.

"No, ma'am."

"Do you have any idea where it is? Did you ever see Connor with it?"

"No, ma'am."

"You better be telling the truth, Lucas," my mother said. "Because this is a pretty serious situation."

"I swear. I'll swear on a stack of Bibles if you want me to. I swear on Grandma's grave. I had no idea there was a gun in Connor's house. I never saw it. I never heard about it. This is all news to me."

I sat still a minute, feeling all four of their eyes burning into me. Then the feeling in the room seemed to lighten a tiny bit. As if they believed me, or some wild outcome like that.

"Hmm," Mrs. Barnes said. "Well, all I know is, it didn't walk away on its own."

"Did you ask him about it?"

"Of course I did. He denied taking it."

I was wondering if she went into his room and looked. But before I could wonder long, she answered my question. It felt as though she could read my mind.

"I spent an hour searching his room, but I never found it. But it has to be somewhere."

I thought about Connor telling me his mother had insisted he go out and lie in the sun. It made more sense in light of this new information.

"I agree it has to be somewhere, ma'am, but I swear, if Connor took it, he kept it as much a secret from me as from you."

It was a strange thing to say, I thought, as I listened to the echo of it. Because I'd accidentally let on that I did think it was possible Connor had taken it.

"Let me ask you another question, then, Lucas. Are you at all concerned about Connor?"

"Concerned, ma'am?"

"Has he been seeming down to you?"

"Down? Well . . . maybe. Maybe some, yeah. But I guess in some ways he's always seemed a little down to me."

"And you don't think it's gotten worse lately?"

"I don't know what to say about that, ma'am. I don't know. Maybe. But then sometimes I think I'm not a very good judge."

"Well, I thank you for your honesty, Lucas." She stood, and straightened out her skirt. Fiddled with her belt for a second. "You've been such a good friend to my son. I believe you, what you say. I'll just go leave you to your day."

My mother said, "Won't you stay and have a cup of tea, Pauline?"

But Connor's mom said, "No. No, thank you, Ellie. I don't want to leave my boy alone too long."

And with that, my mother saw her to the door.

Part of me was so happy to have the ordeal be over. But another part of me said it wasn't over and I knew it. It was my job to be a good friend to Connor. And I had withheld a piece of important information. And I had a sudden bad feeling that too much withholding could be the end of my friend.

My mother walked upstairs, and I sprinted to the door. Slipped out of the house.

I caught up to Mrs. Barnes from behind as she walked down the street. It seemed to alarm her. At least until she saw it was only me.

"One more thing I have to tell you," I said.

We stopped, and she turned to face me on the sidewalk. And she wouldn't look at me. The old Mrs. Barnes had returned. She had screwed up her courage to come into my house and be a new and improved Pauline Barnes, but now that was over. Whatever she had gathered together, she'd run out of it by then.

Either that or she had some idea what I was going to say.

"You asked me if I was concerned about him. He did say something that worried me. But I'd really appreciate it if I didn't have to say word for word what it was. Because there's an honor with guys. He tells me things he wouldn't tell anybody else, and I'm supposed to keep it to myself. That's what best friends do, right? But I *have* been worried about him lately. So if you were thinking it was a good idea to get him some kind of help or keep an extra-close eye on him, well . . . I guess I'd say I think that's a good idea, too."

She smiled the saddest smile I'd ever seen in my days. The saddest I've seen even up until now. She reached out and held one warm hand to my cheek.

Then, without a word, she walked away.

Chapter Ten

Pebbles and Contempt

I didn't sleep well.

It had been all I could do to stop myself from going over to Connor's, and I mean right up until bedtime. But I knew his mom would've been the one to let me in. And she would've immediately known that I'd come to tell him what she'd done—coming to my house, and all. Telling me everything she'd told me.

So I just stayed home and let it ruin my sleep.

I dozed off at about three a.m. and popped awake an hour later. I tossed and turned for what felt like a long time, then got up and got dressed without turning on any lights.

I slipped out of the house and walked over to Connor's without a flashlight. There was a moon, and that helped. But mostly it was just a walk I could have done in my sleep. That is, if I could have gotten any sleep.

I slipped across his front yard, cutting over the grass. His next-door neighbor's big German shepherd, Ajax, heard me and barked a few times. But Ajax barked at everything, so I didn't figure he'd draw much attention.

There was a ring of gravel around a little seedling apple tree near the front stoop. I picked up a couple of the smallest pebbles I could find, working almost entirely by feel.

Then I positioned myself under Connor's window and bounced three pebbles off the window frame. I purposely avoided the glass, because maybe even a small pebble could break a window if you threw it hard enough. Fortunately I was a pretty good shot.

He came to the window and stared down at me, and I stared up at him. It was too dark to see the expressions on each other's faces, but the way he just froze there with his hands on the glass seemed to be a thing that spoke loudly enough.

Then he disappeared again.

I stood still for a minute or two, feeling stupid. Not knowing if I was waiting for anything or not. If he planned to come down, or if he'd just thought, "The hell with Lucas," and gone back to bed.

Then I heard Ajax barking again. A movement caught my eye, and I looked over to see Connor standing in his driveway in the dark, his old threadbare blue robe tied over his pajamas. He tossed his head toward the backyard and we walked down the driveway together.

We pulled two webbed chairs off the back patio and sat next to each other in the grass. Still without saying a word.

I had my head dropped back, staring up at the sky. Man, there were a lot of stars! This was back before the town had much outdoor lighting to pollute the dark sky at night. I saw more stars than I might've thought existed for me to see. I saw the Big Dipper, Ursa Major and Minor, Cassiopeia. I heard crickets for the first time, even though they'd probably been playing their strange music all along.

"Sorry to wake you up," I said. Barely over a whisper.

"I wasn't sleeping," he said.

"Got it. Guess there's a lot of that going around."

Another minute of silent stargazing. Then I figured I'd better get it off my chest, what I'd come to say. Sooner or later I had to.

"Your mom came by to talk to me yesterday."

I didn't look over at him. But from the corner of my eye I saw him drop his face into his hands. I waited. Then he rubbed his face briskly and turned his head toward me. Like he wanted to look at me. But it was a little too dark for that.

"So *that's* where she went," he whispered.

"Yeah. That's where she went."

"I didn't take the damn gun."

I let out a long breath that I must have been holding.

"Well, I'm awful glad to hear it. Because that would be a pretty scary thing, you know."

"What do you think I'm going to do?"

"Well, after that time you said—"

"Don't," he said. "Don't even bring that up again."

We gazed at the sky for a minute more. Or, anyway, I did. I didn't look over at him. I have no idea what he was looking at.

"So here's the thing," I said after a time. "Here's the way it's going to be. I'm just sort of . . . *here* now. I'm just here with you. If I can't get you to go places with me, I'll just sort of be here."

"Twenty-four hours a day?"

"Not sure yet. I don't have the thing all worked out in my head."

"What if I don't want you here that much?"

"Not really sure you get a vote," I said. I was half kidding. I think that came through in my voice. But only half kidding.

Silence while he digested that.

"What about running?" he asked.

"Not going to run on an hour's sleep anyway."

"What about tomorrow's running?"

"I'll worry about that tomorrow."

"What about your girlfriend?"

Yeah, I thought. *What about her? What about calling and inviting her out to eat, then surprising her with a picnic because it's more romantic? What about that?*

"Here's the thing," I said. Then I stopped, and sighed. Because I was letting some pretty important things slip away. Slide out of me. "We've been friends since we were three."

"I know it."

"I just think that counts for something."

"More than a girlfriend?"

"If you're in any kind of trouble . . . then . . . yeah. I'm putting you first. And there's not a whole hell of a lot you can do about it."

We sat there together until the sun came up. Without ever saying another word.

—

It was about three thirty in the afternoon. We were upstairs in his room, playing cards. We were on something upwards of our hundredth game. I'm not exaggerating. I had won about sixty, and he'd won maybe fifty or more.

He looked up at me over his hand of cards and narrowed his eyes.

"Seriously, Lucas," he said. "You need to get your butt out of here and go have that picnic."

Obviously, I had told him a little bit about Libby over the course of the day. Libby past and Libby future.

"Maybe some other day," I said.

"My mom is here. I'll be right here. When you get back, everything will be just the way it is now."

It sounded like a promise. But I was not about to leave a thing like that to guesswork or chance.

"Promise?"

"Yeah. Promise."

I looked at the clock radio beside his bed.

"I don't know," I said. "I think it's too late for today."

"How is it too late?"

"Well, it's supposed to be a picnic lunch. *Lunch.* By the time I put the whole thing together and got over there, it would be time for dinner."

"So? Who says it can't be a picnic dinner?"

"It's sandwiches."

"You can eat sandwiches for dinner."

I looked over at his phone. He had a phone in his room, the lucky dog. The fact that I looked at it meant I was considering it.

He noticed.

"Go ahead," he said. "Call."

I just sat a minute. The tips of my fingers were tingling, but I had no idea why.

Then I got up and walked to the phone.

I knew her number by heart. But I had never called it before. Which means I had memorized it, but not the cool way—by using it. The pathetic way. By staring at it until the numbers were permanently etched into my brain.

"She might have plans," I said. "Kind of short notice."

"One way to find out," Connor said.

"Maybe her parents want her home for dinner."

"One way to find out."

I picked up the phone and dialed.

Mrs. Weller picked up.

"Hello?"

"Oh," I said. "Hi. Mrs. Weller?"

"Yes?"

"It's Lucas Painter. Is Libby in, please?"

"She is, Lucas. And you have very polite phone manners. Just hold the line a minute, and I'll go tell her you're calling."

I shifted from foot to foot. Caught Connor's eye. Nodded.

Then Libby was on the line.

"Lucas?"

"Yeah," I said. "It's me."

"About time you called."

"It's only been a couple of days."

"Oh. Well, it seemed longer."

It made my face hot when she said that. Or maybe it was *the way* she said it. I turned my face slightly away from Connor, hoping he wouldn't see it redden.

"I was just wondering . . ." Then I stalled, and realized I had no idea how to phrase my request. I hadn't rehearsed this part at all. Which, considering how obsessed I'd been with every other aspect of the thing, seemed strange. "Do you have to be home for dinner?"

"Tonight?"

"Yeah."

"Well, I don't know. What did you have in mind?"

"I thought maybe I could come get you and take you someplace."

"I'll ask my mom," she said.

I tapped my foot and waited, and then she was back on the line, her words all in a rush.

"She says it's okay and I accept, what time do you want to pick me up?"

———

I showed up at her house promptly at five, the carefully prepared picnic basket dangling from my hand.

Libby answered the door.

She looked at me. Then down at the basket.

"I hope this is okay," I said. "I hope it's something you'll like. My first thought was to take you out someplace to dinner. But I thought a picnic would be more romantic."

She said nothing for a moment. Just looked into my eyes. But I could tell by her face that I'd done well. I had struck the right note with her. And just in that moment my life was so perfect I could hardly stand it.

"Mom!" she called over her shoulder. Into the house. "Lucas and I are going. See you later."

And then we were walking down the street together hand in hand. And life was just the way you see it in the movies or on TV.

My life. Was all that.

———

"If anybody asks you," I said, "we had this picnic in the park."

We were up in the woods, on the highest hill I knew how to find, looking down through the trees at the town spread out below. I hadn't chosen a spot looking over the river. Libby might have thought it was a nice view, but I didn't. Not since reading that newspaper story.

"Probably smart," she said. "Parents are weird about the woods, and I don't know why."

"I don't know why, either. I like it up here."

I lifted the checkered tablecloth off the basket. Unfolded it and spread it carefully on the forest floor.

"Have a seat," I said.

She settled on one edge of it.

"This is nice," she said, looking down over the town. "I like this."

"I hope it doesn't seem weird to have sandwiches for dinner."

"I don't see why a person shouldn't," she said. "Besides, I didn't exactly think you had a roast turkey or a baked lasagna in there."

I sighed out a bit of tension and began unpacking the food. Carefully laying out two sturdy china plates, cloth napkins. I arranged the fruit and the wrapped sandwiches on a third plate in the middle of the cloth. The cookies were in a plastic storage container, and I set those beside the serving plate.

Then I saw the pink rose, which had apparently fallen to the bottom as I walked. I'd forgotten it. And it was supposed to come first. But anyway, better late than never, I figured.

"Here," I said, pulling it up by the stem. "This is for you."

She took it from me, her eyes soft.

"You're a very thoughtful boy," she said. "You know that?"

It made me blush, so I turned my face down. I pulled the two small bottles of apple juice out of the basket and put one by her plate, one by mine. I never answered. I was too embarrassed by her praise.

"I can't believe some girl hasn't already snapped you up."

Flustered, I became a tour guide for sandwiches.

"This is sliced ham," I said, pointing. "And this is deviled ham."

"Ooh. I like deviled ham. And I haven't had it for ages."

I put that one on her plate. I wasn't sure if I should take it out of the plastic first. Maybe that would have been more polite. But maybe she didn't want my hands all over her food. By the time I remembered I had made the sandwich with my hands, I had already gone ahead with giving it to her wrapped.

"There's also turkey and tuna," I said. "If you're hungry enough for two."

She ignored the statement and stared into my face as she unwrapped her sandwich.

"Have you had a girlfriend before?"

"Not really," I said.

The honest answer would have been not at all. Not in any way. But I thought what I said sounded better.

"I wonder why."

Now we were traveling down a less comfortable road. Were we really going to analyze whether there was something wrong with me? Why I repelled girls like the wrong end of a magnet?

"You do know I'm only fourteen," I said. "Right?"

"I know."

"Does that bother you? That I'm a little younger than you?"

"No. Who cares? It's only a year. And you're very mature. And you seem to know a lot about how to have a girlfriend for a guy who never had one."

I did not wade into the minefield of replies.

We began to eat our sandwiches. I took the sliced ham, since I figured she was less likely to choose it after eating deviled ham. We ate in silence for a time, staring down over the town. The sun was on a long slant through the trees, off to the west. And I felt unbalanced.

Turned out I had no idea what unbalanced even felt like. Not yet. I was right on the cusp of finding out.

"I think I might know why," she said.

"Why what?"

"Why you haven't had a girlfriend."

Her words iced my belly in a heartbeat. Was she really going to tell me what I was doing wrong? After everything had gone so well up until this moment?

"If you want to know, that is," she added.

I didn't. Of course I didn't.

She looked over at my face and seemed to pick up on my discomfort.

"Oh, it's not you," she said. "I wasn't going to say anything bad about you."

I breathed a little. Not much, but more than I had been breathing.

"Okay. I guess I want to know, then."

"It's just that you have to really think about who you want to hang around with. People will judge you by that."

I had a bite of sandwich in my mouth, and I chewed it before answering. I didn't know who she meant. Maybe Mrs. Dinsmore? But how would she even know that? My intention was to ask, but as it turned out, I didn't need to.

She went on to tell me.

"I really think you can do better than Connor Barnes for a friend."

I swallowed hard. The bite of sandwich seemed to hang up on its way to my stomach, and I felt a wave of something like heartburn.

"What's wrong with Connor?"

"He's just kind of weird," she said. "And kind of a sad sack. He always has this big black cloud over his head, following him everywhere he goes. I mean, not really, but . . . you know what I mean. I think you'd have a lot more friends if he weren't with you all the time."

My mind had begun to run circles inside my head. I was trying to get a feel for whether this was a "game over" sort of thing, or if I could still think of her as a potential girlfriend.

"He's been my best friend since we were three."

"Maybe that's too long. Maybe it's time to make new choices."

"Let's talk about something else," I said.

"Okay. I didn't mean to upset you. Just trying to help."

We finished every last bite of that meal without finding one other thing to talk about.

———

I learned something about kissing that day. I learned it can wipe the slate clean of just about everything that came before it.

We were lying side by side on the big tablecloth. The dishes and any leftover trash had been carefully packed into the basket, which I'd placed off to the side. Out of our way.

She moved her face over close to mine, and I kissed her. And suddenly everything felt okay again. I knew there had been something bad back there, behind us. Something had happened and I hadn't forgotten it. Not by any means. But it felt like such ancient history now. Like it couldn't possibly still matter.

I've had the same feeling many times since, over the years, in relationships. Some little tip of an iceberg peeks up above the surface. Then it goes down again, and you think, *Oh good. It's gone. I guess it was nothing.*

Only now I'm not a kid anymore. So now I know.

We kissed for a long time. I have no idea how long. Might have been ten minutes that felt like a second. Might have been a few seconds that stretched out forever.

She rolled over onto her back and sighed. Not a bad sigh. More of a contented one. She laced her hands together behind her head and looked up at the late afternoon sky through the trees. So I did the same.

"This is nice out here," she said.

"Yeah. I like it out here in the woods."

"You seem to know these woods pretty well."

"I run out here."

"Oh. Right. I heard you were a runner. I heard you scored a place on the track team for the fall semester."

Suddenly, in my head, I was on the team for the first time ever. Really on the team. Not resisting. Not planning to weasel out of it.

"You run through these woods all by yourself?" she asked. Before I could think how to answer.

"No. Not usually alone. I have a couple big dogs who run with me."

"I didn't know you had dogs."

"They're not mine."

"You run with two dogs that aren't yours?"

"I do."

"Whose are they?"

"You know that lady who lives out here in the woods?"

The silence that followed my question felt weird. It felt much too silent.

"You mean . . . ," she began. But then she didn't seem to want to ask me who I meant.

"Zoe Dinsmore," I said.

Looking back, I'm not sure why I felt safe enough to say it. I guess all that kissing had softened up my brain. I had misplaced all my best walls and boundaries.

She sat bolt upright.

"You *know* her?"

"A little. Do you?"

"No. But I know who she is. And I'm shocked that you know her, Lucas. I'm . . . shocked."

"Why?"

"Because she's . . ."

But then she seemed unwilling to finish her thought again.

"What? She's what?"

"She's a killer."

I sat bolt upright, too.

"She's not a killer," I said.

"She killed two kids. That makes her a killer."

"She didn't kill them."

"So why are they dead?"

"An accident killed them."

"And she caused the accident."

"But it was an accident."

"But she caused it."

I could feel that we were going around in a loop, like that traffic circle in Blaine, but I couldn't find a place to turn off.

"Sometimes things happen," I said. "It's not like she did it on purpose."

"She showed up to work on hardly any sleep. And drove innocent kids around. Why didn't she call in sick to work? Why didn't she pull over when she knew she was sleepy?"

"Maybe she didn't know. My mother fell asleep at the wheel once. With me in the car. I think I was about seven. We were coming back from the north county, and her head nodded, and then she drifted over the centerline and scraped a car going the other way. Just sort of scraped the trim off the guy's door. She kept saying the same thing over and over—that she hadn't had any idea she was so tired. She hadn't known she was about to go to sleep. She couldn't feel it. Every night I lie in bed and try to go to sleep. And then the next thing I know, I'm opening my eyes and it's morning. I never feel myself fall asleep. Ever. Do you?"

We sat there for what felt like a long time. Staring down at the town, which I thought looked less welcoming than it had a minute ago. She never told me if she could feel herself fall asleep.

"Why are you defending her?" she asked after a time.

Her voice was like glass. Whatever door she had opened into her life for me was closed and locked now. And you didn't have to be an expert on girls to know it.

"I just think things happen sometimes and it's not really anybody's fault."

"*I* don't," she said. Still like glass. "*I* think we have to take responsibility for what we do."

"So if my mom had hit that guy's car head-on, and somebody in the car had died, you'd think my mom was a killer?"

"Of course not," she said.

Now she really had my mind spinning in circles. Uncomfortably so. It was dizzying.

"What's the difference?"

"Your mom is a good person."

"You know my mom?"

"Not really. But I know she is."

That was the moment when *my* door closed.

I locked it.

I could have continued to argue. I could have pointed out that she had decided my mother was an angel and Zoe Dinsmore was the devil without knowing either one of them. And that her worldview made no sense.

I didn't. Because I knew she was not my girlfriend and she never would be. So why even bother trying to get through?

That disastrous conversation had allowed me to look through the window of her and see the space inside. And it was not a nice place. And I no longer wanted to go there.

"Let's go back," I said.

I got to my feet and began to take up the tablecloth to fold it. Which involved more or less pulling it out from under her. I was upset, to put it mildly.

"Wait," she said. "Give me a minute to get up at least."

I waited, and she did.

I folded the cloth, hoping she wouldn't keep talking.

She kept talking.

"See, this is just what I was trying to tell you before. You have to be careful who you hang around with. People will judge you by who you hang around with. And then they might not want to be around you, either."

"Stop," I said. And I looked her right in the face. She was shocked that I had spoken to her so abruptly. I could tell. "Stop talking. I don't want to talk about this anymore. I just want to go home."

"What about our date?"

"It's over."

"Just like that?"

"Just like that."

She snorted. Literally snorted through her nostrils like an angry bull. Then she stomped off toward town.

"Wait," I said, picking up the basket and following her. "Let me walk you home at least."

"I don't need you to walk me home." She threw the words over her shoulder, like something she spat out.

"You might. It's easy to get lost in the woods."

"I can see the town."

I was nearly jogging to keep up with her.

"But when you get down off this rise, you won't. And it's easy to get turned around."

"I'll manage," she said.

But I followed her. To make sure she would find her way out okay. I didn't try to talk to her again. I didn't want to talk to her again. But I followed her until she stepped out onto my street and turned toward home.

Then I followed her home.

She glanced once over her shoulder at me as she disappeared into her house. Then she slammed the door hard.

And that was it. My first girlfriend. My very first relationship. Two whole days of it, and that was that.

—

I showed up at Zoe Dinsmore's cabin at what I guessed was about seven o'clock in the evening, judging by the sun. I was out of breath from running. I was deeply feeling my lack of sleep. But I was far too upset to go home.

I pounded hard on the door. Raised my fist high over my head and banged with the outside edge of it. The dogs were inside, and they barked a few deep barks, because they couldn't see it was only me.

"Who is it?" she called through the door.

"It's Lucas."

The dogs stopped barking at the sound of my voice.

The door opened and they came spilling out, lashing me with their wagging tails. For the first time ever, I paid them no mind.

Zoe Dinsmore looked into my face in the fading light.

"Uh-oh," she said.

"Why do people do that? Why do they need to make you wrong? Or make you out to be some kind of bad person? Everybody knows bad things happen. I know we're not supposed to talk about this. I know you don't want me to. But I'm talking about it. I'm just talking about it. Because I need to know."

In the moment of silence that followed, I watched her face. She was looking down at the threshold and her own bare feet. She didn't look angry that I had asked. She didn't look much of anything.

"I suppose you'd best come in," she said.

———

"Here's the thing," she said. "If they admit to themselves that what happened couldn't have been easily prevented, then they're admitting it could happen to them."

"But it could."

"But they don't want to admit that. Until it actually *does* happen to them, they want to be completely sure it can't."

It was a good while later. The sun was nearly down. We were sitting on the floor of her cabin, our backs against the end of her bed. She had started a fire in the woodstove to get her through the night, and we were staring at it. The little cast-iron door was open, and we were sitting there transfixed by the fire.

I wouldn't have thought it would be cold enough for a fire in June. But then, I didn't live in an unheated cabin in the woods. She obviously knew more about it than I did.

I had long ago told her about my date. I had spared not one ugly detail.

"So they would do that to you? Just to make themselves feel a little more comfortable?"

"Apparently so."

"Even though it's just a lie in their heads and they're not really safe at all?"

"They've been doing it to me for seventeen years, kid."

"Everybody?"

"No. Not everybody. Some are more understanding, but the way they look at me is almost worse. I swear I'd rather have the contempt."

"Why did you stay?"

That fell to her floor and lay there for a moment. I swear I felt like I could look down and see the question lying—uncomfortably—on the floor near the sleeping dogs.

She didn't answer.

"Your daughter told me that everybody thought you should go far away and start again somewhere new. Someplace where nobody knew you. And that nobody knew why you didn't do it. Not even her, and she's your daughter."

"I was born in this town, kid. Lived here all my life. Everything I know is here."

"So? If you'd gone someplace else seventeen years ago, you'd know that place like the back of your hand by now. There has to be more to it than that."

"I don't think you'd understand."

"Try me."

The fire crackled and snapped while I waited for her to try me.

"I didn't think I deserved it," she said. "There. Is that honest enough for you?"

Chapter Eleven

The Dark and Uneven Path

I've lived my whole life in a small town, but in the days after my uneasy breakup with Libby Weller, I was stunned by the downside of small-town living. Even though I had nothing to compare it to. It didn't matter. The problems were simply glaring.

It was the second morning after the dreadful picnic. I came down into the kitchen early, hoping to scarf down a bowl of cereal and go running before anyone else was up.

Instead I found my mom sitting at the kitchen table, talking on the phone. The cord that hooked the receiver to the phone base was ridiculously stretched, and my mom was curling a little section of it around her finger as she listened.

She looked up and caught my eyes, and I knew all was not well.

"Speak of the devil," she said. Into the phone, as far as I could tell. "I'll have to call you back, Marilyn."

She got up to hang up the phone.

"I'm going running," I said, and tried to break for the door.

"The hell you are," she barked. "Sit."

I did as I'd been told. She rarely if ever used that voice with me, though she used it with my father all the time. I found it best to freeze like a deer in the headlights at times like that. Say nothing, do nothing. Almost like playing dead. My father had a different set of theories.

"How do you know Zoe Dinsmore?" she asked, sitting across the table from me.

"She has these two really nice dogs," I said. I had an angle. I was going to play on her guilt over the fact that I'd always wanted another dog and she'd always refused to get me one. "And you know how I feel about dogs. I got sort of attached to them. They go running with me in the morning."

Then I stopped talking, and realized my mistake. If I'd left the dogs out of it, I could've pretended I somehow knew Mrs. Dinsmore from town. That I kept bumping into her at the library or something. But I had tipped my hand regarding my life up in the forbidden woods.

"I thought I told you never to go in those woods."

"Yes, ma'am. I guess you did."

"And do you want to tell me why you went and defied me?"

What I said next might have been another angle. In the back of my mind, I might have been trying to play the guilt card to get myself off the hook. But it was also the damn truth. Why go further into motives when somebody asks you for the truth and you give it?

"I think because it's so quiet up there. It really gets to me when you and Dad fight."

I waited for her reaction. I guess I was assuming she would take that into herself in some way. Feel the pain I had just described and understand that she had caused it. I didn't get what I was waiting for.

"I told you, you could get lost up there."

"But I never do. I know it like the back of my hand."

I waited again. Nothing happened.

"You really can't get lost," I added. "I don't know why you think so. The whole place is only about two or three miles wide. On one side you can see town, and on the other side you can see the river. I don't know what you think the problem is."

"The problem is," she began, her voice booming, "your little cousin got lost up there, and it scared the hell out of everybody. He was gone overnight. He was only nine. We thought he might've been kidnapped. We thought he might be dead. And when the search party finally found him, he had hypothermia. He had to be in the hospital for a day. It was terrible. I never want to go through a thing like that again."

My cousin—well, I had three, but only one was a "he"—was five years older than me. So this must've happened when I was four. Which explains why I didn't remember.

"But he lives in Oregon," I said.

"They were here for a visit. You were too little to remember. I felt totally responsible, because they were staying with us. If they hadn't found him, I don't know what I would've done. I'd have never gotten over it, I can tell you that right now."

We sat quietly for a few seconds. In my head, I was going over what I had learned. Not in words, exactly, but I felt it.

Here are the words I have for it now.

When somebody holds a view that seems to make no sense, know that it makes sense to them, but for reasons you don't know anything about yet. And I guess in a lot of cases, you never will.

I wanted to answer her, but I wasn't sure what to say. So in my head I went to Mrs. Dinsmore's cabin. I just thought to myself, *What would the lady tell me to do?*

"I'm really sorry you had to go through that," I said. "It sounds scary and terrible."

"It was."

"But I'm not nine. And I really know my way around in there. And I promise I'll be fine."

I got up from the table, thinking I could make my break.

"Wait," she said. "There's more."

I didn't sit down again. I didn't want to commit to much more listening. I just hovered over her, feeling tall. Too tall.

"What?"

"I don't want you anywhere near that Dinsmore woman."

"Why not?"

"She's just not a suitable friend for you."

"I wouldn't say we were friends," I said. But it was a lie. I would say it. Only, not to my mother. "I just really like those two dogs."

"She's not a good influence on you. On anyone. I don't want any more phone calls from people telling me you're spending time with a person like that. It's not appropriate."

"I don't understand how you can say that. Just because she had a bad accident?"

"Oh, honey. That's not all. There's a lot you don't know about that lady. She drank, and she took tons of drugs. Showed up different places in town out of her mind. They say it started *after* the accident, but I don't know. It just sort of made everybody wonder. Some say she cleaned up her act and stopped. Others don't believe it. I don't know what to believe. I just don't want you near any of it. I don't know why she stays in this town, but she obviously wants to be left alone. So leave her alone. You understand why I say that to you?"

"Yes, ma'am. I understand why."

I did understand why she'd said it to me. I just had no intention of following her order.

I slipped out the door, and only as I was jogging down the street did I realize I had skipped breakfast. But I just kept running.

———

When I got to Connor's house, things only went from bad to worse.

His mom came to the door, then turned and walked away down the hall without saying a word to me. I had no idea what that meant. But she left the door standing wide open, so I came in and closed it behind me.

I walked up the stairs to Connor's room. Slowly. Like I wasn't sure what waited for me up there. Because, truthfully, I was less sure with every passing day.

I rapped on his closed bedroom door.

"What?" he said from inside. From the tone of his voice I gathered that, whatever it was, he didn't want it.

"It's me."

No answer. I turned the knob and pushed the door open.

Connor was sitting in the same chair he almost always sat in, but it wasn't pulled over to the window. It was facing a blank corner of the room. He was literally making himself sit in the corner. It was very strange.

"What are you doing?" I asked him.

"What does it look like I'm doing?"

"It looks like you made yourself go sit in the corner."

"Well, there you go."

He said nothing more, so I perched uncomfortably on the end of his bed. I stared at the back of his head as he sat perfectly still and said nothing at all. Just in that moment I saw Libby's point about his dark cloud. You could almost see it. The rest of her observations could go take a hike as far as I was concerned.

The silence lasted for a minute or two, and seemed to get darker.

Then Connor spoke. His voice was quiet but hard edged.

"Why didn't you tell me you broke up with her over me?"

For a moment I couldn't find it inside myself to answer.

I'd told him about my disastrous picnic date the day before, when I'd come and sat with him just about all day, whether he wanted me to or not. But I'd left out what Libby had said about him. Of course I had. Who reports on a thing like that when they could just as easily keep it to themselves?

"Because I didn't. It wasn't about you."

"That's not what I heard. I heard I'm holding you back. That you'd have lots of friends and girlfriends if you didn't have me standing in your way."

I lost it in that moment. It was a buildup of stress breaking free, I suppose. I raised my voice to him, which I don't think I'd ever done before.

"Who are you talking to, Connor? Who are you hearing this from? You won't even go out of the house. Where are you getting all this information?"

Then I stopped myself. Breathed. Tried to drop my shoulders. I was still staring at the back of his head. If it upset him to be yelled at, he was doing a good job of keeping it to himself.

"Somebody told my mom about it at the market yesterday. She didn't say who. Might've been Libby's mom. Or maybe everybody in town has heard all about it by now."

So that explained why his mom had been acting strangely at the door.

I almost walked around and sat in front of him. Because it felt weird to explain a whole big thing to his back. But he hadn't left much room in that corner, and I knew he probably didn't want me to, so I didn't.

"Look," I said. "It went down like this. We were having a perfectly nice picnic. And then she said that stuff about you. And I told her we'd been best friends since we were three. And then she said something else. I don't remember exactly what. And I told her I didn't want to talk about it anymore. I wanted to talk about something else. At that point I wasn't going to break up with her. I was just going to keep being friends with you, and she could keep her feelings about it to herself. But then later she went off on Mrs. Dinsmore, and wow, Connor. It was weird. It was ugly. She said the lady was a killer. That she killed two kids. And that's when I realized she's just not a very nice person. Libby, I mean. I just didn't know it until we talked a little. She's just kind of awful. But she was wrong, Connor. She was wrong."

"About Mrs. Dinsmore? Or about me?"

"Both."

"No," he said. His voice sounded weirdly firm. "She was right about me. I'm just holding you back. I release you from this friendship, Lucas. Go have lots of friends and girlfriends."

"No," I said. "I'm not going anywhere."

"I want you to."

"No," I said. "I'm staying right here."

"Then you're an idiot."

"Well." I paused. And sighed. "You can call me any name you want. But I'm staying right here."

———

I stayed there with him for most of the day, and I have to say it was just numbing. I don't know any other word for it. We barely talked. The time crawled by. But I was afraid to leave him alone.

Then, sometime after lunch, I began to realize the hopelessness of my mission. I couldn't watch him every minute. Nobody could. Even if I stayed through dinner and spent the night, he could do something stupid while I was sleeping. Hell, he could excuse himself to go to the bathroom and do something stupid before I figured out he'd been away too long.

"I guess I'm going home," I said. "But I'm still your friend."

"I can't imagine why," he said. "But it's obvious I'm not going to change your mind about that."

I walked down the stairs slowly, wondering if I was ever going to see him again.

When I got down to the long hallway, I saw Connor's mother in the dim living room. The shades were all drawn, as usual. She was sitting in the chair Connor's father used to sit in. The last place I'd seen him.

Her head was dropped back, just the way his had been. But no ice pack. She just had her eyes closed.

I moved to the living room doorway and leaned there, wondering if I dared speak to her. I thought she didn't know I was there. So when she spoke up, it startled me.

"What is it, Lucas?"

"I just wanted you to know, ma'am . . . Libby Weller did say some things about Connor that were not very nice. But I never did. I said he was my friend, had been since we were three. And when she kept at it, I told her to stop talking about it. And I'm not going to be seeing her anymore anyway."

At first, nothing. Maybe she was waiting to see if I was done.

"I appreciate your telling me that," she said after a time.

"I hope you'll keep an eye on Connor."

"Of course I will," she said. But with not an ounce of life in her words.

I turned to walk away, but she had one more thing to say. She called it down the hall after me.

"I can't watch him every minute, though."

It was hard for me to know how she meant that last thought. Was she resigned to the danger of the thing? Already terrified by the guilt she would feel? Or was she just like me: overwhelmed by how helpless we are to change the fate of the people we want to help?

"Yes, ma'am," I said, because I didn't know what else to say.

I slipped out the door and ran home.

—

Once again I woke up well before the sun.

I had an idea, but it was a weird idea. It was powerful, but it was weird. I knew it would change things. Maybe change them in a good way. Maybe make everything worse.

It was either the best or the worst idea I'd ever had.

Trouble was, the more I thought about it, the more I knew there was no way to tell which way it would fall. Not in advance. The only way to know best from worst was to move forward and give it a try.

Now, this next little bit is going to sound like déjà vu, and in a way I suppose it is.

I got up. Slipped out of the house without waking anybody. Without turning on any lights. I walked over to Connor's house in the dark and bounced pebbles off the window of his front bedroom.

The neighbor's dog barked at me.

When Connor came to the window and put his hands on the glass, I felt a load of anxiety drain out of me. I wasn't too late.

I walked around to the backyard and met him coming out the mudroom door.

"This is getting old," he said. Quietly.

"Come somewhere with me."

"This time I was sleeping."

"I'm sorry. Do this for me. Please."

"I thought we weren't going to do this anymore. You said you'd stop asking me to go places with you."

"Just this once. I promise you we won't see any of the other guys from school where we're going."

He sighed, and said nothing. And I knew I had won.

"Go get dressed," I said.

And he did. Without any questions.

———

"I just like being home," he said as we walked down the dark sidewalk together.

He had his hands stuffed in his jacket pockets. He had his shoulders up around his ears, like that would somehow keep the world away.

We were headed for the woods, but he didn't know it.

"You can't always be home," I said.

"Why can't I?"

"You have to go back to school in the fall."

He clammed up then, and stopped talking. I wasn't quite sure what to make of that. But it sure didn't feel like a good sign.

It was barely light when we hit the path I liked to use to get into the woods. The one I figured was the most direct route to the lady's cabin. It was the very beginning of civil twilight. We could see the trees just well enough that we stood a good chance of not slamming into one.

I took a few careful steps down that uneven footing.

"Why are we going in here?" he asked.

His voice sounded too far away, so I turned around to see why. I saw why, all right. He wasn't following me anymore. He was still glued to the sidewalk.

"I want to take you someplace."

"Why?"

"Because I do."

"That's not really a reason," he said.

I sighed and picked my way back to where he stood.

"Look," I said. "I'm working really hard to be a good friend here. And I normally don't ask you for much. But I'm asking you to do this one thing, and if it doesn't work out, I won't ask you to do anything else ever again."

Then we just stood there in silence for a moment, unable to see the expressions on each other's faces. I was wondering why I'd given away the store for this idea, promising him it was the last time I'd ever try to do something to help him. Especially since it could've turned out to be the worst idea I'd ever had.

"Whatever," he said.

And he took a step on the dark and uneven path.

—

The sun was not yet up when we got to Zoe Dinsmore's cabin, but it was pretty light.

The dogs came spilling out of their doghouse to greet us.

"Holy crap!" Connor breathed. He grabbed a handful of my sleeve. "They're so big!"

"They won't hurt you," I said. Then, to the dogs, "Rembrandt. Vermeer. Come meet my friend."

They wiggled over with tails swinging, and Connor petted their heads. I could tell he was still a little bit intimidated by them. But it's hard not to pet a dog who's looking up into your face and wagging.

"Is this who you wanted me to meet?" Connor asked. He sounded hopeful. Like maybe he could be done now. Maybe he could just go home.

"No."

"Oh," he said. "That's too bad."

We walked up onto the porch and I rapped on the door.

"Mrs. Dinsmore? Are you dressed yet?"

No answer. For one horrible moment I thought I might've brought Connor out here to witness the aftermath of the suicide of the lady I was hoping could help him.

Then the door swung open.

She looked at Connor. Then at me. She was wearing her overalls on top of a solid-gray flannel shirt. Her feet were bare and her hair had been freshly braided.

"And who do we have here?" she asked, indicating Connor with a flip of her head.

"This is my friend Connor. He's the one I was telling you about."

"I see." A pause. A sigh. "Well, you two boys come in."

But the minute we stepped inside, she grabbed me by the shoulder and steered me back out the door.

"A private word with you outside," she said. Then, to Connor, "Make yourself at home, son. We'll be back in just a few."

She pulled the door closed behind us, and we stood on the porch together. The sun was just coming up over the rise, between the trees. It burned into my eyes when I tried to look at her.

I had the definite sense that I was in trouble.

"You mind telling me what exactly *I'm* supposed to do with him?"

"Um," I said. Not a great start. "I was hoping you might . . . help him."

"Help him how?"

"I'm not sure. But you always help *me*. And I don't know how you do *that*. You just do, somehow."

I watched her eyes narrow. I had to squint to see it, because of the way the rising sun was shining into my own.

"Let me get this straight," she said. "You're worried your friend doesn't want to live anymore. So you bring him to talk to the one person in the world you know *for sure* doesn't want to. Is there a logic in here that I'm missing?"

"Maybe," I said. "I don't know." I dug deep. If there was ever a time to dig deep, if there had ever been such a time in my life, this was it. "I think . . . sometimes I'll think bad things about myself. Like I'll think I'm stupid or I can't do anything right. But if Connor told me he was stupid and couldn't do anything right, I'd stand up for him. Sometimes it's easy to want something for somebody else, even if it's more than you want for yourself."

"Interesting," she said.

I hoped she would go on to say more. She didn't.

"Do you think I'm right?"

"Kid, I have no idea."

"It's dicey," I said. "I'll grant you that. All morning I was lying in bed thinking of that room with nothing but mirrors inside. Remember that? It was in that traveling art exhibit that we all went to see when it stopped in Blaine."

"I didn't go to see it," she said.

"Oh."

I should've known. She wouldn't have wanted to mix with all those locals. Also, now my point was lost. I knew I could never put it into words.

"I know what happens, though," she said, "when you have a mirror on both sides of you. It reflects out to infinity."

"Right!" I said. "That! I was lying in bed worrying that if you met Connor, his troubles and your troubles would reflect out like that. Multiply. Off into infinity, like you said."

She screwed her face up into a cartoon of criticism.

"So then you got up and brought him here."

"Yeah. Sounds weird, I know. But I was still hoping for that first thing, where you want him to stay even if you don't want to stay yourself. I knew it was either the best or the worst idea I'd ever had. And I tried and tried to figure out which it was. But I couldn't. There was just no way to know."

"Big chance to take," she said.

"Yeah. I know. But I was out of ideas."

We stood that way for what felt like the longest time. I figured she was thinking. I didn't want to move or speak, because I didn't want to interrupt her thinking. In case it was about to come down in my favor.

"I think you're crazy," she said. "And I think I'm crazy to let you talk me into having any part of it. But go on ahead and take your run and leave him here. I'll see if he wants to talk."

"Thanks," I said. "I really appreciate this. I owe you one for it."

"You don't owe me crap," she said. "And vice versa."

Then, just as I was stepping down off her porch, she said one more thing to me.

"Hey. Lucas. Sorry I cost you that girlfriend."

I stopped. Turned back. The dogs were disappointed, I could tell. But they waited.

"You didn't," I said. "She just turned out to be . . . not who I was thinking she was."

"Yeah," she said. She had her arms crossed over her chest. "Relationships are like that. You have to hang back for a time. See what you've got and what you're getting yourself into."

I nodded, and began my run.

What she had just said about relationships—I chalked that up as one more thing I couldn't possibly have known if I hadn't had Zoe Dinsmore to tell it to me.

———

When I picked Connor up again, it was full-on light. Hot, almost.

I'd purposely taken a very long run.

He marched out of the cabin in perfect silence, his eyes trained down to the porch boards. Like his mother.

I looked past him to the lady and mouthed the words "Thank you" without making a sound.

We walked through the woods toward town together, my best friend Connor and me. Or I guess it should be "Connor and I."

We walked a quarter mile or so without any words spoken. I was beginning to think bad thoughts based on the silence.

"What did you think of her?" I asked when I couldn't stand it anymore.

I wanted to ask what they'd talked about. But I knew it wasn't any of my business. It hurt to know that, but it was still the damned truth.

"It was interesting," he said.

Then he acted like he planned not to say another word.

"Good interesting?"

"Not sure."

We walked in silence until we could see town stretched out below. Connor stopped, as though taking in the view. So I stopped, too.

"We don't talk like that in my family," Connor said.

"Like what?"

"I don't know how to say it. It's like, at my house, the more it matters, the more we don't talk about it. That lady, she'll say anything. She'll talk about anything. The hardest thing in the world, she just spits it right out. It was kind of . . ."

I waited. For an uncomfortable length of time. To find out what it "kind of" was.

". . . upsetting," he said at last.

I started to say I was sorry. But I never got that far. He spoke again, interrupting my thoughts about apologies.

"Will you take me out there again tomorrow? I don't think I could find the place just all on my own."

"Sure," I said. "I'll take you out there any day you want."

I had a dozen questions, but I didn't ask any of them. I didn't want to jinx it.

Chapter Twelve

That's Not Him

It was at least two weeks later, and it might even have been three. It was one of those mornings when—after I'd done my run and taken the dogs home—I was jogging down the path toward town and ran into Connor walking up the same path to the lady's cabin.

He stopped when he saw me.

"Hey," he said.

"Hey," I said in return.

I always wanted to ask him a million things. What they talked about. Whether it was helping him. What it meant that he kept going there on his own. If there was any room for me in this new equation.

Yes, much as I hate to admit it, I was feeling jealous and left out. It's not pretty, but there it is, and it's the truth.

"You doing okay?" he asked me.

He. Asked *me.* If *I* was okay.

Just for a minute I almost blasted out the truth: That it was killing me. That I felt like I'd given him the best tool I had to understand my life, and now I no longer had it for myself, because how could I ask the poor lady to save two pesky young guys at once? And that I couldn't stand not knowing how it was going, what was being said. It was my thing, my idea. And I didn't even get to ask if I should feel good about it. It was driving me crazy. Stone crazy.

"Yeah," I said. "I think so."

In my defense, I kept my crap to myself. At least I was that much of a friend.

"Good," he said.

"You?"

"Not sure. I'm here, anyway."

I didn't know if he meant here on this path through the woods, going out to talk to the lady again. Or here on the earth in general. And I didn't ask.

"Know what I was thinking?" I asked him.

"No. I don't. What were you thinking?"

"That your grandmother used to be like that. She would say anything that came into her head. She didn't hold back."

"Oh yeah," he said. He clearly had not thought of that on his own. "She did. Didn't she?"

Connor had adored her. But then she went and died when we were seven. The fact that he had no living grandparents might have factored into my thinking about taking him to meet Mrs. Dinsmore. But it had not occurred to me at the time that she had a lot in common with the grandparent he'd loved the most.

I waited to see if he could make some kind of connection. Maybe realize that he liked her for that reason. But he didn't seem to want to talk about it anymore, and I couldn't tell if he connected those details or not.

The conversation stalled. Connor shifted from foot to foot, and I could see he wanted to move on.

"Maybe I'll come by later," I said.

"Yeah, good."

But I didn't go by later. Because my whole world had changed by later. Hanging out at Connor's house was soon the last thought that was likely to cross my mind.

—

When I walked through the kitchen door, my father was home. And it was a weekday. A working day. So that was strange. But not as strange as the fact that my parents were talking to each other. And quietly at that.

They were sitting at the kitchen table, leaning close together. As though there had already been someone in the house who might overhear.

I heard my father say something about a general discharge, and how it follows a person through the rest of his life. I didn't know what he meant. It sounded like a medical condition.

Now, I'm not one to talk much about people's energy, or aura, or whatever you want to call it. I just take people straight on without all those extra levels of . . . whatever. But I still have to say it: In that moment, there was something invisible hanging in that room that just bowled me over. I could feel it. And it nearly knocked me down.

They looked up and saw me standing there.

"Lucas," my mother said.

I wanted to ask what was going on. What was wrong. But I didn't. And I think the fact that I didn't had something to do with the whole Connor and Mrs. Dinsmore thing. I had begun to assume that pretty much nothing was any of my business. I had started to keep my questions to myself.

"I'm going upstairs," I said.

"Wait," my father said. His voice was booming and big. Deep.

I stopped in midstride.

"Before you go up there," my mother said, "we need to tell you something."

I walked to the table. It was only a few steps, but I remember a distinct feeling like I was walking up to a hangman's noose or a guillotine. Marching to my own execution.

I sat.

"What?" I said.

My mother spoke first.

"Your brother is home."

"What?" There was no delay, not even a fraction of a second. It just burst out of me. *"How? How* is he home? How *can* he be?" It sounded like I was arguing, but the more I talked, the more I was getting excited. In the back of my mind I was beginning to wonder why they weren't treating this like a good thing. "He wasn't supposed to be able to come home for . . ." Then I hit a big question. Not the biggest. The biggest hadn't made it through the jumble of my thoughts yet. But big. "Wait," I said. "Did you *know* about this?"

My mother looked down at the table in shame.

"And you didn't *tell* me?" I shouted, raising my voice in a way I never did to my mother.

Well, from that moment forward I could never again claim that I'd never yelled at her. Everything was changing in that moment.

"It was just a few days," she said. "We were trying to figure out the best way to tell you."

I sat a minute with my mouth hanging open. I had all these things I wanted to say, and might well have said. How it really isn't so hard. How she maybe could have used the words she'd used a minute ago. "Your brother is home." See? Easy.

I didn't say any of those things. Because, before I could, the biggest question came up through my thoughts.

I asked it. I couldn't not ask it.

"Did he get injured?"

A pause. One I didn't like. It wasn't what I would call long, but it was long enough to contain some news I didn't want to hear.

"He . . . ," my mother began, ". . . hurt his foot."

My father lost it and started yelling at her.

"Oh, for heaven's sake, Ellie, how can you say a thing like that? Why do you talk in euphemisms? Just tell the boy the truth. He doesn't have a 'hurt foot.'" He said those last two words in a high, mocking voice, showing us both what he thought a foolish woman sounded like. "Half of it is blown off."

My ears tingled while I sat and digested that, and listened to them fight.

"Now see here, I won't have you telling me how to raise my son! I raised those two boys into fine young men, and where were you? Working every minute!"

It struck me that almost every important development of my life had sounded something like this. That I had absorbed almost every piece of family news over this blaring backdrop of rage.

"If they were both fine young men, he wouldn't have done what he did."

"Don't you dare, Bart! Don't you dare say a thing like that to me! You have no idea what he went through over there!"

"Well, you don't either."

"But you're the one making judgments based on what you don't know."

The volume of their voices was starting to hurt my eardrums.

In my head, in the privacy of my imagination, I took a brilliant stand. Literally and figuratively. I stood, towering over them, and told them to stop. Now and forever. Just stop fighting. I told them it was killing me. At a moment like this, when I should be upstairs welcoming my brother home, it was a crime to be expected to sit here and listen to all this screaming. I told them it had been this way as long as I could remember, and I couldn't take much more. I asked them if they knew how much it took out of me.

In the real world, I stood. Just like I had in my fantasy land.

Then I walked out of the room.

Because in the real world I couldn't even have shouted them down. They never would have disconnected from their fighting long enough to give me their attention.

Besides. I had more important things to do.

I walked up the stairs, still hearing them shouting.

"It was irresponsible!" My father.

"I won't let you speak that way about him! He's my son!" My mother.

Their voices got quieter as I walked upstairs. Not because they lowered their volume. Because I was walking away.

"*Your* son? Not *our* son?"

"Well, isn't it always moments like this when you foist them off on me?"

I stepped up onto the landing and looked in the direction of Roy's bedroom door. It was closed. It had never been closed while he was gone. Not one time.

I walked to it, a dizzy feeling in my head. Like I was dreaming. Was it possible that all this was only a dream?

I steeled myself and knocked.

"Who is it?" I heard. A weak, mushy sort of voice through the door.

"It's me, Lucas."

"Oh. Okay. Come in."

I opened the door.

The first thing I saw was the foot. It was bandaged, of course. So I wasn't literally seeing the foot. But I was getting a good look at where it ended.

My brother was under the covers, but his foot was outside them, and propped up on a pillow. I guess even the weight of blankets would have been unbearable on that wound.

It wasn't really half the foot gone, like my dad had said. More like a third of it. More like from the ball of the foot, I was guessing, where the big toe joints into it at the base. From there forward, nothing. Air. It reminded me of Libby Weller's brother Darren, and how *nothing* can be more shocking than just about anything. No amount of wounding of a human body part could be worse than the utter absence of it.

He noticed me noticing.

"Hey buddy," he said, his voice fuzzy.

"Land mine?" I asked. That's what had gotten Libby Weller's brother. A land mine.

"Gunshot."

I looked at him then. At his face. And I got a second major shock.

I thought, *Wait. That's not Roy.*

I thought, *They sent us back the wrong brother.*

I mean, the shape of his face was familiar. And his hair was the right color of sandy dark blond, though it was much shorter than I had ever seen it. It wasn't that he had some major feature that identified him as someone else entirely. He just wasn't quite Roy.

It was like seeing someone on the street that I thought might be Roy, and waiting for that click of familiarity. And never getting it.

I figured it would come along in time. But, the problem was, I had no idea *how much* time. In that moment I'd have guessed fifteen or twenty minutes would solve the issue. It ended up being closer to fifteen or twenty years. But I don't mean to get off track.

"Sit down," he said. And his voice sounded like his voice, only with most of the life gone out of it.

I pulled up a chair.

The room was dim. Weirdly dim, like Connor's house. The curtains were drawn tightly closed. And yet he was staring toward the window as if he could look out of it, which struck me as strange.

"You look so different," I said.

"Must be the hair."

He lifted a hand to run it over his buzzed head, but he almost missed. He had to adjust the path of that hand to guide it to his own scalp.

I could still hear our parents fighting downstairs. But I couldn't make out individual words, which was a blessing.

I thought about the letter. My last letter. The humiliatingly mushy one. How long ago had I sent it? More than three weeks ago. Maybe a month. I had no idea if he'd gotten it. It was impossible to know with APO mail. Sometimes it was two weeks. Sometimes two months. One letter my mother sent him never got there, as far as we could tell.

I was hoping he hadn't seen it.

Sitting there with him, looking right into his face, I couldn't imagine saying the things I'd said in that letter. Sad, but true. It just felt too personal. It felt like the truthfulness of the words would rip me open, exposing a part of me that might not survive out in the air. It was all just *too* important.

And yet some part of me had to know.

"I sent you a letter," I said. "After I answered the last letter you sent me. It was just an extra one. It was short. But probably you'll never get it now. Which I think is okay because—"

"I got it," he said.

Then we just sat there in silence for a minute. Really, a full minute or more. And while we were sitting, I felt my face get redder and redder and redder.

"Why do you think it all came down the way it did?" he added.

"I don't know what you mean. I don't know how it all came down."

"Oh."

More silence.

"What were you trying to tell me?" I asked him, anxious to change the subject. "In that last letter? Something you saw, but it got all blacked out."

"No." His voice sounded firm for the first time. Almost normally firm for Roy. Not quite, but at least in the right ballpark. "No, you don't need to hear that. The minute I sent that letter I was sorry. The minute it was out of my hands I would've done anything to take it back. When I found out you couldn't read it, I was so relieved. I never should've put that on you. Once a thing like that gets into your head you'll never get it out again. Never."

He dropped into silence. Then, much to my alarm, he began to cry. Really sob openly. Roy was five years older than me, and I had never seen him cry. At least, not that I could recall.

"I just wanted to get home to you," he said. "When I got that letter. But I didn't want to let the guys down. It still kills me that I let the guys down."

I had no idea what he was talking about.

"Oh hell," he said. "I'm sorry. I'm on so many painkillers. I mean, they've got me so doped up, buddy. Morphine up the wazoo. Not literally. I just mean I'm on a lot of it."

He fell silent. I waited while his sobs wound down. A long, slow, painful wait.

I felt a little better knowing he was on heavy meds. Because otherwise his behavior was scaring me. But knowing he was on a lot of morphine really helped explain things. He had been given a huge dose of truth serum. He would come around when it wore off. Go back to seeming like himself.

"I should probably get some sleep," he said.

"Sure. I'll just leave you be. We'll have plenty of time to talk later."

I let myself out of his room.

My father had left to go back to work. Or, anyway, he'd left. I could hear the tires of his car crunching on the gravel of the driveway. The part about his going back to work was just a guess.

I was hungry, but I didn't go into the kitchen. Because my mom was still in there, and I was afraid she would tell me more. I was pretty sure, without ever talking to myself about it, that I wasn't ready to know more.

———

I managed to wait about two hours before running back to Mrs. Dinsmore's cabin—mostly to avoid cutting into Connor's time with her. I did not manage to stay away completely.

The dogs ran to greet me, and I was so happy to see them that I started to cry. Well, I suppose it wasn't just the dogs. I had a lot going on to put those tears in me. The dogs were more like a fuse into all that gunpowder. But it did strike me that they were the only . . . well, I started to say "people," but they weren't people. They were the only beings in my life who loved me and had no trouble saying so.

Now, if there was one thing I hated as a kid, it was anybody seeing me cry. Dogs not included. That's another thing that's great about dogs.

I thought I'd just put the tears away again. I wrestled with them as I stepped up onto the lady's porch. I figured I would win, because I usually did. But that day they flipped me and pinned me. Got me in a headlock I knew I could not escape. This time I'd get my freedom back when the tears told me I could have it back and not a moment sooner.

I sat on the edge of the porch with the dogs and cried into Rembrandt's short silver coat. Every time I lifted my head Vermeer tried to lick the tears off my face.

I heard a voice from behind, and it startled me.

"This can't be good. You don't ever come a second time unless you've got something bad going on."

I didn't answer.

She came and sat on the edge of the porch with me. I kept my face pressed into the boy dog's coat, so she wouldn't see I was crying. But then a little hiccupy sob broke through the gates.

"Oh dear," she said in that signature gravelly voice. "You'd best tell me what's on your mind."

I raised my head. The jig was up anyway.

She was wearing jeans with a big, oversized, untucked blue work shirt over them. Sleeves rolled up to her elbows. Her hair was down and freshly combed. It struck me that she had been a pretty woman, once upon a time. Before she'd decided she didn't want to be anymore. Before she'd decided she didn't want to be anything to anybody.

"Spill it," she said.

"It's too much, though."

"What's too much?"

"For you, I mean. First me and then Connor. Both needing you and leaning on your time like we do. It's too much. Isn't it?"

I was looking off into the woods as I asked it. But I heard her sigh.

"Well, it's a lot," she said. "But I don't know the magic boundary on what's too much."

We sat for a minute, saying nothing. Vermeer was still licking my face.

"Now you know why I have dogs," she said.

"Yeah. They help. Wish I had one." Another awkward silence. "I never asked you what kind of dogs they were."

"Weimaraner and Great Dane."

"Oh. That explains a lot. That's how they got so big." I paused. Cannonballed into the deep end of the thing. "My brother's home from the war."

She gave me space to say more, but I didn't use it.

"And, obviously," she said, "there's a reason why that's not such a happy thing like it's supposed to be. How bad did he get hurt?"

"Lost half his foot. Well. A third of it, anyway."

"Land mine?"

"No. He says it was a gunshot."

"Yeah. I guess that makes more sense. Land mine wouldn't leave you any foot at all. So, listen. It's bad, I know. I'm not saying it's not bad. But it may turn out to be a small price to pay. I mean, you get your brother back, and if he'd stayed over there, maybe not one bit of him would've made it home."

I didn't answer. I was staring off into the woods, thinking I wouldn't bother her with the rest of my troubles. How much of other people's problems can one poor woman take?

"There's more," she said. "Am I right? It's written all over your face."

"I just don't understand why my folks are upset with him. They're acting like it's his fault or something."

"Hmm."

We sat for the longest time. Minutes. I got the sense that she had all kinds of things to say but hadn't decided whether or not to say them.

"My ex had guns," she said after a time. "I'm not a fan of them myself. But he had a deer rifle, and then a pistol for home protection. That's what he called it, anyway, but it always seemed to me that bringing a gun into a house is more likely to do the opposite of protecting it. Case in point, he was cleaning it. Thought he'd taken all the shells out, but he'd left one in the chamber. Shot himself in the foot. Still walks with a bad limp to this day. Not that I've seen him any too recently."

I waited. I was wondering if she was going to tell me what this had to do with my situation. It did seem like a weird coincidence that we both knew someone who had taken a gunshot to the foot. Maybe that was her only point.

"Here's the reason I'm telling you all this." She paused. And I knew that something big was coming. And I knew I didn't want it. "Kind of hard to shoot a person in the foot from some distance. More likely you'll get them somewhere between the legs and the head. For that foot injury, seems like the gun would have to be right above the foot, pointing down. Now, I can't say that for an absolute fact. I've never been in combat, and I suppose weird things happen. I'm just talking likelihoods here. You understand what I'm saying to you?"

"Yes, ma'am."

I wasn't feeling much. At least, not in the way of reactions or emotions. The inside of my head seemed to be stuffed with cotton. The inside of my guts felt like concrete. My mouth was painfully dry.

"But you don't want to go there just yet."

"No, ma'am."

"Fine. I won't bring it up again."

We sat in silence for a time. Then I guess she got tired of that, because she spoke up.

"Well, if you got nothing else you wanted to say . . ."

"I need to ask you about something."

"Okay . . ." But she sounded skeptical.

"I've been working really hard not to ask anything about Connor. Because I figure what he talks about with you is none of my business. But I just wanted to know if he told you this, because it's one of those life-or-death things. Did he tell you his father's gun went missing? And his mother thinks he took it?"

"Yeah. He told me he didn't take it."

"Oh. Okay. Good."

"You think he took it?"

"I don't know what to think," I said. "About anything."

And, with those words, it came over me how tired I was. Bone tired. It was like a wave that broke over my head and then took me.

Something came out of me that I wasn't expecting.

"You still take drugs?" I asked her.

"Excuse me?"

"I heard you drank a lot and took a lot of drugs. Showed up places around town pretty much out of your mind, so then maybe a lot of people who wanted to be on your side, maybe after that they couldn't be. But I never saw you out of your mind, so I was thinking maybe that's a lie. I guess I was hoping it was a lie."

"You saw me in a coma from an overdose of pain meds."

"Oh," I said. "Right. Well don't I feel stupid now?"

She didn't say more for a long time. I could feel her gathering up for something. Maybe to talk to me about it. Maybe to go back inside the cabin. Maybe she hadn't even decided yet herself.

"After the incident," she said, "I drank and used. And, yeah. It got pretty bad." Her voice sounded unusually quiet. As though she'd lost all her energy. "Then I got clean and sober. Went to meetings and everything. For years—over ten years. Then I started needing some pain meds for an old back injury. From the accident. And then I got carried away on those. Which leads me to the time you met me."

"You could go back to the meetings."

"Maybe," she said. "I'm still kind of on the fence about that. About whether there's any point. Now if you'll excuse me, that's more than I usually tell anybody, even those I've known forever. And I think it's more than enough for one day."

She got up stiffly. As though her back was hurting her. Or at least as though something was. She walked back into her cabin and closed and locked the door behind her.

I stayed and hugged the dogs for a while longer. But sooner or later I had to go home, and I knew it.

Chapter Thirteen

Picking Up Stuff

Oddly enough, the first outside visitor to come around and see my brother was Connor. And I hadn't even told him Roy was home.

He showed up sometime after breakfast. I wasn't out running because, for the first time since I'd picked up the habit, I didn't feel like I wanted to. I just couldn't bring myself to do it.

I heard the knock at the door, but I waited for my mother to get it. Normally she would get it. This time she never did.

I trotted downstairs and threw the door wide, and there he was. It was surprising to see him at my house, to put it mildly. I'm not sure if that showed on my face. Probably it did.

I almost said, "What are you doing here?" but I caught it just in time. Realized how rude it would sound.

Instead I said, "Sorry about yesterday. You know. How I said I'd come by and all."

"Well, I wondered," he said. "But then I found out about Roy."

So that's a small town for you.

"You want to come in?"

"Yeah," he said. "I'd like to see him."

That was the first I realized he'd come here for Roy and not me. Which was fine. It just surprised me. Looking back, I'm not sure why. For all the time he'd spent at my house over so many years, of course he knew my brother. Cared about my brother. But somehow I'd gotten so wrapped up in what Roy meant to *me* that I wasn't including anybody else in the picture.

I waited until we were walking up the stairs to say, "I'm not sure if he's awake." Purposely waited. I didn't say it at the door, because I didn't want him to go away and come back later. If we had to wait, I wanted him to wait with me. I wanted him to talk to me. I felt like we hadn't talked in ages.

I wanted to know if he was okay.

Bumping into him relatively often outside his own bedroom seemed to be a good sign, but I wanted to hear it straight from him.

I knocked on Roy's door.

"Oh thank goodness," I heard Roy say from inside.

I didn't know what that meant, except it meant he was awake.

I opened the door.

"Oh, it's you," he said. He sounded disappointed.

"Yeah, me," I said, talking over my hurt. "Can Connor come in and say hi?"

We stepped inside without really waiting for an answer.

I pulled up a chair, and Connor sat on the end of Roy's bed. Carefully.

"I thought you were Mom with my pain meds."

"No," I said. "Just us."

"Where *is* Mom?"

"No idea. She might not be home. She usually gets the door when she's home."

"Do me a favor, buddy."

My eyes had been gradually adjusting to the dim light, and I noticed that he was sweaty. As though he had a fever. Which worried me.

"What?"

"Mom has my pain meds in the downstairs bathroom. Kind of dumb if you ask me. Run down and get them, okay?"

"Yeah," I said. "Okay."

I left Connor and Roy alone to talk and ran down the stairs. I called for my mom three times, but never got an answer. So I walked into the downstairs bathroom and grabbed the only prescription pill bottle with Roy's name on it from the medicine cabinet.

I have to admit it: I had a little tickle of doubt, or dread. Or both. Because my mom may have been many things, but she was never dumb a day in her life.

But I couldn't look into Roy's face and refuse him something.

I carried it up the stairs and stepped back into his room.

Connor and Roy had been talking, but quietly, so I couldn't hear what about. Roy stopped when he saw me and reached his hand out for the pills.

"I forgot water," I said.

"I don't need water."

"How can you take a pill without water?"

"I do it all the time," he said. "Learned it over there."

I watched him shake two of the tablets from the bottle into his palm. I almost said something. Because I had read the label coming up the stairs, and it very clearly said to "take one every four hours as needed." But I didn't say anything. Because it was Roy. Who was I to tell Roy what to do?

He popped them into his mouth and chewed them.

"You chew those up?" I asked.

"They hit you faster that way."

"Don't they taste awful?"

"Pretty damn bad, yeah."

I walked into his bathroom to get him a cup of water to wash away the taste. Roy had his own bathroom off his bedroom. I had to use one down the hall. The perks of being older, I suppose.

"Thanks," he said when I handed it to him.

And I noticed again how much he was sweating.

"You want me to open a window or something?"

"No!" he said, all sharp and sudden. "I'm freezing."

That was when I started worrying he might be sick. I sat on the edge of his bed, as close to him as I could, and watched him. He did seem to be shivering some. I wanted to reach out and put a hand to his forehead the way our mom would do if she thought we had a fever, but I could never bring myself to do it.

So I just stared at him, and listened to him talking to Connor about more or less nothing. Connor's school, and his family. I couldn't help noticing that Connor was painting a rosy picture of his life while Roy was gone. Then again, what did it really matter? It was just small talk and we all three knew it.

After a time I saw Roy's shivering start to ease, so I figured the sweating and shaking was more about pain and maybe not an actual illness. I felt my shoulders loosen up, and I was shocked by how tightly I'd been holding every muscle in my body. I made a conscious effort to let everything soften up.

A few minutes later, as Roy asked questions of Connor, he began to slur his words. And yet he reached for the pill bottle again. I'd left it on his bedside table, not realizing that might have been a mistake. Once he was under the effect of the drug, he might not understand that he was taking too much. Maybe that had been the method behind my mom's madness in keeping them downstairs.

I grabbed it up before he could get to it.

"I think you should wait," I said.

I stood and carried the pill bottle into his bathroom, where I stashed it in his medicine cabinet. When I got back out, Connor was talking to Roy, but Roy was clearly nodding off.

I stood and watched, and Connor paused to see if his words were getting through. When it seemed we had lost Roy, he got up off the end of the bed.

"I should go," he said.

We walked to Roy's bedroom door together.

"No, stay," I said. "Stay and talk to me. We haven't talked for a long time."

"Nah. Maybe later. I haven't been to Zoe's yet."

We stepped out into the hall together. I confess I was feeling stung. Partly because talking to me seemed to be no priority for him. Partly because I'd never called Zoe Dinsmore by her first name. Not once. It's hard to admit, but it made me a little jealous. Suddenly Connor was closer to the lady than I had ever been.

I walked him to the door. And, as I did, I expressed none of what I was feeling. You know, the usual. The way we always did things.

"Maybe I'll come by later," he said, but he didn't sound like he meant it. I wasn't expecting him, based on the way he said it.

"Right. Whatever."

Which was the closest I was going to come to saying I was upset.

I closed the door behind him and turned around to see my mother standing in the kitchen doorway, her hands on her hips. I could tell she was angry. About something. In that moment I couldn't even have ventured a guess.

"Okay, where is it?" she asked.

"Where's what?"

"Roy's pain meds. I know he didn't come down the stairs and get them himself."

"He asked me for them and—"

"*Never* do that again!" she shouted. The first word, "Never," was so sharp and loud it made me jump.

"He said he needed them."

"It was too soon! You can't put them where he can get to them. Promise me you'll never do that again. Where are they?"

"In the medicine cabinet in his bathroom."

She clucked her tongue at me as she climbed the stairs. I couldn't help noticing that she hadn't waited and forced that promise out of me. What would I do if he asked me straight out for them again?

I decided my only real hope would be to lie and say Mom had hidden them but even I didn't know where. Or maybe I'd get lucky, and by then it would be the truth.

"I'm worried he might be sick," I said to her retreating back.

"He's not sick," she said, and kept climbing.

I just stood there in the hall for a moment or two.

Then, as I was walking up the stairs, I passed her coming down. She didn't say a word to me.

As I closed the door to my room, I heard the kitchen door slam, and her car start in the driveway. She never bothered to tell me where she was going. She didn't even call out the word "Bye."

———

Roy's second visitor arrived by cab about three hours later. I was looking out my bedroom window, and I saw the yellow cab pull up. That was an occasion, to see a cab in this town. We actually didn't have a taxi service in Ashby. Somebody must've called one to come over from Blaine.

The driver jumped out and came around to the curbside rear door. The way a gentleman will open the door for a lady. But it wasn't a lady I saw climb out of the back seat. It was Darren Weller.

He handed his crutches out to the driver, then carefully positioned himself so his one good leg was out of the cab, shoe sole down on the sidewalk. The driver reached a hand out to help him up, and handed him back his crutches one by one, until Darren was standing steady.

I watched Darren slip the driver some kind of bill and then make his way, slowly, obviously painfully, up our walk.

He looked different than last time I'd seen him. His hair was freshly combed, slicked back with some kind of men's hair product that left wet-looking comb marks along his scalp. He was wearing neatly pressed chinos and a white long-sleeved shirt. The partly empty leg of his slacks had been carefully folded up and pinned.

I was pretty sure my mom wasn't home, so I went downstairs to let him in. I respected him too much not to go let him in. Though, truthfully, I was also afraid of him now. Or still. But more so now, because I thought he might punch me for not being nicer to his sister.

I opened the door, and we looked at each other for a minute. Well, a few seconds. It felt long. He didn't look angry. He looked more sad than anything.

"He taking visitors?"

"He might be kind of doped up on pain meds. I could go see." Another awkward few seconds. "Oh," I said. "I'm sorry. Come in."

He did, easing along on his crutches. I could tell how much it hurt him. I could see it in his face. Every time he rested his weight on them, I saw the wince. I remembered what Libby had told me about shrapnel in the muscles of his chest.

"Maybe you could go up and see what's what," he said. He was looking up the stairs as if the second floor was the summit of a mountain he was only half sure he could climb.

"Sure," I said. "I will." But then I stuck where I was for a moment. "Are you mad at me?" I asked him.

His face looked completely blank.

"About what?"

So that was obviously a good sign.

"Things didn't exactly work out between me and your sister."

"Aw, hell," he said. "I know what a pain in the ass she can be. I know it better than anybody."

—

The logistics were tricky, to put it mildly. But here's how we worked it out: Roy came down. He came down the stairs with one hand on the banister, the other on my shoulder. I walked a couple of steps ahead of him and below him, careful to stop if he seemed wobbly.

When we got to the bottom of the stairs, Darren swung over on his crutches and offered my brother what I can only call an embrace. The word "hug" would not be expansive enough to cover it. I could hear them speaking quiet, almost reverent words into each other's ears, but I couldn't hear what words they were.

Then Darren clapped Roy on the back a couple of times, and they broke apart.

"Hey, buddy," Roy said, turning his attention on me. "Run upstairs and bring me down my crutches, okay?"

I did as I'd been asked.

Then I watched my brother and my ex-girlfriend's brother disappear—slowly—into my father's den.

I wanted to follow, but I didn't. I wanted to rate, but I didn't. I ached to be a member of the authorized personnel—figuratively speaking—who could walk through that door marked "Authorized Personnel Only." But I wasn't.

You had to have survived a war. Watched parts of yourself separate away. Actual parts, and maybe invisible parts as well.

You had to know things I couldn't possibly know.

—

Darren came out about an hour and a half later. By himself. I tried not to think about everything he had likely been told, and how much I wanted to know it. At least, I think I wanted to know it. Sometimes it's hard to be sure until it's too late.

He came over slowly on his crutches. It was clear he was tired from so much moving around. He put a hand on my shoulder. He never had before.

"Where's Roy?" I asked.

"On the couch in the den. He's not feeling good about getting back up the stairs. When your dad gets home, you can tag-team the thing."

"Okay."

If he ever got home. You never knew in those days.

"Now do me a favor, okay, Lucas?"

"Sure," I said.

He led me farther away from the den door. He leaned in as if to say something important. Then he seemed to go an entirely different direction in his brain.

"Wait," he said. "Let me call my cab first."

I sat on the living room couch with my heart pounding and my fingers woven together, fidgeting.

He came out a couple of minutes later. When he eased down on the couch next to me, he made a long noise. A cross between a sigh and a grunt. It reminded me of my grandmother before she died—of the noise she made every time she sat down. But Darren was only twenty.

"I need you to do something to help your brother," he said. His face was leaned in close, his voice quiet.

"Anything. What?"

"Find out where there are some meetings in town. Or in Blaine. Or wherever the hell you have to go. If AA is all you've got, it'll do. But try to find NA if you possibly can. Try to find what they call an open meeting. That way you can go, too. And then get 'im there. And sit with 'im so he doesn't walk out before it's over. So he at least has to pretend like he's listening. And if he says he'll just go to that VA drug counseling instead, don't go that way. Trust the VA with his injury—what choice do you have? But don't give 'em his heart or his soul to heal. Hell, most of 'em haven't even healed their own."

I could hear a pulsing of blood in my ears. It was loud, and pretty distracting.

"I don't know what NA is."

"Like AA, but for drugs."

"What's the *N* stand for?"

"Narcotics."

"Oh." I sat quietly for a minute. Then I said, "Is this because he's taking too many of those pain pills? Because I think maybe he just got high on them and forgot how many he was supposed to take."

"Nah," Darren said. "It's not about that."

I wondered if I wanted to ask what it was about. Then I wondered if not asking would keep me safe from Darren's telling me anyway.

"He's only been home since yesterday," I said.

I think I was fighting back against the idea that Roy needed to go to meetings. In fact, I'm sure I was. I wanted Darren to be mistaken about that.

"This is not about what he's been doing since he got home. It's about what he did over there. Guys pick up stuff over there. It happens a lot. Because stuff's easy to get, and because it makes everything almost bearable. It's usually a situational thing. Guy needs it till he gets home. Then he doesn't need it anymore."

"Maybe he won't need it anymore," I said.

"Well. Thing is, he might've said something to suggest he's one of the ones who can't put it down without help."

"What did he say?"

It was a brave question. But I think I figured if I knew, I could find a flaw in Darren's conclusion.

"He asked me if I knew how to get 'im any."

"Oh," I said.

I couldn't find a flaw in that.

We sat in silence for a time. And the silence had a burn to it. I wasn't sure if it was a temporary break in our conversation, or if we were just waiting for his cab to pull up and honk.

"Did you pick up stuff over there?" I asked.

It was another bold question. But I needed to know.

"I did," he said.

"But then you set it down when you got home?"

"I did, yeah. But not everybody can. And it doesn't make me bigger or stronger or braver or better. Different people have different reactions to things. That's all."

"What if he won't go with me?"

"Then you call me up and tell me, and I'll come over and help you sort things out. Okay?"

"Okay," I said. But it sounded like a lot of responsibility.

We sat in silence for a while longer. And, in that silence, I stepped back in time in my head. Back to before Roy came home. When I'd thought everything would be so simple. I'd thought Roy would just come home, and then everything would be great.

I think I grew up a lot in that moment.

"How old are you now?" he asked, knocking me out of my thoughts.

"Fourteen."

"That's good," he said. "Four years. Maybe we'll be out of that damn war by then. But if not . . . well, you'll have to make up your own mind what to do. You can't just do what I think you should do. But I'll tell you this. If I had it to do over again, I wouldn't go."

"I have a choice?"

"Everybody has choices. Always. Just, sometimes they don't like 'em. You can go where the draft board sends you. Or you can go to Canada. Or you can go to jail. If you ask me, jail is the more honorable way to go. You can look the guys who did fight straight in the eye and say, 'Yeah, I sacrificed, too. I didn't have it easy.' But think carefully before you get yourself into a thing like a war."

"Maybe it'll be over by then," I said. Which had already been said. So it would've been more honest to say, "Oh dear God, please let it be over by then."

He opened his mouth to answer, but just then his cab honked in the driveway. And that was it for our visit.

—

I knew when my mom was home because I heard her holler my name. I don't usually use the word "holler." But in this case it feels like the only one that'll do.

"Lucas!"

I came to the railing on the second-floor landing and looked down, wondering what I had done wrong this time.

"What?"

She looked up at me, her face livid. If my life had been a cartoon, she would've had smoke coming out of her ears.

"What did you do?" she shouted.

She had a pill bottle in her hand that I could only assume was Roy's medication. She held it up as Exhibit A in the trial that would likely end with my death penalty.

"I didn't do anything," I said. "I didn't touch it."

"Four pills missing! Four! You think I don't count them? I know he didn't walk down the stairs by himself and get them."

"Oh," I said. In that ugly moment the truth stretched out in front of me like a mile of bad road. One I would have no choice but to navigate. "He . . . we . . . I helped him come downstairs. Because Darren Weller came by to see him. It would've been harder for Darren to get up the stairs than for Roy to get down them. I never thought about the pills. I'm sorry."

She peered up at me for a moment. Her anger seemed to be draining away, but I swear she looked as though she was trying to keep it.

"I'm hiding these where only I know where they are."

"Yes, please," I said.

Sooner or later he was going to ask me to get him some. And when I said I didn't know where they were, I wanted it to be the truth.

She narrowed her eyes at me. Trying to figure me out, I guess. I remember vaguely wishing in that moment that she saw herself and me as being on the same team. But that was not my mom, or my life.

Then she turned and stomped away.

Chapter Fourteen

My Name Is Roy And . . .

I beat Connor out to the lady's cabin the following morning. Purposely.
I figured she might still be sleeping, but I was wrong on that score. She
was sweeping off her front porch with an old broom. A *very* old broom
It was missing a lot of its straws.

"Hey," I said, patting the dogs' heads as best I could while they
jumped and danced around me.

"You're early."

She stopped sweeping and leaned on her broom. She was a lot of
woman and it was not much broom. It didn't look like it wanted to
hold her.

"I need to ask you about meetings," I said.

"Meetings," she repeated.

"Like for people who're addicted to drugs. You said you used to go
to them."

"Yeah. I guess I did say that."

For a moment she just stared at me. I was guessing she was curious
as to whether I was asking for myself or a friend. So I answered what
was in my head, even though it might not have been in hers at all.

"And it has to be an open meeting. Because I need to be able to go, too. And I'm not . . . you know . . ."

I hated to use that word. The A-word. It seemed harsh.

She turned and walked into the house, leaving the door open. I stood there feeling like a fool because I didn't know if that had been an okay thing to ask or not. But I figured if I had offended her, she would have slammed the door behind her. Or at least closed it, shutting me out.

She came back a minute or two later with a little paper booklet in her hands. Maybe only four pages, or maybe six. She sat on the edge of the porch with it, and I sat down next to her. The minute I dropped my face to their level, the dogs smothered me with wet kisses.

When I was able to open my mouth safely—which involved holding Rembrandt at arm's length with one hand against his chest—I asked about the booklet.

"We have so many meetings in this town that you need to sort them all out on paper?"

"Hardly," she said. "This is for the whole tricounty area. Okay. The one at the bank is still going on. That's the only NA that's right here in Ashby. Monday, Wednesday, and Friday, 6:00 p.m. Monday and Friday are open meetings. Wednesday is closed for addicts only. It's in that community room at the First Bank."

"Oh yeah. I know where that is."

We sat in silence for a moment. I expected her to ask me who I was wanting to take to meetings, but she never did.

I figured that was the difference between Zoe Dinsmore and myself. She didn't seem to burn to know things. She seemed to be able to leave everything alone in her head.

Either that or it was easy enough to figure out on her own.

"Can I say how I feel?" I asked after a time.

"You always did before."

That stung me a little. But I kept going. Zoe Dinsmore was pretty damned beelike, and if you were going to shrink back every time you got stung, well . . . I figured it would be a waste of time to come out to her cabin in the first place.

"I feel like I'm having to save too many people at once here." At the corner of my eye I saw her nod slowly. "I mean, I'm not even out of high school. What am I doing trying to help all these people? Three people all at once like this. That's a lot, don't you think?"

"You can take me off your list," she said.

"But then I might lose you."

A pause.

Then she said, "Okay. Seriously. Want me to tell you how to take the pressure off yourself?"

"Yes, ma'am. I sure do."

"You've just got to stay out of the outcomes, Lucas. It's not that you walked Connor out here to meet me that's weighing you down. It's the fact that you're holding yourself responsible for whether it works out or not. You can take your brother to some meetings without turning yourself inside out. Trouble is, you take on the responsibility of being the one who sees to it that he recovers. Want to know why that stuff takes so much out of you? Easy. It's all stuff that's out of your control. You're trying to change things that're not within your control to change. And whenever you try to do something that's impossible to do, you're going to find yourself a little on the tired side. Make sense?"

"Yeah," I said. "It does."

It did. Actually. Though I'm not sure that was the good news.

"You don't sound too sure."

"It's just that . . . what you just said . . . it's that kind of advice that lets you know what to do but not how to do it. I mean, how do you not take that stuff on?"

"Right. I'll grant you that. It's easier said than done. But practice at it. You'll get better at anything you practice."

We sat quietly for another minute.

Then she said, "Here," and held out the meeting schedule to me.

"You should keep it," I said. "You told me you might think about going back."

"I know where those three meetings are if I want them."

I sighed. Took it from her. Folded it up and stuck it in my shirt pocket.

"How's it going with Connor?" I asked.

"That's not what you were going to practice, now is it?"

"I just thought maybe if I knew more, I could worry less."

"Oh, I doubt that," she said. Then, "I can't really tell you how it's going, because I don't really know. He's talking to me. Talking is better than not talking. But beyond that it's hard to say."

"I wish I knew why he couldn't talk to *me*."

"Because you take it on."

"What do you mean, take it on? I don't even know what that means."

"It means you care too much about him to stand back from the situation. If he tells you he can't take much more, you freak out and feel like you need to do something. Me, I just hear him out. I just let him get it off his chest."

"Nothing wrong with caring," I said. I sounded a little on the defensive side. Probably because I was.

"Never said it was wrong. You asked the question and I answered it."

"Yeah. Okay."

We sat another minute. Vermeer sighed deeply, finally accepting that the run was unavoidably delayed. She curled up in the dirt at my feet, and Rembrandt took her cue and followed suit.

"Look. Here's what I don't get," I said. "He's so close to his mom. And she depends on him so much. Especially now that his father is gone. I just can't understand how he could even consider such a thing. You know. Knowing what it would do to her and all."

"But can you understand that he feels a lot of rage toward his mom? *Because* she depends on him too much? And because he has to consider her feelings first in everything he does?"

I opened my mouth to answer, but no answer had formed yet in my brain. And, before one could, I looked up to see Connor walking up the path toward the cabin. So I knew this conversation was over.

It was time for me to practice relaxing about the things I couldn't control.

—

When I'd finished my run and jogged home, I found more opportunities to practice.

My mom was gone. Where to, I had no idea. She was starting to be away more and more. She said nothing about it, and I couldn't imagine even wanting to know the story behind it. I figured if I knew, I wouldn't like what I found out. Call it a hunch.

Roy had managed to come downstairs on his own and was limping around on his crutches, obviously looking for something. And what he was looking for was obvious.

I stepped into the hall just in time to see him leave the downstairs bathroom and make his way into our parents' bedroom. I followed him. Stood in the doorway and watched him pull open the top drawer of my mom's dresser and rummage around in there.

"What're you doing?" I asked.

It startled him so much he almost lost his balance and fell off his crutches.

I'd meant to say it casually. Not so much as an accusation. More like "Hey. What's up?" I don't think I succeeded.

"Oh. Hi. Buddy. You scared me. Listen. Mom took off and forgot to give me my pain meds."

I doubted that. She had a written schedule. She checked off the doses with a pencil. I didn't say so.

"So . . . ," he continued, ". . . you know where she's keeping them now?"

"No."

"Help me find them. Okay, buddy?"

"No."

My brother seemed to freeze in time. Really, the whole world seemed to. The utter silence was shocking. I remember thinking the birds had stopped chirping outside the window because of what I'd said to Roy. Though, looking back, it's possible they'd just flown away by then. For their own reasons.

I heard him clear his throat carefully.

"Thought you cared enough about me to do me a favor, buddy."

"I can't do that one, though." I wanted to say I couldn't do it *because* I cared about him, but I couldn't bring myself to talk like one of those corny made-for-TV movies where people say exactly what they're feeling, as though there was nothing difficult about that at all. As though people did that correctly every day. "As a matter of fact," I said instead, "I was going to ask a favor of *you*."

"What?"

"I want you to come someplace with me."

"Where?"

"I want you to not ask where."

"When? Now?"

"No. Later on this afternoon."

"Weird that you won't even tell me what it is."

"I know. But I'm just going to ask you to trust me. You trust me, don't you? And if you do this for me, I'll do something for you. I'll ask Mom to show me where she keeps her schedule of your meds so I can look over her shoulder and catch it if she ever forgets and skips a dose."

I waited for a minute. Watched as he rolled that around in his head. It was a useful offer only if she really was forgetting. It was no use to him if he only wanted to take more than what had been prescribed.

Meanwhile he seemed as though he never planned to answer.

"So will you go with me?"

"On one condition. That Mom or Dad won't drive us."

"How are we supposed to get there if nobody drives us?"

"Well how do *you* get places? You never ask them to drive you."

"Walk. Or take the bus. But I don't have a hurt foot."

"I'm good on my crutches now. They're mad as hell, and I'm not getting stuck in a car with either one of them lecturing me."

"Okay," I said. "Suit yourself. We'll take the bus."

—

I bolted down as much dinner as I could stomach, then took a plate up to Roy and told him to hurry. Told him we had to leave in twenty minutes.

When I got downstairs, my mom was doing up the dinner dishes.

"Roy and I are going out," I said.

I had to run it by her. No way I could get him out of the house without her noticing. But it was dicey, and I knew it. She was a brick wall between me and our getting where we needed to go, and I knew I might not get through her. I could feel a little vein pulsing with tension near my ear.

"*What?*" She said it not like she hadn't heard me. More like she'd heard it but she couldn't believe it. "No," she added. "No, no, no. I don't like this one bit. I don't trust either one of you."

That was a sad truth, but I believed her. In fact, I'd already known.

"But—"

"I need that boy here where I can keep an eye on him."

I moved closer to the sink. I needed to confide in her quietly. And I think she knew it. I think she could see honest information coming. She seemed to withdraw into herself. To move out of the way of the honesty. She never moved her feet, though. It was all an inside job.

"I'm taking him to an NA meeting," I whispered.

"What *is* that?" she asked. As if it irritated her not to know. "I don't even know what that is."

"Like AA, except for drugs."

"How do you even know about a place like that?"

"Darren Weller told me. I promised him I would do this for Roy. So please, please don't stop me from doing this. Okay? It might help. And I promised."

"Oh."

I watched her face change. Watched her feelings about the situation evolve—possibly against her will. It always seemed to bother her to let her anger drop away. It was something she seemed to want to hold tightly.

"Well I guess I underestimated you," she said. "I'll drive you boys."

"No. We have to go on our own. He agreed to go with me on the condition that it would be just the two of us. And he doesn't know where we're going, so don't spill the beans, okay?"

A long pause.

Then all she said was, "You need money for the bus?"

"It would be nice, yeah."

I'd been hoping Roy had some. If not, we were on foot.

I followed her to her purse, where she dug out a handful of change. She dropped it into my palm, staring into my face the whole time. It made me uncomfortable. It made me need to look away.

I felt her hand on my cheek.

"You're a good boy," she said. "Take care of your brother."

Then she hurried off. Before I could even answer her. Before she'd be forced to confront the fact that she'd said a kind and loving thing.

———

We got off the bus on Main Street, near the end of the business district. It turned residential farther down.

It was almost six, and I wanted to walk faster. I didn't want to be late for the meeting. But I had to slow my steps for Roy.

The sun was on a long slant behind us, but it was still hot. Weirdly hot. I could feel it baking the back of my neck. I could feel sweat trickling down into my collar.

"Where are we going?" he asked.

I figured this time he meant it more logistically. Like "Which way should I walk?" At least I hoped so.

"The bank," I said.

"Isn't the bank closed after five?"

"The community room."

The community room was a separate room in the back with a separate entrance. It made no difference if the bank was open or not.

"Oh," Roy said.

I could feel him wanting to ask more. But, to his credit, he didn't.

We walked around the corner of the bank. I was still shortening and slowing my strides for Roy, who seemed to be tired already on his crutches. We walked down the side street and into the parking lot.

The door of the community room was standing wide open, and the light that spilled out of it felt welcoming. I could smell cigarette smoke and coffee.

A big handful of guys and one lady were standing around in the parking lot smoking and talking. Two massive chopper-style motorcycles sat parked among a smattering of cars. The guys nodded to us as we walked slowly by.

Then, just at the doorway, Roy stopped cold.

I had already walked into the room, where tables had been arranged in a big square. It took me a second to realize that Roy wasn't with me anymore.

I backtracked, and found him staring at a handwritten paper sign taped to the wall next to the open door.

It said: **NA MEETING IN PROGRESS—PLEASE DO NOT DISTURB.**

"No," Roy said when he saw I was there. Not really in a defiant way. More like he was churning things around in his head, and this was the only thing he could push out.

"But you already promised."

I watched him chew that over behind his eyes, still staring at the sign. As if it took many minutes to read every word.

"But I didn't know what I was promising."

"But you promised to do whatever it was without knowing what it was."

A pause. I felt like my whole life was resting on that pause. Bowing everything under the weight. Ready to snap something at any minute.

"Tell you what," Roy said. "I'll go to the meeting. But only if I can do it by myself. You have to go home."

"But I promised Darren Weller I'd stay with you."

"Oh," he said. "Darren Weller. Got it. That explains a lot. Look. Seriously. Buddy. This is not the kind of thing a guy does in front of his little brother. Can you understand that? I'll give the meeting a try this one time, but first you have to go home."

I sighed. I saw no way out.

I dug in my pocket and counted out change for the bus trip home. He took it from me.

"You have enough for the bus?" he asked me.

"I do, but I can just walk. Or run it. It's not even two miles."

"Oh. Right."

The people who'd been milling and smoking brushed past us into the room. Through the open doorway I could see the clock on the wall at the end of the long tables. It was straight up six o'clock.

"You'd better go in," I said. "I think it's starting."

He limped in on his crutches, and I closed the door behind him.

I almost went home.

I walked out to the street. It was absolutely abandoned out there. Everybody in town was home for dinner. It felt weird, like standing in a ghost town.

For a minute or two I just stood there and looked around. Then I decided I would wait for him. I didn't know how long the meeting was. Maybe an hour. Maybe even an hour and a half. But I decided I owed it to my brother to be there when he got out.

I would sit on the curb outside the community room door, leaving him alone to do his meeting thing in privacy. But when the meeting let out, I would walk him to the bus stop and we would ride home together. And if he wanted to, he could tell me how it had gone.

Yeah. That felt right.

I walked back around the building. Sat on the curb where the sidewalk leading to the meeting room door met the tarmac of the parking lot. My back to the door, I watched the sun through the trees, careful not to stare long enough to burn out my eyes and go blind. But I wanted to see if I could actually watch it go down. Or if time moved too slowly for that.

A couple of minutes later, long before I got the answer about the sun, I heard the door swing open behind me. I didn't even have time to turn around and see who was coming out. Before I could, a knee crashed into my back, and the person attached to the knee went flying over me.

"Ow!" I shouted out loud.

I watched my brother Roy fall onto his crutches on the tarmac. It was weird how the moment seemed to play out almost in slow motion.

"Ow!" he shouted.

So we had that in common, anyway.

I lurched up and forward to get to him. I tried to help him up. But for the moment he seemed to accept being down.

"I didn't see you there," he said. "The sun was in my eyes."

"You okay?"

"I think I bruised my ribs falling on this damn crutch."

"You sure you didn't break any?"

"Not positive," he said. "No."

"Did you hurt your foot?"

"Oddly, no."

"Where were you going?"

He never answered the question. Then again, the longer the silence held, the more the question answered itself.

"Come on," I said. "You have to get up."

He sighed deeply. Then he let me help him to his feet. I handed him back his crutches.

I thought he might challenge me and walk off toward the bus stop. He didn't. I think he might have been too humiliated for that.

He walked back to the door, and I held it open for him. And then I followed him in. And sat with him.

He never offered a word of objection.

—

It was somewhere near the end of the sharing, when I'm pretty sure everybody else had spoken. The leader of the meeting—a big guy with a leather vest and tattoos all up and down both arms—asked my brother Roy if he wanted to say anything.

He didn't call him by name.

He just said, "Maybe our newcomer would like to share?"

Roy pressed his lips into a tight line and shook his head.

Everybody stood up and closed the meeting by holding hands around in a circle and reciting the serenity prayer out loud. I had been sitting next to Roy, so I was holding his hand on the left side, which felt weird. Actually weirder than holding the hand of a total stranger on my right.

I didn't know the prayer, so I just moved my lips a little and listened. Soon I would know it backward, forward, and upside down.

Chapter Fifteen

What Might Be Coming Next

Connor showed up at my house early the next morning. Very early. Before my run. Before my parents were awake.

I let him in through the kitchen door and we tiptoed upstairs. I had a little bit of churning going on in my stomach, because it seemed like he had come to tell me something, and I worried it might be something bad.

I closed us into my room, and we sat on the bed, both of us staring down at the spread. We were just fascinated by that spread.

"I came by yesterday afternoon," he said. "But your mom said you were out."

"Yeah. I had to take Roy somewhere."

"Really? That seems weird."

"Why does it seem weird?"

"I don't know exactly. Just seems like *parents* take a guy his age someplace. Not his little brother."

"Well, this was a little-brother thing."

I was hoping he would ask no more about it, and I got my wish.

We sat a minute in silence. Connor was wearing jeans with a hole worn in the knee, and he was rolling the loose frayed threads between his fingers. Funny how desperate a person can get for something to focus on. For something to do with his hands.

"I came by to tell you I was sorry," he said at long last.

"What for?"

We were keeping our voices down. Almost to a whisper. Because my brother and my parents were sleeping in rooms down the hall.

"Because I haven't been talking to you much lately. I go out and talk to Zoe, and then I come back and I don't even tell you what we talked about. And the whole thing was your idea. I wouldn't even know her if it wasn't for you. But . . . it's kind of hard to explain. Have you ever been sitting on a bus bench with some total stranger and started thinking that you could tell them your whole life—everything you were thinking—even though you couldn't tell your best friend?"

Unfortunately, the answer to his question was no. I hadn't had that feeling. But I wanted to be encouraging.

Then I remembered how it was easier to hold the hand of a total stranger in an NA meeting than to hold hands with my own brother. It was less embarrassing somehow.

It was confusing, so all I said was, "I'm not sure. Tell me more about it."

"It's like you can talk to somebody who's completely outside your life, and it feels safe. Because then when you're done, you just go back to your life and there's still nobody there who's heard about all those feelings. It's just feelings, Lucas. It's nothing you don't know. I'm not keeping any big secrets from you."

I was looking out the window at the birds. There were some birds— I think they were swallows—that had been making nests in the eaves right over my bedroom window. I like to watch them swoop and dive.

"I didn't figure it was any big secret," I said.

I mean, I knew his life. And what I knew felt bad enough. Then again, it didn't seem much worse than mine. But I guess you never can tell. You know. From the outside like that.

I remembered something Darren Weller had said to me. *Different people have different reactions to things. That's all.*

"You seem like you feel better," I said after a time, when I was pretty sure he wasn't going to answer. "I mean, I see you outside your house and everything. Do you feel better?"

"Kind of yes and kind of no," he said. "You put all that stuff out, and then it's not really very different. But I guess at least it's out. I'm not entirely sure what that does, just getting it on the outside of you like that, but it seems like it does something. But I did figure out one thing for sure."

He fell silent for a minute. I watched him fingering the loose threads around the hole in his jeans, and I didn't ask. I didn't dare ask what was the one thing he'd figured out.

"It's like . . . ," he began. Then he faded, and I thought I might never know. "Zoe almost died. Well, you know that. You know it better than anybody. I guess she felt like nobody needed her around. But *I* do. *I* need her around. But she didn't know it yet because she hadn't even met me. But she was just about to meet me. All those years thinking nobody needed her or wanted her around, and she was just about to meet me and she didn't know it. You get what I'm driving at?"

"I'm not sure," I said.

"Well . . . now I'm starting to think . . . you don't know what might be coming next. And it might even be something nice. Something good, even though everything before it wasn't good at all. You see where I'm going with this?"

"You're saying you have to stick around to see what happens next."

I watched his face light up, and I knew I had hit it.

"I knew you'd get it," he said.

It was a moment the likes of which we hadn't had in a very long time. If we had ever had a moment like that one.

He seemed satisfied that we had covered that topic, so he flew in an entirely new direction.

"I'm trying to talk my mom into getting me a dog. Wouldn't that be good?"

"Yeah," I said. "It would be great. Think she'll do it?"

"Not sure. She's trying to talk me into a cat instead. She's really paranoid about a dog doing something nasty on the rugs. She figures a cat would be trained to a litter box. I guess a cat would be okay, but . . . you can run with a dog."

"You're thinking about taking up running?"

"Yeah. Maybe. It sure did *you* a lot of good."

I took a deep breath and said something I really wanted badly not to say. But here's the way I looked at it, and I still see it the same way now: you're either a guy's friend or you're not.

"You could always try running with Zoe's dogs."

It actually hurt coming out. But I don't think that mattered. I think what mattered is that I said it. No matter how it felt.

"Nah," he said. "That wouldn't be right. I couldn't do that to you. It's enough that you shared Zoe with me. Running with those dogs, that's your thing. I couldn't horn in on that."

"Thanks," I said, and didn't elaborate. Or need to.

"I'm going to go out there now," he said. "But I figured it was high time I came by and talked."

Speaking of talking, I think by then we had forgotten to whisper and had begun to talk in our natural voices. Because my bedroom door flew open. Suddenly and almost violently. My mother stuck her head into the room as if she could catch me in some dastardly act. What act, I still don't know. Did she think I had a girl in there?

"Oh," she said. "It's you, Connor."

"I was just leaving," Connor said.

"Probably just as well," she said. "Not that you're not welcome here. But everybody else is asleep." Of course, she said it pretty loudly. That was my mom for you.

So that was the end of that talk. But it was okay, because we'd said enough. Really, we'd said everything we needed to say. At least for the moment.

—

When Wednesday came around, I walked up to my brother Roy's room to ask if he wanted me to go with him on the bus to the meeting. It was really a polite way of letting him know that I was pushing him to go, whether I was welcome in the Wednesday meeting or not.

"You said you couldn't go on Wednesdays," he said. "You told me the Wednesday one was a closed meeting."

He was lying on his bed, bare chested, on his back. Curtains drawn closed. Hands linked behind his head. He seemed to be keeping himself busy by staring at the ceiling in the strangely dim room.

"I'd still go with you," I said. "I just wouldn't come in. I could just sit outside and wait for you."

Speaking of waiting, I waited for him to tell me all about how it was an utterly ridiculous idea. I waited for him to say, "Why on earth would I need you to go back and forth on the bus with me just to sit outside?"

He didn't.

"Yeah," he said. "That would be good."

I was surprised, of course. But I didn't argue.

—

The first time we'd ridden the bus to the meeting together, we hadn't talked much. This time was a slight improvement, because this time at least *I* talked.

I told him about how I'd been running in the woods almost every day. And how I'd earned myself a place on the track team come fall, if I wanted it. But that I still didn't think I wanted it.

I told him about the guys on the track team who had given me trouble, and even about how Connor had gone after them.

I told him about Libby Weller, though I didn't state the exact reasons for our breakup. I just told him I learned pretty suddenly that she wasn't a very nice person.

I was purposely leaving out any mention of Zoe Dinsmore, because if it turned out he didn't approve of her either, well . . . that just felt like more than I could take.

I talked until I felt weird about doing so much talking. About filling the air of the mostly deserted bus with so many words. Especially since he was saying nothing in return.

I watched him look out at the passing houses. His eyes were turned away from me, but I could see a perfect reflection of them in the bus window. He seemed to be focusing intently, but I had no idea on what. Maybe what I was saying. Maybe something else entirely. I got the sense that he was either listening carefully or not at all.

I stopped talking. I think I'd run out of things to say.

I got that feeling again—like I was looking at my brother but he wasn't really my brother. Close, but not quite. I thought maybe when his foot was healed and he didn't have to take the pain meds anymore, I would get him back.

Maybe that's why I'd gotten so wrapped up in the idea of his recovery.

He turned and looked right into my face. Possibly for the first time since he'd gotten home.

"Why didn't you tell me all this?" he asked.

"When?"

"In your letters."

"Because it wasn't important."

"Who says it wasn't?"

"How could it matter? You were seeing horrible things, and you had bullets whizzing by your ears. What difference did it make if I got a place on the track team or not? It's stupid. It's nothing. It wasn't even worth wasting your time with stuff like that."

"But that's the stuff I wanted to hear about. You know. Regular stuff. From home. Normal stuff, like my life was before."

"Oh," I said. And then I felt absolutely horrible. "I didn't think of that. I'm sorry."

He turned away and looked out the window again.

"Whatever," he said. "Don't worry about it. You didn't know."

———

I sat on the curb outside the meeting room door, watching the sun go down. The more it went down, the more I could stare at it without burning out my eyes and going blind.

I couldn't hear what was being said inside the meeting room, with one exception. When a person said his name, or her name, the whole group said hi back to them. I couldn't hear the first part. I couldn't hear anybody named Joe say his name, but I could hear the group say, "Hi, Joe." And three or four minutes later, "Hi, Evelyn." And five minutes after that, "Hi, Carlo."

Once, at what I thought was getting near the end, I heard everybody say, "Hi, Roy."

But if my brother was sharing, I never heard what he said.

Maybe five minutes later the door flew open behind me. Light spilled out, followed by the sound of voices, followed by people. I got up and dusted off the seat of my jeans.

Roy came limping out on his crutches and we walked off toward the bus stop together. Slowly.

"Did you talk?" I asked him.

"No."

"Oh. I heard them say hi to you."

"Yeah. That guy Joe called on me to share. But I didn't want to. But he said, 'Well, anyway, who *are* you?'"

"Oh." I tried not to let on that I was disappointed. I was guessing I failed. "Well, at least you said your name was Roy and you're an addict. That's something."

"I didn't say that. I just said my name was Roy."

"Oh," I said. "Okay."

We traveled the rest of the way home in complete silence.

—

"That guy Joe" was leading the meeting on Friday. The one where I got to come in and listen again.

He was a compact little guy with neatly combed hair and wire-rimmed glasses. Sort of the opposite of the tattooed motorcycle guys. Joe looked like more of a college man or a bookworm. Somebody you wouldn't expect to see at an NA meeting, except for the fact that I was already learning not to cling too much to types. Addicts were more different kinds of people than I might've imagined.

"My name is Joe and I'm an addict," he said, when it was time for him to lead the sharing.

Everyone in the room said, "Hi, Joe." Even me.

That is, everybody except Roy.

"I don't usually tell my whole story," Joe began. "Because it's a small town and I figure you guys have heard it, like, a gazillion times. But we have a newcomer, so . . ."

His eyes flickered up to my brother Roy. Roy's eyes did not flicker back. They remained glued to the table in front of us.

"I never touched drugs 'til I was nineteen," Joe said. "Never wanted to touch them, and never thought I would. And then I was in Nam. Sixty-five and sixty-six."

At that, Roy's eyes flickered. They darted up and met Joe's for just a fraction of a second, and then both guys looked away again. Quickly. Like the way you recoil after touching a hot stove.

"You hear a lot about the drugs guys do over there, and everybody always figures you're talking street drugs. Well, there was plenty of that, and I'll get to it. But it didn't start with that. It started with the drugs the army gave me.

"I probably should've mentioned that I was never drafted. I joined up and volunteered to go. I thought there was something going on over there that was worth getting behind. I thought my government knew exactly what it was doing, which I guess is why, when they issued me drugs, I thought they must be okay. I mean, they wouldn't give them to us if they weren't okay. Right?"

He paused for just a brief second, and I could feel Roy hanging on the pause. He was listening in a way I hadn't seen him listen before. I could see it on his face.

"When we'd go out on a mission, they'd issue us Darvon and codeine, which I didn't much use. They were for the pain, and I was lucky enough not to have gotten injured. And then they gave us Dex. You know. Dexedrine. Heavy-duty speed. Really good-quality stuff straight from Uncle Sam. And sometimes they'd give us a steroid shot. We kind of knew what they were doing. They were experimenting with supersoldiers. Pharma-created supersoldiers. I didn't get tired so easy with Dex. I could do so much more in a day and hardly feel it. But it wasn't just about physical energy. The Dex made me feel powerful. Hell, it made me feel invincible. I could face anything on that stuff.

"I didn't find out until about a year after I got home that there was another reason for all that 'better living through chemistry' stuff. They were trying to get on top of combat stress. They figured out that drugs could help guys hold it together through the worst Nam had to offer. Guys break down under the stress, and this was mostly keeping it from happening. I had a counselor at the VA after I got home, and

I don't know if he was supposed to tell me this or not, but he told me the breakdown rate was ten percent in World War Two. Four percent in Korea. But Nam? One percent. Better living through chemistry, like I said. But then he told me the downside. What they learned in the long run. You give a guy enough drugs to hold it together during combat, it doesn't keep him from the effects of the trauma. Just postpones it. It's all there waiting for him when the drugs wear off. But, hell, I didn't need him to tell me that. I was a case study in it by then."

He stopped to take a breath, and you could've heard a pin drop in that room. And everybody but Roy and me had heard this a gazillion times before.

"So I started doing a ton of Dex," Joe said. "You would think there'd be a limit to how much I could get, but there wasn't. There was an amount the army recommended, but in my unit they were handing the stuff out like candy. I don't know what it was like in other guys' units, but that stuff flowed like a waterfall in mine. But the problem was, it wore off. And when it wore off, you felt *so bad*. I mean, you just wanted to chew somebody's head off. So here we are, a bunch of guys with guns who were just about ready to murder somebody over nothing because it's so hard to come down off that stuff. The more Dex I took, the worse it felt at the end of the day. And I couldn't sleep. I tried the Darvon and codeine, but it wasn't enough. So that's when I started smoking scag."

I thought he would say what scag was on his next breath, but he didn't. So I missed a sentence or two of his sharing, catching Roy's attention.

"What is that?" I whispered in his ear.

"Heroin," he mouthed back. No real sound.

". . . like, two dollars for a hit of really pure stuff, and it was everywhere. So I leave to go over there like this perfect Boy Scout, and I come back stateside addicted to both speed and heroin. Lost my marriage and my little boy. My wife took him away and never told me where. I have no way to get in touch with her and tell her I have seven months clean and sober. I've been looking for them this whole time, but nothing so far. But my sponsor's always telling me it takes time to clean up the wreckage of my past. Anyway, I have a decent job now, and a car that runs about ninety-five percent of the time. And that's not bad for seven months. And I can get to sleep at night without using anything. I still don't usually sleep too long, though. Like, two hours at a time. If I get down too deep, the nightmares start to get their hooks in."

His eyes tracked over to Roy again.

I wondered if Roy had nightmares. If so, he had them quietly.

"That's all I got to say for now," Joe said. "Roy? You got anything you want to share?"

"No," Roy said.

This time Joe did not even push him to say his name before the sharing moved on.

—

"Give you guys a lift home?"

We were walking through the parking lot when we heard it.

I stopped and turned. Roy kept going.

It was Joe.

"Roy," I called. "Wouldn't it be a whole lot easier on your foot to take the ride?"

I watched him teeter to a halt on his crutches. Secure his balance. I watched his resistance crumble.

"I guess," he said. "Yeah."

I knew he didn't want to get into a car with Joe, so I took his agreement to mean that he was in even more pain than I realized.

We moved off toward Joe's car together. Slowly.

Joe drove a powder-blue Corvair, which was a model of car my mother once told me she would never so much as go near. Apparently they were not big on safety, those Corvairs. I didn't care. I could tell Roy was tired and discouraged, and I just wanted to get us home.

Joe slid the seat way back on the passenger's side to accommodate Roy's crutches and bad foot. He helped my brother ease in. Then he came around the driver's side and held his seat forward, and I had to practically fold myself in half to fit into the tiny back seat.

He started it up, and it was loud. It either had those old glass-pack mufflers on it, or maybe even no mufflers at all.

"You guys brothers?" he asked as we drove out of the bank parking lot.

I waited for Roy to say something, but he didn't. I caught Joe's eyes in the rearview mirror.

"Yeah," I said. "Brothers."

"Where do you guys live?"

"Over on Deerskill Lane. Last block before the dead end."

"Sure," he said. "I know where that is."

We drove in silence for a time. Joe rolled down his driver's window and lit a cigarette, which he held in his left hand, his forearm resting on the edge of the door. The air that flowed in felt hot and summery, even though it was heavy dusk. It smelled of cigarette smoke and contained a light stream of sparks. I couldn't stop staring at them.

"How long you been back stateside?" he asked my brother.

At first, Roy said nothing. Then, when I guess the silence grew too heavy even for him, he said, "Not long."

"I'm gonna write down my phone number," Joe said. "In case you need someone to call."

"I won't," Roy said.

"Never know what you're gonna need."

He pulled up in front of our house when I pointed it out to him. My mom had left the porch light on for us. I could see moths playing in the beam of it. Or maybe it wasn't play to them. Maybe it was desperate. Some crazy way to satisfy a need.

Roy threw the passenger door open and jumped out. Right, I know. I would've thought the word "jumped" was a stretch, too, if I hadn't seen it with my own eyes.

"Here's my number," Joe said to me, scribbling on the inside of a cardboard matchbook cover with a pen that didn't seem to want to write. "Give it to him when you get in the house."

"I don't think he'll call," I said.

"No. I don't think so, either. But you never know. This way at least he'll know he can."

"Thanks," I said. And took the matchbook from him.

I pushed the passenger seat forward to let myself out. But then I stalled and didn't move for another few seconds.

"How did you know?" I asked him.

"How did I know what?"

"That my brother was in Vietnam?"

"Oh. That. Well, I didn't know, now did I? I couldn't really *know*. I just took a guess. Seriously injured is a clue, but he could've been in a car accident or something. Mostly I just had a good long look at his eyes and took my best shot."

———

My mom was sitting at the kitchen table, drinking something that looked and smelled alcoholic. She looked up at me as though I'd wakened her from a dream.

My dad seemed to be absent. Again. I almost opened my mouth to ask if he still lived here. Really, officially lived here. But I never got the chance.

"So, how's that going?" she asked me.

"The meetings, you mean?"

"That's what I had in mind, yeah." A little bit sarcastic. As always.

"Not sure. Maybe not great so far. But I think maybe it takes more time."

She stared down into the brown, liquid eye of her glass again.

"Connor came by. He wanted you to come over. He said he had something he wanted to show you. But then I told him when you'd be back, and he said you'd best wait until morning."

"Okay," I said.

I walked upstairs, knowing that now I would have to lie there and try to get to sleep, wondering. Wondering what Connor could possibly have to show me that I hadn't seen a million times already.

Chapter Sixteen

Promises and Repayments

I showed up at Connor's house a little after six a.m. I could see lights on inside, so I knocked on the door. I thought his mother would scold me for coming by so early, but I had to do it. The suspense was killing me.

Instead she answered the door with a smile on her face. I was stunned. I don't think I had ever seen such a thing before.

"Oh, Lucas," she said. "Good. You're here. Connor will be so glad. He can't wait to show you his kitten."

"Connor has a kitten?"

"He does! We picked her out yesterday afternoon. And she's just the cutest little thing you've ever seen. Snow white, with the most beautiful . . . oh, but why am I telling you? You're just about to see her. Go on up."

I walked down the hall and was dazzled by something like . . . light. When I got level with the living room, I saw she had just one curtain open in that one room. On the side with a view of no neighbors. Just the woods.

I walked up the stairs and knocked on Connor's door.

"Mom?"

"No, it's me. Lucas."

"Oh, good. Come in, but quick. Don't let the cat out."

I dashed through the smallest space of open door I could possibly manage, then closed it behind me.

Connor was sitting cross-legged on his bedroom rug. He was holding what I thought was a pretty inventive cat toy. It was just a little fabric mouse, but he had tied it on the end of a string and tied the other end of the string to a stick, so he could dangle the mouse like a caught fish on a rod and line.

Just for a moment I saw nothing else. No kitten.

I had a sudden panicky thought. What if there *was* no kitten? What if Connor and his mother were all happy and excited about something that turned out to be . . . you know . . . completely imaginary? How horrifyingly weird would *that* be?

A split second later a completely nonimaginary kitten came zooming into view.

She had apparently been crouched under Connor's bedside table, gearing up to attack. And hoo boy, did she ever attack. She flew across the rug and leapt into the air, jumping maybe three or four times her height. She swung at the mouse. Missed. Landed on her feet. They say cats always do. Then she spooked at nothing. A ghost. Her back arched up wildly high, like a cat on a Halloween decoration, and she crow-hopped sideways at nearly the speed of light until she was under the bedside table again.

Connor and I both laughed out loud.

"She's a riot," he said. "I've been laughing pretty much since we brought her home."

I sat on the rug near him. He reached over and scooped the cat out from under the table and held her close to his belly, and I petted her. I was surprised when I touched her, because so much of what I'd thought was cat was just fur. She barely seemed to be under there at all.

She was snow white, like Mrs. Barnes had said. Her ears were a delicate pink. I felt as though I could see right through them. Or almost.

Her eyes were the most brilliant shade of blue. Like the sky on a summer afternoon. The contrast of those eyes on the otherwise white canvas of fur was really stunning. I couldn't take my eyes off her.

"She's so pretty," I said.

"Yeah, she is. She'll be a gorgeous cat."

"Why do you think your mom broke down and got her for you?"

"I think she figured it would keep me home more."

I instinctively lowered my voice. "Oh. Right. Where did you tell her you've been going?" I had purposely resisted asking.

"Just that I've been taking a long walk in the morning. Which is true. Well. True enough, anyway. In a way she's been happy about it, because I guess she figures it's a good sign that I want to get out of the house more. But I also think it makes her a little nervous. Here," he added, "you want to hold her?"

I took the kitten from him and held her against my own belly, and I swear she felt like she weighed nothing at all. But she was real, all right. I could feel her tiny heart beating. And when I scratched her behind the ears, she purred.

I confess I was a bit smitten. I could only imagine how Connor must've felt about her.

Connor accidentally moved the toy. She saw the movement and scrambled to get down, nearly scratching me with those tiny razor claws. I let her go.

She ran for the space under the bed, but Connor expertly used the dangling mouse to change her mind and draw her away.

For a space of time—I could not have told you how long a time it was—we just watched the cat attack that dangling mouse. Every time she did something wild and outrageous, we burst out laughing. Which was nice. I wondered when Connor and I had last laughed together. How long it had been.

Then he got to his feet and handed me the stick.

"I have to go to the bathroom," he said.

He moved off in that direction. Connor had a bathroom attached to his bedroom. Apparently everybody did. Except yours truly.

The kitten ran under the bed, and I didn't react fast enough to stop her.

"Don't let the cat go under the bed," he said before closing the bathroom door.

I lay down on my belly and looked under at the kitten, and she looked back at me with those astonishing blue eyes.

"Why not?" I called in to Connor. "What happens if she goes under the bed?"

"It's just really hard to get her out again."

"Can't you just pull the bed out from the wall?"

"You can put the bed anywhere you want, but she'll stay right under the middle of it where you can't get to her. I think it's like a game to her."

"So how do you get her out once she goes under there?"

"You have to crawl under there on your belly."

I sighed. And began crawling.

The kitten evaded me by running to the top end of the bed. Which was a tactical error, because a wall stopped her. She sat hunkered against a heat vent, looking ready to fly away again. But I caught her before she could.

Feeling more than a little claustrophobic in that tight space, I gently pulled her away from the vent.

That's when I saw it.

At first I wasn't even sure what I was seeing. But I knew it was something. Something that was not supposed to be there. It was inside the vent, behind the metal grate. Nothing is supposed to be back there except air. So when you see something, whatever you think it is, it's going to stand out as a thing out of place.

I held the kitten close to my shoulder and tried to take a minute to let my eyes adjust. There wasn't a ton of light under Connor's bed, of course. And there wasn't any inside the heating duct.

Still, I could see the corner of something. A small box, maybe. And a bit of curved something that looked like polished wood or some other hard substance.

I had a bad feeling about what it might be. I could've been wrong, but I had to know.

I wiggled out from under the bed and pulled the head side of it back from the wall. I wasn't sure what to do with the kitten, so I put her inside my shirt and she held still there. For the moment, anyway.

I dug around in my pocket, where I knew I had a little bit of change. Found a dime. I used it as a screwdriver to take out the two decorative screws that held the duct cover in place. They were loose. Somebody had obviously taken the cover off recently.

I laid the two screws on the carpet and pulled off the grate. Reached my hand in. Pulled the two items out into the light.

A brand-new, unopened box of one dozen bullets. And a handgun.

I got to my feet, holding them. Staring at them in my hands.

I heard Connor's voice. He was back in the room.

"Oh, you pulled the bed out," he said. "I told you, that never works."

I looked up from my hands to see why he was not reacting to my discovery. He was looking down, still tucking in his shirt.

I said nothing.

A moment later he looked up.

We both just stood there for a minute, almost meeting each other's eyes but not quite. It was one of those near misses we'd learned to do so well.

The moment stretched out.

The cat began to wiggle in my shirt.

"I know you might not believe this," Connor said. His voice sounded like half himself, half somebody else. Like Connor fully grown, maybe. "But I haven't been lying to you about any other things. This is the first lie I told you since we were, like, ten."

I looked directly into his face. He looked away.

"What did you lie to me about when we were ten?"

He surprised me by laughing. Not the way we laughed at the kitten and her wild hunting antics. There was nothing merry about it. It sounded more like a comment on the ridiculousness of our situation.

"I don't even remember," he said. "Can we stay with what's important here?"

"Promise me you won't lie to me for the rest of this talk."

"Okay. I promise."

"You were serious about this."

"At one point, I think . . . yeah."

"But that's over now?"

"Yeah."

"You sure?"

He actually stopped to think for a minute. That was interesting. I guess it could have meant he wasn't completely sure. But I took it to mean he was taking seriously his promise to tell me the truth.

The kitten thrashed violently in my shirt, scratching my belly.

"Ow!" I shouted, and tried to fish her out of there. But she was on the move.

"Why is the cat in your shirt?"

"It's a long story. *Now* who's having trouble staying with what's important?"

The kitten had scrambled around to my back side, and her thrashing was untucking my shirt in the back. I tried to catch her with one hand—the other one was full—but she was too fast for me. She leapt to her freedom, landed on her feet on the rug . . . and ran under the bed.

"Okay," Connor said. "You're right. And the answer is yes."

"I think I forgot the question now."

What I really meant was that I had lost track of how it had been phrased. Whether a yes answer was the good news or the bad news.

"Yes, that's over now."

I breathed out a boatload of tension and anxiety, and felt like over-cooked noodles without it. I sank down onto his bed, still holding those alarming items. I could feel my hands shaking. I guess the shock was wearing off. I guess it was finally dawning on me that I was holding something in my hand that kills people. Something that almost took my friend Connor right out of the world.

"So . . . ," I began. I think my voice might've been a little shaky, too. "If we get rid of this, you won't just find another way?"

"No," he said. "I won't. I promise."

He sat down on the edge of the bed with me, but not too close. A respectful distance away. I say respectful because he was giving me space to be angry. I could tell. I could feel him braced against my possible anger.

I didn't answer. I was just staring at the polished wood handle of his father's gun.

"When I came over to your house the other morning . . . ," he began. "When was that? When I came over to talk to you about how it was going over at Zoe's? I'd already changed my mind by then."

I breathed for a minute. Deeply. Trying to feel less shaken.

It's weird how you know something, but you don't *really* know it. You have a sense of it inside your gut. And then all of a sudden you find out it's real. You see it, right in front of your eyes. And part of you thinks, *What are you so shocked about? You knew this all along.* But when the gun is lying in your hands, let me tell you . . . that's a whole different brand of knowing.

It cuts right through the middle of you.

"So we get rid of this," I said.

"Okay, yeah. That would be good."

"You want to give it back to your dad?"

"No! He can't know I had it. My mom can't know I had it either. Let him think he lost it, or it got stolen. He can buy another one. He can afford it. He probably already did."

"Okay, fine. So we dump it. Get me some kind of bag or something. To put it in. I can't just carry it down the street like this."

For a minute he rummaged around. Opening drawers, staring into his closet. I think he was a little bit in shock, too. Bottom line, most people don't keep bags in their bedroom.

"Use the pillowcase," he said, pulling it off his bed pillow. "I'll tell my mom the cat shredded it and I threw it away."

I took it from him, and put the gun and the box of bullets in the bottom of it. And I tied the whole thing in a big, soft knot.

I stood there staring at it for a minute. The kitten peeked out from under the bed, maybe wondering why nobody was trying to catch her.

"That'll look too weird," Connor said.

"That's what I was thinking."

He hurried over to his closet and took his school backpack down off a hook on the inside of the door. It was empty because it was summer. I put the weird knot of pillowcase into the bottom of it and shrugged the pack onto my back.

"Thanks for doing this for me," he said.

"Thanks for not using it on yourself."

It was a pretty direct statement. It burned coming out. Probably burned him to hear it. It hit me that I had been talking around the thing. With both Connor and Mrs. Dinsmore. Using soft, not very exact words, like "not staying." But damn it all to hell, sometimes you just have to call a thing what it is. And if they're harsh words, maybe it's because it's a harsh thing. And maybe it's better to recognize that. I'm not sure what I thought I was accomplishing by trying to make it sound nicer than it was.

I snuck down the stairs and made it out of the house without running into Mrs. Barnes. I trotted down their porch stairs and broke into a run on the sidewalk. But the load in my pack bounced around too much. It was small as loads go, but weirdly heavy.

Then I decided running would draw too much attention to me anyway. Because nobody runs with a backpack.

I made a beeline for the woods. And, because it was an entry point I had never used before, and a part of the woods I didn't know like the back of my hand, I promptly got lost.

Score one for my mom.

—

It had been just long enough to worry me. I'd been backtracking, and thinking I was on the right path, and then finding out it was the same path I'd been lost on all along.

I was starting to get scared.

Then I remembered to use the sun.

It was well up now, shining into my eyes. Which meant I was facing the same direction I'd be facing if I were sitting on Zoe Dinsmore's porch. Which meant I wasn't running the long way through the woods, and I wasn't facing town. Which meant if I just kept going, I would hit the River Road.

Problem was, there was no real path in that direction. But I pushed on anyway.

It was slow going because I had to pick my way through tree roots and underbrush. My legs were getting scratched up. I'd have to wear long pants for weeks to hide the damage. In the middle of a hot summer. But I just kept going.

Sweat poured down my legs and down my neck into my collar, and it tickled. But I just kept going.

And then I burst out onto the road. Suddenly. Somehow the brush had hidden it until the last minute, and I hadn't seen it coming.

I crossed the road and looked down into the muddy, fast-flowing river. And I cursed it. Actually cursed it out loud.

"You son of a bitch," I yelled at the river, which couldn't have bothered to be insulted by my words. "You swallowed up everybody's peace of mind in this town. Least you can do is take a problem off our hands for a change."

I dropped the backpack onto the ground. Looked around me 360 degrees. There was not a soul to be seen. Well, a soul. But not a person. A buck stared at me from the shoulder of the River Road, as if trying to figure out what I was so upset about. Then he trotted away, his hooves clattering over the tarmac.

I took out the knotted pillowcase. Swung it around like winding up for a pitch. But just before I let it go, I had a bad thought. Imagine if I threw it too far and it landed on the bank on the other side. Exposed.

The nearest bridge was probably three and a half miles away. And what if I got to the other side and couldn't find the spot where it had landed?

I did a light underhand swing, but before I could let go, I was struck with another bad thought.

Imagine if I threw it not far enough, and it landed on this near bank. This muddy, slippery, very steep bank. I'd have to scramble down there and try to get it. But one false move and that river might take *me* away.

I put it back in Connor's pack and ran three and a half miles down the road shoulder to the bridge.

It was a one-lane bridge with a high iron structure to support it, built for cars but also built back when cars were a lot smaller. There was a car coming; I could hear it. I ducked into the woods and leaned on a tree until it had crossed the river and gone on its way.

Then I walked out of the woods and onto the bridge with the terrifying bundle under my shirt. On every step it poked at the place where the kitten had scratched me.

I stood a minute, just looking down and watching the water flow. But there was a method to my madness. I was straining my ears to be sure there was no one coming. When I was sure I heard nothing but silence, I looked around. All around. But if there was ever a deserted part of the developed world, I was standing in it on that crazy morning.

I slipped the pillowcase out of my shirt and let it fall straight down into the river.

"You owe me one," I told the river. Quietly this time. "You owe us all one. You hide that for me. You make this one thing right, at least."

I looked around again, but thankfully I had not been seen. There was simply no one there to see me.

I ran back down the road toward my familiar entrance to the woods on the river side. The one that would take me in a fairly straight line to Zoe's cabin.

When I passed the cemetery, I could see fresh flowers on the two graves. Matching red flowers on long stalks. But I was too upset to think much about it, and I didn't go closer. I slowed my feet for just one beat, staring at them.

Then I ran as fast as I had ever run in my life. Or maybe faster.

———

She was on her way back from the outhouse when I burst over the rise, still sprinting like a maniac.

"What the hell got into *you?*" she asked when I was close enough to hear her.

I stopped in front of her. I could barely speak I was panting so hard.

"He was really going to do it."

"Who was really going to do what?"

"Connor."

I stood a minute. Panting. Watching the news settle on the inside of her. Of course I was only watching the outside of her, but I could still see. It was on her face. I didn't know where the dogs were, so they must have been inside the cabin. Nothing else would stop them from greeting me.

"He *did* have his father's gun," I said. "He lied about that."

"Does he still?"

"No. I threw it in the river. He said he doesn't want it anymore. He said he changed his mind."

"Good."

For a minute we just stood there. Looking at each other. Really looking at each other. None of that "near miss" business.

"You know what this means," I said. "Don't you?"

"I'm not sure what *you* think it means."

"You saved him."

"I don't know about that."

"You did. You kept a person here in the world. You saved a life. So that's like . . . I don't know how to say it. It's like a repayment. It's like . . . one down and one to go."

She didn't hear it the way I'd hoped she would at all. I watched her face harden. I watched her recoil from the idea.

"That's not the way the world works, my friend."

Her voice was all armored. But at least I liked the way she'd called me her friend.

"Why isn't it?"

"You want to go tell Freddie's or Wanda Jean's parents that this makes up for their loss?"

"I didn't mean it did. That wasn't what I meant."

"Well, what did you mean, then?"

She had her arms folded across her broad chest now. Just below the top of the bib of her overalls.

I felt like she'd just thrown me a hard essay test, and I didn't have any answers. But then one came to me. And I thought it was good. I thought I'd get an A on this test.

"I guess . . . ," I said. "I guess I mean if you can save somebody . . . I mean, isn't that a good enough thing? Isn't that enough reason to stay?"

I thought it was a better answer than she did, apparently.

She shook her head. Let out a little low chuckle that seemed to be at my expense.

"Ah, youth," she said. It reminded me of something my mother had said to me. "When everything in life is so damned simple."

Then she walked up onto her porch and opened the door to her cabin. As she walked in, the dogs came spilling out and ran to me.

And jumped on me. And whimpered at me. And kissed me.

So at least I had that.

I fell to my scratched-up knees and held the dogs around their necks and spoke hurt words into their ears.

"Well, she *did* save him," I said to them. "And that *is* a good reason to stay."

They gave me sympathetic looks. They couldn't possibly have known what I was so upset about. But to me their looks seemed almost to say, "Well, we all know how she is, don't we? We know how she can be, but we love her all the same."

Or at least that's how I interpreted their gazes, and I have some solid truth to back it up, because that's what you really do get from dogs. And it's no small thing to be loved all the same, let me tell you.

—

When I got home, and stepped into my kitchen, my mom was holding the receiver of the phone. Waiting to see if it was me coming in.

Really, who else could it have been?

I knew I had a phone call, and I knew it was Connor.

She covered the mouthpiece with the heel of her hand.

"It's Connor," she said. "It's the third time he's called for you. I hope nothing's wrong."

"No. It's fine. Nothing's wrong. He's just really excited about his new kitten."

It bothered me to lie so smoothly and so easily. But I did it for my friend. I couldn't look her in the eye, though, which might have made her suspicious. Then again, I didn't look her in the eye very often.

I took the phone from her. I was hoping she would leave the kitchen. She did not leave the kitchen.

"Hey," I said to Connor.

"Everything go okay?"

"Yeah. Fine."

"Oh, thank goodness. Wow. Whew. I've been jumping out of my skin here. Nobody saw you?"

"No. It's fine."

"Where did you put it?"

I could feel my mom standing close. Feel her listening. But I didn't look up at her, because I didn't want her to know it was a problem.

"It's fine," I said again.

"Oh. Is your mom right there?"

"Something like that, yeah."

"Okay. Good. Because I'm going to tell you something, and this way you just have to listen and you can't argue with me. So just stand there and don't say anything, okay?"

There was a pause on the line, and I thought he might really be waiting for my permission. So I said okay, even though it made me nervous. It sounded like he was about to read me the riot act for everything I had ever done wrong to him in our lives. Every time I hadn't been what he needed.

I could not have been more wrong if I'd been trying.

"You've been a really good friend," he said. "And I haven't."

"No, you are."

"Just listen," he said. "Don't talk."

"Okay."

My mom moved across the kitchen to the fridge and started rummaging around in there. But I had to assume she was still listening.

"Not lately I haven't been," Connor said. "Lately you've been bending over backwards to try to help me, and I haven't been much good at all. And I'm not saying it like I did last time—like you shouldn't even be friends with me. I'm not saying that. I want you to be. I just want you to know that I'm going to do better now."

A pause while I waited to see if he was done.

"It's a deal," I said.

"I'm sorry for the way I've been."

"You don't have to be."

"Well I am. Thanks for what you did for me today."

"Anytime," I said.

Then, strangely, we both burst out laughing.

"Well, not anytime," I added.

We said our goodbyes, and the incredibly stressful part of that incredibly stressful day got to be over.

I looked up at my mom, and she looked back at me. Probably to see if I would tell her what all that had been about.

"He just really loves that new kitten," I said.

Chapter Seventeen

Tell Them Your Story

Come Monday, my brother and I were halfway to the bus stop together after dinner. On our way to the meeting. I walked. He limped along on his crutches.

At first we didn't talk.

The sun was on a long slant, but it was still hot. Now and then a neighbor had driven by and honked a hello to us. One, old Mr. Harrigan, had rolled down his window and given Roy a big thumbs-up. Probably for serving in the war and then getting home. I could tell that one made my brother uncomfortable.

When Roy finally opened his mouth, I thought he was going to talk about that. But he took us in an entirely different direction.

"Why don't you want to be on the track team?" he asked me. Like he was seriously interested in my answer.

He hadn't seemed seriously interested in anything since before he left for the war. Except for his meds.

"I don't know. It's kind of hard to explain. I just . . . when I run in the woods, with those dogs, I just feel . . . like . . . completely free. And when I run on the track at school, I'm with these other guys who don't really like me. And the coach is watching. And everybody would be judging me. Or at least I'd feel like they were. And it's just the complete opposite. It's like being in a cage or something."

"But you could do both," he said.

By then we'd arrived at the bus stop. There was no one else around. I sat. He just stood there, leaning on his crutches. I think getting up and down was hard for him. Once he got up, he didn't tend to sit unless he figured he could stay a while.

I looked up at him, but he was staring off into the distance, and I don't think he noticed. I got this feeling, like that moment perfectly summed up everything between me and my brother since he got home. Me staring at him, hoping to see something. Find something. Him a million miles away in his head.

"I guess I could do both," I said. "But why do the school part at all? I mean, if I don't like it much."

For a time, he didn't answer. Then he looked down into my face, which felt surprising. Jolting, actually.

"I don't usually say things like this to you," he said, "but here goes. I would appreciate it very much if you could see your way clear to take that spot on the team as a favor to me."

He looked away again. We both looked up to see the bus coming, but it was many blocks down the street, and it had just missed one of the only two stoplights in town.

"Why would that be a favor to you if I did?"

We just kept staring at that bus, stopped at the red light, like we'd never seen anything so fascinating in our lives.

"I tried out for track," he said.

"You never told me that."

"I didn't make it. I wasn't fast enough. You don't just come home from school and tell your kid brother, 'Hey, today I tried to go after something I really wanted and fell flat on my ass.' And now I can't even run *badly*. I'll probably never run again. So if I could go to a track meet and see you doing it . . . taking that spot on the team I could never snag, well . . . I would like that."

The light turned green, and the bus made its noisy way to us.

"Okay," I said. "Then I will."

—

"How long do we have to keep going to these meetings?" he asked me.

We were on the bus. Counting the stops until it was time to get off. Or I was, anyway. That might have been the last thing on his mind. He might have been leaving all such logistics to me.

"I don't know. I'm not sure. Maybe till it's not so uncomfortable for you to go?"

"That's bizarre," he said, his eyes still off in the distance.

After our brief track team moment I had lost him again.

"Why is it bizarre?"

"So long as I hate going, I have to go. Then, just as I figure I don't mind it much anymore, I'm off the hook."

"You can still go if you want. I think some of those people have been going for years and years. Sounds like it, anyway, when they share. And you can get a sponsor like people do, so you'll have somebody to talk to outside the meetings."

The word "sponsor" sounded weirdly commercial, but it was, in program terms, more like a personal mentor.

"Why do you hate it so much?" I asked, when he didn't answer.

"I don't hate it. I just figure they're waiting for me to tell them my story."

And that was the end of that conversation. Because I couldn't tell him he was wrong. I couldn't say no they weren't. Of course they were waiting for him to tell his story. And so was I.

And I, for one, was getting stretched pretty thin waiting to hear what had happened.

We rode and walked the rest of the way to the meeting in silence.

———

We were in the part of the meeting when it was almost time for the sharing to start. That's when it happened. That final tilt of the teeter-totter that puts you fully on the other side. The final huge tipping point of the summer of 1969.

We had done all the readings. The leader had asked if there were any newcomers in their first thirty days. Roy hadn't raised his hand. Roy never raised his hand. I don't think he was trying to pretend he had been clean longer. At least I chose not to believe that. I think he wasn't going to call himself a newcomer in his first thirty days until he was off the pain meds. I think he was claiming no clean time at all.

The leader had run through the process where they give out these little key tags they called "chips" for anyone who had thirty, or sixty, or ninety days. Or six months, or nine months, or anybody who was celebrating an anniversary of a year or multiples of years.

Only nobody was. But they went through the list every time, call-ing off all those milestones to see if anybody wanted to raise their hand and take a chip.

I saw a few sets of eyes flicker over to the door, so of course I looked where they looked.

Zoe Dinsmore was just stepping into the room, closing the door behind her.

She either hadn't seen me yet, or had seen me and her eyes had moved on. She was looking at Roy, and Roy was looking back at her.

And, now, this part was weird. At the time.

She nodded to him. And he nodded back.

I couldn't have told you exactly what the nod meant, but it was an acknowledgment of something. Something they shared between them. Which was absolutely stunning to me, because I had no idea they'd ever shared anything between them. But I could see it was not the kind of nod you exchange with a stranger. It was a nod to some level of mutual history. It was an understanding. Some things don't need explaining. Some things are just plain on their surface.

They broke off their gazes, and Zoe found herself a seat.

She sat across from us, and her eyes came up to mine. Just very briefly. She offered me one weak, sad little smile, then looked down at the table.

The leader, this guy named Jeff, spoke directly to her.

He said, "We just finished giving out chips, but I'll ask again. Anybody here in their first thirty days of recovery?"

Zoe raised her hand, still staring down at the table.

"My name is Zoe, and I'm an addict," she said.

And instead of the usual group response, which would have been "Hi, Zoe," just about everybody in the room said, "Hi, Zoe. Welcome back."

———

"I'm thinking there's not a single person in this room who doesn't know my story well enough to tell it themselves," Zoe said when she was called on to share. "Am I right about that?"

Her eyes scanned the room. No one spoke. No faces seemed the least bit confused.

"Good," she said. "Then I won't waste your time with that, because you know it, and I hate like hell to talk about it anyway. I'll just tell you this. If you're thinking of going out again, don't. Don't even mess with it. Just consider that I did the research for you and it still stinks out there. And the addiction problem you used to have hasn't gotten any better while you were recovering in these rooms. If anything, it's gotten worse. It's like you're in here thinking you have all this insurance, but meanwhile your disease is out there doing push-ups on the porch. You think you can let it out of the box and then put it back in again when you're ready because you did it the one time, so maybe you get overconfident and think you did that with your own superior will. So you let it out, and then you look at it, and you look at the box, and your disease is like a thousand times bigger than the box, and you can't for the life of you figure out how you ever got it to fit in there in the first place.

"I almost didn't make it back here," she said, her eyes flickering somewhere close to mine. But no direct hit. "I almost took myself out instead. But I guess that wasn't what my higher power had in mind for me. I guess the plan is for me to stay around and try to do some good.

"So all I want to say, and then I'll pass it along . . . I just want to say it's a hell of a lot easier to hold on to your seat in this room than it is to give it up and think you can get it back again. If we do get back to the rooms, the wear and tear on our bodies and souls is considerable. And then there are the ones who don't make it. And I was almost one of them. So take my advice. There's nothing for you out there."

A pause. No one filled it. No one spoke while a person was sharing, and everybody waited to be sure they were really done. Until the sharer passed the torch, so to speak.

Zoe opened her mouth again. "I want to hear from . . ."

She pointed directly at my brother. I could see the alarm on his face.

"I forget your name, son."

"Roy," he said.

"I want to hear from Roy."

A long silence. Like, really uncomfortably long. But no one filled it. It was Roy's turn to share and that was that. He could say he chose to pass, or he could start talking. But the meeting was not going to go on until he decided.

"My name is Roy," he said.

My body and brain tingled, waiting to see if he would say it.

"And I'm . . . well, I have no idea what I am. No, I do. That's not really true. I think I know I'm an addict, but I just don't want to say it out loud, because then it will be the truth about me and I can never unsay it. And it'll never stop being true. But I guess I pretty much just said it anyway, didn't I?"

He paused. Sighed.

"I just got back from overseas." His eyes came up to where Joe was sitting at the far corner of the table. "Like that guy, only my story just about couldn't be more different from his. No disrespect to him. Just the opposite. He's the one who deserves the respect. My story is a disaster. There is *nothing* about me to respect."

He paused again. Long enough that I wondered if he'd ever restart himself. Long enough that I found it hard not to shift in my seat. Everybody else seemed to manage to hold still and wait. Then again, they weren't his kid brother.

"I can't believe I'm about to do this," Roy said, "I really don't want to do this."

But then he did.

"I didn't enlist like this other guy," he said. "You could've held a gun to my head and I wouldn't have gone over there. If I hadn't been drafted, I mean. And I didn't get hooked on the drugs the army gave us, either. I hated speed. I wouldn't even take it. I didn't tell anybody I wasn't taking it. I'd just hide it in my cheek and spit it out later. It made me all jangly and nervous, like the top of my head was about to come off. Like I couldn't make my stomach hold still. Hell, I felt that way anyway over there, all the time. I didn't need something to make it worse.

"It was all street drugs for me. Except the word 'street' is an exaggeration. Most of the places they had us stationed didn't even have streets. But you could always get scag, and it was strong and it was cheap. And it was heaven. You could be right in the middle of hell and smoke that stuff and feel like everything was just fine. And I *was* right in the middle of hell, so that was handy."

He stalled again. Everybody waited.

My stomach knots were twisting into stomach double knots.

"I hate to say all this in front of my brother. I think he sort of looks up to me. And believe me, he never will again. Not after he hears about this mess. But I guess sooner or later I was going to owe it to him to tell him how it all went down.

"Okay. Here goes. Man, I hate this.

"I was smoking all the time. Not just to wind down at night like most of the guys. All the time. Even when I knew there might be enemy fire. I just couldn't face it any other way. I knew I was a sitting duck, loaded like that. Sometimes I could barely raise my arms, so I wouldn't have been any too quick to fire back in my own defense. I guess I just got to the point where I didn't even care anymore. Like I *couldn't* even care. I just didn't have it in me to care. I was scared out of my skin, and I just wanted to go home.

"What I finally ended up doing, I'd almost done it a dozen times before. Just so I could go home. I just wanted a quick ticket out of there. But I didn't do it. I mean, until the day I did. Because of the guys. The other guys. I figured I owed it to them to stay. Anything less just seemed so selfish."

I got that all-over tingle again. Waiting to hear what "it" was.

"But then I got this letter from my kid brother, saying he loved me and wanted me to come home safe. He'd never talked to me like that before. I guess war pulls all kinds of stuff out of you that you didn't even know was in there. Even if you're not actually over there fighting it. It just takes a toll on everybody."

Something came into my head. Something my brother had said to me the first day he was home. After he told me he'd gotten the last letter I sent him. The one he was telling everybody about now.

Why do you think it all came down the way it did?

That's what he'd said to me. And then he'd gone on to avoid telling me how it all came down. I almost thought I knew parts of it, especially after I'd had that conversation about it with Mrs. Dinsmore. But I had not been able to bring myself to ask the details of how it all came down. I guess I figured I had no right to ask. It was his life. If and when he wanted me to know, he would tell me.

Now he was about to tell me. Now he was about to tell everybody in the meeting.

I thought, *Oh, holy hell, it was all my fault. Whatever he's about to say, it was all my fault.*

"So, we got pinned down and ambushed, and I was loaded. *Really* loaded. I was flying. We were taking fire from what felt like every direction, and I could just as easily have passed out as fired back. And then somehow my unit got on top of the thing, and whoever was shooting at us stopped shooting and retreated, and I was alive, and, like . . . entirely unhit. And I still can't figure that out. I mean, is it true what they say about God looking after fools and babies? Or was I keeping my head down without even knowing it because I was so loaded? I honestly have no idea.

"The details are just really fuzzy, and not because a little time's passed. It was fuzzy while it was happening. I just remember I was sitting there on the ground. Afterward. And my rifle, my M16, was on the ground beside my right leg. For some reason that part was clear. That part is, like, tattooed into my brain. I had my right hand on the rifle. And there was a dead guy on either side of me. Both of them were guys I knew. Not like my best friends or anything, but I knew them. I knew they'd been scared, like me, except I think they both handled it better. But maybe I only think that because I'd been on the inside of myself and on the outside of them. But I knew they'd wanted to get home, just like me. And they had parents, and brothers who wanted them to get home. Well, the one guy, I think he only had a sister, but my point is the same. I thought about how their families would get a letter or a call or somebody would come to their house, and then I thought about my own brother, and then what I wanted to do didn't seem so selfish anymore. I could tell myself I was doing it for him. That might have been a story I told myself, though. I mean, it was true and it wasn't true. I was just at a breaking point. Even so loaded I could hardly move my arms and legs, I just knew I couldn't take it anymore."

He pressed his eyes against the heels of his hands. Rubbed them hard.

I thought I was going to explode waiting to hear. Even though most of me already knew.

"I can't believe I'm doing this," he said, dropping his hands to the table again. "This is so stupid. I can't believe I'm about to tell a bunch of people that I did something this stupid. But I guess this is the place for it, right? Because it was definitely the drugs that made what I did so extra stupid. My life would be so different right now if I hadn't been so loaded in that moment. But I was, and time is never backing up again, and I'm never getting my foot back, and I just have to live with that.

"Here's the part where the scag messed me up. Here's what I thought I was about to do. I thought I could put a bullet hole through my foot. You know. Just a hole. And in time it would heal. Maybe I'd have to have surgery to sew all those muscles and tendons back together. And physical therapy to walk normally. But I figured it would be enough to get me home. And I'm not saying I thought very clearly about all those details right then, but hopefully you know what I mean. I just figured I could hurt myself bad enough to get home but not enough to totally change my life forever. But it was a really stupid, really loaded set of thoughts. Because here's what I forgot to consider. It was a point-blank shot. I'd seen bullet holes made by M16s. More than I could count. If I hadn't seen so many of them, I might not've been so desperate to get out of there. But I wasn't considering that those bullet holes were shots fired from a long distance. They were not point-blank shots. This was a point-blank shot. I was too loaded to understand that it was about to shred my foot so badly that some amputation would be required.

"And there's another thing I messed up on. I didn't take into account that it would be pretty obvious what I'd done. Somehow I thought I'd be scooped up with the other wounded, and that would be that. We'd all be treated as having been injured in the firefight. But I guess the army's not that stupid. And also it's possible I might not've been the first guy to go to such lengths to get out of there."

I sat, listening to an invisible echo of his words around the room. I looked at the faces to see if they were judging my brother. They weren't. Not as far as I could tell. They were listening. Just listening.

My brain filled with the image of myself in Connor's bedroom, holding that gun and box of bullets in my hands. I remembered that feeling—the one where you'd thought you knew, but now that you really knew, it was just a whole different game of cards.

But my brother was still sharing.

"So that's my message about drugs if there's anybody in this room who needs one. Probably mostly just me, right? I mean, they really make you that stupid.

"But, you know what? It's a weird thing to say, but I think if I had it to do over again, I'd still do it. Bad discharge and all. Permanent maiming and all. Because I got home. I might not've gotten home if I hadn't. I think about it sometimes, and I feel bad for the other guys. The ones I left behind over there. I feel like I let them down. And it's true, I did. But I made this huge sacrifice to get out of there. If they decided it was worth half their foot, they could get out, too. Sometimes I think that. Other times I think I'm the biggest jerk in the world, and I'm not sure which is true. Both, maybe. Maybe both parts of the thing are true. But it's not like I left them undermanned over there. They'll just draft somebody else to take my place . . ."

He trailed off, and his face looked shocked. Like I was watching the blood drain out of it.

"Oh hell," he said. "I never thought of that. That's another thing I get to feel terrible about. I'm not trying to justify myself to you. You can think whatever you need to think about me. Hell, there's nothing you can call me that's any worse than what I call myself every day. But I'm just going to say this, and it's not an excuse. It's just the damn truth. What did they think would happen? Take a bunch of guys straight out of high school and send them into that hell. Take away everything that was ever familiar to them and tell them to kill and die, to watch their friends dying in horrible ways all around them. We were kids. We thought we were men until we got there, and then once we were there, it was so clear that we were just kids. I know there are plenty of guys who handled it way better than me. But how can you put kids in a situation like that and not end up with a total mess in at least a lot of their cases? It just doesn't make any sense to think so."

He pressed his eyes with the heels of his hands again. I thought he might be crying and trying to hide it. But when he dropped his hands, his eyes were dry. I wondered if he'd cried over there. If the war had used up every tear he'd ever had in him. Or if that was the place where he'd learned not to cry, no matter how bad things got.

"The reason I haven't been raising my hand as a newcomer is this," he said, seeming more settled in his brain. As if he'd come home to the US in his head and could speak more calmly. "Here's the thing about that. I'm still on a lot of pain meds for the injury. I'm taking them as prescribed now, because I really don't have any choice. And I know from hearing you all share that you can still call yourself clean if you're taking necessary meds the way the doctor prescribed them. But I don't want to do it like that. When I'm really clean, I'll come in here and say so, and we can start counting my time from then."

He stalled again. Looked around the room. He seemed to have just wakened up somehow. He seemed vaguely surprised by everything he saw.

"Of course I'm totally humiliated because I told you all that," he said. "And I'm done talking now. I'll just sit here and let somebody else share and wonder why I said all that. I guess I got tired of knowing it would come out sooner or later. I guess I got to the point where maybe it was easier just to get it over with. Speaking of which, I call on Joe. The guy who served so much more honorably than I did. Who's probably over there thinking I'm like something disgusting to scrape off the bottom of his shoe. Because if he's thinking that, I want to go ahead and hear it now. I'm not good with waiting for terrible things to catch up with me. I'd rather just get them over with."

He paused, but nobody spoke.

"I'm done," he said.

Everybody in the room said, "Thanks, Roy."

Including Zoe Dinsmore. Who I'd temporarily forgotten was there.

I looked at her and she looked at me. Her eyes held no judgment. Neither did they seem to want to console me. There was something very matter of fact in her gaze. As if she were telling me, "Yes, this is the world, Lucas. I've been dealing with it since before you were born."

Joe said, "My name is Joe and I'm an addict."

Everyone said, "Hi, Joe."

He looked right at my brother, who refused to look back.

"Thanks for your share, Roy. In case you don't know it yet, you're not the only person in this room who's done something stupid behind drugs, and you're not the only person whose fear got the best of them. So far as I know, there's not a person in this room who cares what you did when you were out there using. We all mostly care what you're going to do now."

Then he went on sharing about his own situation, and the meeting just moved along. The focus never fell on my brother Roy again.

It was as if the drama he'd just shared was no better and no worse than anybody else's drama. Or maybe there was no "as if" about it. Maybe that was just the truth of the situation.

—

Zoe Dinsmore came up to us after the meeting. Met us at the door.

"You boys want a ride home?" she asked.

But my brother Roy said, "No, thanks. Thanks anyway, Mrs. Dinsmore. My brother and I can take the bus."

He didn't seem to be afraid of her, or avoiding her. I didn't hear a lot of subtext. It sounded like he just figured we were okay. And maybe like he even enjoyed those little bits of time we spent, just the two of us, making our way back and forth to the meetings.

But I might've been reading that last part in.

As I followed Roy out the door, I looked at Zoe Dinsmore and she looked at me. And she nodded at me, the way she'd nodded at my brother. A nod to a lot of history. I nodded back. Maybe to acknowledge that it was a huge deal that she'd showed up in the meetings again. And also that it was a huge deal that my brother had unburdened himself and joined the group for real.

And maybe those two things weren't even entirely coincidental to one another, though I wasn't sure where that thought had come from, or if there was anything to it.

I turned and stepped out into the dusky parking lot, hurrying to catch up with Roy. I was thinking I knew approximately what history Zoe Dinsmore and I were acknowledging with our nod, but what could possibly have transpired between her and my brother?

I'd been so shocked and saddened and compelled by Roy's story that I'd forgotten to wonder.

We walked side by side toward the bus stop.

"You know her?" I asked.

"Just a little. I know who she is."

"How do you know her?"

"Don't you remember my first real girlfriend?"

He was struggling now on his crutches. I could tell he was tired. Part of me wished he would have agreed to the ride. But then we couldn't have had this talk. I was torn.

It was an evening of feeling torn.

"Yeah. I remember her. Mary Ellen. Right?"

"Right. Mary Ellen Paulston."

"Oh. I didn't remember her last name. That sounds really familiar. Why does that sound so familiar?"

It may seem like a strange thing to have said. Because it was his girlfriend's last name, and I'd known her. I must've known her last name at one time. But that name was familiar in a whole different sense. I knew it from somewhere else, and the context felt strangely important.

"Wanda Jean's little sister."

"Oh crap," I said.

"Yeah," he said. "Oh crap."

"Do you hate her? Is that why you didn't take the ride?"

"No. I don't hate her. I just wanted to take the bus home with you. I wanted to see how you were doing after . . . you know."

But I didn't want to talk about that yet. I wanted to talk about this Zoe Dinsmore connection.

"Did Mary Ellen's family hate her?"

"No. They didn't hate her. They avoided her because it brought up too many feelings and they didn't know what to say to her. But they didn't hate her. They knew she didn't do it on purpose."

"So did you meet her back then? Or did you just know who she was?"

"I met her once, but it was years after the thing happened. I think it was after she got clean for the first time and was going to meetings. I think she wanted to make amends to the family. You know. Like the ninth step of the program. You know which one that is?"

Of course I knew. I'd been sitting in meetings. The twelve steps were read at the beginning of every meeting. I had them memorized. I heard them in my head as I was trying to fall asleep at night.

Nine. We made direct amends to such people wherever possible, except when to do so would injure them or others.

Roy kept talking.

"But I guess you're not supposed to do that if it would only hurt people more. Or maybe she was just respecting the family by staying away, I don't know. Or maybe she was scared. I know I would've been. But she knew I was Mary Ellen's boyfriend. Everybody in town knew that. So she saw me at a bus stop one day. She was in the market and she saw me waiting for a bus, and she stepped out and came over and told me who she was. But I already knew. And she asked me if I would give a message to the family for her."

He limped along in silence for a time. The bus stop had just come into view, and not a moment too soon.

"And did you?" I asked, when I could tell he was not going to continue on his own.

"I did."

"Oh," I said.

I figured I shouldn't ask. It felt wrong to ask.

We reached the bus bench at long last. He settled himself on the seat, even though he might not be there for long. I knew he was really tired.

We sat staring off into the distance together, as though we could make the bus materialize by watching hard enough.

"Was it private, do you think?"

It surprised me that I asked. I hadn't known I was about to ask.

"Was what private?"

"The message."

"Oh. We're still talking about that. Well. I don't know." Then he veered in a slightly different conversational direction. "Do *you* know her? How do *you* know her?"

"That's a really long story. Longer than we've got." I flipped my chin in the direction of the bus, which had just come into view. A little dot several blocks down. "But I *will* tell you, just . . . when we've got more time. But you can never, ever tell Mom about any of it."

"Okay," he said. "I guess I can wait."

We stared at the bus, watching it grow larger in the distance.

Then, just out of nowhere, he said it.

"'Tell them my heart is broken, too.'"

"What?" I had no idea what he was trying to tell me.

"That was the message. 'Tell them my heart is broken, too.'"

"Oh," I said.

I tried to imagine the scene as he passed those words along. He was likely around my age when he was given that task to perform. I wondered how it felt to say a thing like that to the family. I wondered if they said anything in reply. If they cried.

But I never asked. To this very day I've never asked. So that was one part of the story that will stay with only the people involved. And maybe that's okay, because maybe it's theirs alone. Maybe nobody else has a right to one damned second of it. One damned feeling.

"I let you down," Roy said.

"Is that another part of the message?"

"No, I'm saying that to you right now."

"Well, don't ever say it to me again."

And he never did.

We're not dead yet. And he might have some more apologies for me on his deathbed, but I hope not. He doesn't owe me any. But up until now he's done as I asked.

Chapter Eighteen

Worth

"Why didn't you tell me you knew my brother?"

It was the following morning. I had just come back from running with the dogs and hadn't seen her on the way out. It was astonishingly hot for not even eight o'clock in the morning. I could feel sweat running down every part of me. My chest, my back, my face and neck. Every limb.

For a minute she didn't answer. Just stood on her porch and petted her panting dogs. I thought maybe she hadn't understood the question because I'd been breathing so hard when I asked it.

She straightened up, and the dogs trotted around the side of the cabin to drink from their bucket.

"Honestly?" she asked. "I didn't remember his name after all this time. Even back then I mostly knew him by sight. I saw him around town with one of the families. I knew he was dating that girl. The sister. Until I saw him with you in the meeting last night, I never put two and two together."

"Oh," I said.

I had been mad, and now I felt silly because of it. I felt deflated, feeling all that anger drain away. She might've noticed; I'm not sure. She seemed to be watching my face as though it was an interesting process, whatever was happening there.

"Don't be too hard on your brother," she said. "We're all just doing our best, even if it doesn't look so good from the outside. Try not to judge him."

"I'm not judging him," I said.

To the very best of my understanding, I think that was true. I wasn't angry about what he'd done, and I didn't blame him for it. The whole thing just made me incredibly sad.

"What will you do when you're eighteen?" she asked me. "And it's time to sign up for the draft?"

"Hope the war'll be over by then."

"And if it's not?"

"Cross that bridge when I come to it."

I walked home. I did not run.

I was still feeling pretty sad.

———

I think it was two days later when my mom flipped out about Roy. About his suddenly being gone.

I was up in my room, lying on the bed, because right in that moment there'd been nothing else I could find to do. And I guess without realizing it, I'd fallen asleep.

See what I mean? You never know you're falling asleep. You only realize it later, when something wakes you up.

My mother came barging into my bedroom, pushing the door so hard it slammed back against the wall.

"All right, where is he?"

I sat up. Swung my legs over so my bare feet touched the rug. Sat on the side of the bed—but I swear I was still sleeping. The image of my mom in the doorway seemed to be an extension of whatever I'd been dreaming.

"Wait. What?"

"Where. Is. He. Don't mess with me today, Lucas. I'm in no mood for it."

"He who?"

"How many are there? How many people could I be talking about?"

I shook my head hard, as though that might help put things in order up there. It didn't.

"Well. Dad. And Roy."

"I know where your father is. He's at work. Now where is Roy?"

In a weird, sleepy moment, I wondered if she really knew my dad was at work. He'd become quite the missing person around our house. I heard him come in sometimes at night, but later and later. Sometimes I didn't know if I'd slept through his coming home, or if he'd never come home. I actually wondered, I think for the second time, if he still actually lived here. I didn't say any of that.

"If he's not in his room," I said, "I have no idea."

She stormed over to the bed and grabbed my chin in her claws. She had these long nails, and they tended to dig in when she grabbed me. I was alarmed, but not awake enough to react much. At least, not on the outside.

"You look me right in the eye," she demanded.

I did.

I watched her face change. Soften.

I think I was finally waking up by then.

"Oh," she said. "You really don't know. Well, I'm going to get in the car and go look for him. You should get up and put on your running shoes and run all over town and see if you can find him."

"But I already ran today."

"Well do it again. You won't die."

She was halfway out my bedroom doorway before I could pull together an answer.

"Wait!" I said. And it came out loud. Too loud. Like I was yelling at her. I adjusted my tone and went on. "Why are we doing this? If he left the house on his own, won't he come back on his own?"

She narrowed her eyes at me.

"That's a very naïve statement," she said. "He's injured, and taking pain medication. So he's off somewhere not using his best judgment. And with the problems he's been having with . . ."

But then she couldn't seem to bring herself to say it.

"I'm not too worried about that," I said. "I think the meetings are actually going pretty well."

"Glad to hear it." The words sounded quite sincere. Especially for my mom, who was not the sincerity queen. To put it mildly. "Now put on your running shoes and go see if you can find him."

———

I was running by the ice cream shop, the Place, when I saw her. I looked through the window of the store, but my view through the glass was partly obscured by reflections. But I saw the familiar face of Zoe Dinsmore, sitting at a table, one hand wrapped around a mug of coffee. Well. The coffee part was a guess. But it was definitely a mug of something.

I stopped running.

I looked in at her, and she looked out at me. And we locked eyes as best we could through all those reflections.

It seemed strange to see her downtown, like any other resident of the little town of Ashby. I knew she came into town now and then—she had to, for supplies if nothing else—but it felt strange to see her sitting at a table in a public shop, enjoying a hot cup of something, like any other townsperson. Like she belonged anywhere she cared to go.

It also felt nice, though.

Then I shifted back a step, and that was when I recognized Roy's crutches. He was sitting with his back to me, mostly obscured by the reflection of a light-colored brick building across the street.

I turned back toward the door and walked inside.

Roy looked around and watched me coming. Zoe must've told him. Or maybe he saw on her face that someone was there.

I sat down at the table with them.

My brother was drinking some kind of ice cream float, stabbing at it with the paper straw in between sips, as though breaking up ice floes.

"Hey, buddy," he said.

"Mom's flipping out."

"What is it this time?"

"You."

"Right, I figured, but what did I do?"

"You left."

"Don't I get to leave?"

"I don't know."

"I'm nineteen."

"Right. I know. I tried to tell her that. Well. Something *like* that. But she worries about you now. I think she figures you're somewhere . . . you know."

"I *don't* know."

"Up to no good."

"Right," he said. "Got it." He frowned into his glass for a few beats. "But I plan to go out a lot more, so she's going to have to get used to it."

"Maybe leave a note?"

"Yeah. I could do that, I guess. I guess I didn't know it would bother her so much. I went out yesterday, and she didn't care. Oh, but come to think of it, maybe she didn't even know. She was away. I got it in my head that I had to have one of the root beer floats they make here. I swear I was thinking about them when I was overseas. Hardly a day went by I didn't feel like I could taste these root beer floats. And I figured I need to get better on the crutches anyway, so I walked down here."

He stopped. Took a long pull through the straw.

"Only I saw him going down Main Street," Zoe said, seamlessly taking over where he'd left off, "and I stopped and asked him if he needed a ride, and the next thing we knew, we were having a soda together. And we had a good talk."

And now here they were, doing it again the next day. There was some kind of subtext in all this, but I swear I didn't know what it was.

I think she saw the confusion on my face, because she looked at Roy, a question in her eyes. He nodded, and she offered it up without my having to ask.

"Your brother asked if I would be his NA sponsor. Which I think your average recovering person would consider a very dicey choice, if not absolute insanity. Partly because men usually get men sponsors and vice versa. But that's just so there won't be any weird emotional attachments, and with me being somewhere between old enough to be his mother and old enough to be his grandmother, I guarantee that's not going to be an issue. More to the point, I don't have any more clean time than he does."

"But you had a bunch of years before," Roy said. "You know a lot more than I do."

"Other people know more," she said.

"That's not the point, though," Roy said. "Here's the point. When she walked into that meeting the other night . . ."

That's when I realized he was talking to me. He wasn't looking at me. But when he called Zoe "she" rather than "you," I got it.

". . . it just changed something for me. Because I knew what she had in her past was so hard, you know? One of those things you never stop regretting, that never really leaves you alone. So I figured if she could pull it together and commit to getting clean again and keep going, so could I. It sort of gave me hope for my situation. That's why she thinks I need to count my clean time from that night."

"Whatever," Zoe said, shaking off his praise. "Bottom line, we're looking to give that a go, no matter what anybody around us might think of the idea." Zoe turned her attention directly onto me. "Would that be weird for you? If I was Roy's sponsor?"

"No!" I said. Shouted, almost, though I hadn't meant to. "No, it would be great." I felt as though a huge weight had been lifted off me. I didn't realize how much the weight of saving my brother had been crushing me until Zoe lifted it away. "If you helped him half as much as you helped Connor . . ."

"I didn't do anything special with Connor," she said. But I knew that wasn't true. "Don't invest too much in me, kid, like I'm magic. That boy just had some stuff he needed to get off his chest. That's all that was."

I heard the distinctive sucking sound of a straw running dry. Hitting the bottom of its drink. I looked over to see that Roy had rushed through the bottom half of his soda and was pushing to his feet.

"I'll go home and tell Mom I'm alive," he said.

"She might be driving around looking for you," I said. "Don't be too surprised if you run into her accidentally."

He didn't answer. Only shook his head. Because . . . you know. That was our mom. What could you do but shake your head about her?

"You need a ride, son?" Zoe asked him.

"No, ma'am. Finish your coffee. I need to practice walking anyway. You two sit. I'll go sort it out with Mom."

I watched him swing along on his crutches, headed for the door. Watched a local man with two little kids hold the door open for him. The man nodded at my brother proudly, as though Roy were some kind of war hero.

I wondered if Roy would get to keep that. Or if, in a town this size, the truth would find its way out.

I looked back at Zoe, and she looked at me. We'd been doing that a lot lately, I'd noticed. Looking each other head on, both at the same time. Like we weren't afraid. Like we had nothing to hide and nothing to lose.

At least, not from each other.

"What did you do that helped Connor so much?" I asked her. "I'd really like to know."

"I just told you."

"But there had to be more to it than that. You couldn't have just sat there and said nothing while he talked."

"Now and then I might've said something in reply."

"Like what?"

She sighed. Rolled her eyes at me, like I was still the little pest I'd always been. But not really in a bad way, if such a thing were possible. Then she surprised me by offering up a serious answer.

"Like when he talked about his mom, and how much she smothers him, and depends on him too hard. I just told him he wasn't wrong for minding. Kids get to feeling like they ought to be everything a parent needs, and they feel guilty if they fall short. But I told him anybody in his position would feel the same way, and it's normal to feel it. And his dad leaving the way he did. I just told him it was between the man and his wife, something that'd been going on years before he was born, and it didn't have nearly as much to do with him as he might've thought. People need help with perspective sometimes. If they're all alone in their own head, they can lose perspective. Sometimes you need to use somebody else like a mirror. Let them reflect back to you the way the world really is."

"Thanks," I said.

"Not a problem."

"Did he tell you about his kitten?"

"Oh yeah. At great length. It's not hard getting Connor to tell you about his kitten. The problem would be getting him to *stop* telling you about her."

But I could tell by the expression on her face that she really didn't mind at all.

—

I didn't want to go home, because I figured Roy and Mom would need some time to have it out. And if they were fighting, I didn't want to hear it.

So I went over to Connor's.

I must admit, in addition to his being my friend, I really wanted to see that kitten again.

Connor surprised me by answering the door.

"Oh," I said. "It's you. Where's your mom?"

"Not sure."

I followed him down the long hallway and up the stairs, and I didn't need time for my eyes to adjust. There was light. Lots of it. Apparently, after his mom left the house Connor had gone around and opened all the curtains.

"She goes out now and doesn't tell you where?"

We slipped through his bedroom door carefully, so we didn't let the kitten out. He never answered. Well, not never. But he moved on to a different topic in that moment.

"Uh-oh," Connor said. "She's under the bed. Well, the best plan is to just sit on the floor and pretend you don't want her to come to you. And then she will."

We sat cross-legged, facing each other. Just for a second we smiled. Then we looked down at the rug, the way we usually did.

Baby steps.

"She calls it 'Me Time,'" he said.

I had no idea what he was talking about. I thought we were still talking about the cat. And if that had been the case, his comment would have made no sense.

"What?"

"My mom."

"Oh. Your mom."

"She doesn't say exactly what Me Time is, but once she made some comment about needing someone to talk to. So she might be going to talk to a friend, though I'm not sure who that would be. Or she might actually be in counseling. I'm thinking counseling, because if she had a new friend, I think she'd tell me more about that. She wouldn't treat it like some kind of secret."

"Oh," I said. "Well. That would be good, if she was in counseling. I mean . . . wouldn't it?"

The kitten stuck her head out from under the bed. And my mood just soared when I looked at that little face. Those pink ears and those tiny, round blue eyes.

She looked at my hand where it sat on the rug, and did that gearing-up-to-attack thing kittens do. Front end hunkered down. Tail end in the air. Eyes all intense. A little swish of her body back and forth. Then she came barreling across the rug, bit my finger with those needle-sharp baby teeth, and ran under the bed again.

Connor laughed. I laughed, too. It hurt, but not so much that it wasn't still funny.

"I think it's good," he said. "It's good to talk to somebody."

"Speaking of which. Speaking of talking to somebody. You're not going to believe this. Zoe Dinsmore is going to be Roy's sponsor in the program. But don't tell anybody. It might not be the right anonymity thing, and maybe I shouldn't have told you. And besides, I don't want it getting back to my mom."

Connor and I had talked once, briefly, about whether Roy would ever get serious enough to get a sponsor. So Connor knew what that meant.

"Wait. Zoe's back in the meetings?"

"Yeah. Didn't I tell you? I'm sorry. It was just a couple of days ago, and I guess I haven't seen you since then."

"That's good," he said. "I'm really glad to hear that. Good for her. And that's good about her taking Roy under her wing, too. I think she'll help him."

"Yeah. I think so, too."

Then we had one of those long silences. Like the old days. The kind that get stronger and more thick and solid the longer they go on, and you start feeling like you can't break through them.

But I didn't want the old days anymore. I wasn't going back there. So I broke through.

"She really helped you, didn't she?"

"Yeah," he said. "She did."

"What was it about talking to her that helped you so much?"

He didn't answer right away. But I didn't feel like he was holding back or holding out on me. He seemed to be really thinking about what he wanted to say.

"Sometimes it's hard to put those things into words," he said.

"Yeah. Sometimes it is."

"I think . . . she made me feel like I was worth having around. And for a while there I didn't really feel like I was."

"It's good that you believed her."

"I didn't," he said.

The cat ran, pretty much sideways, in a wild arc between us and then back under the bed. We were too caught up in what we were saying to laugh.

"Oh, I don't mean that quite the way it sounds," he said. "I just mean . . . I felt like I wasn't worth much, and sometimes on a bad day I still feel that way. But here's the thing. *Zoe* felt like *she* wasn't worth much, and like nobody wanted her around, and she almost killed herself over thinking that. But I know she's worth a lot, and I know I want her around. So I know she was wrong. So now when I feel bad about myself, I think about that, and I think maybe I'm wrong. Maybe things aren't as bad as I thought. So that's one of those thoughts that, once you have it, you don't ever really forget it. Just that idea that when you feel like everything is terrible . . . it might not be the truth. Once you get that in your head, you don't want to do something based on those feelings if it's something you can't ever take back. And this may sound like a strange thing to say, but . . ."

I waited. But he seemed less and less inclined to go on.

"Go ahead," I said.

"No. Never mind. It was nothing."

"Really. Go ahead and tell me. I won't tell anyone."

"No," he said. "I know you won't. I was just going to say that I think maybe I helped her, too. Because she said something like that to me once. Something like . . . like she didn't believe in herself, but she believed in me. She even told me some stuff that was hard about *her* life."

That made me feel bad. A little, anyway. But all I said was, "Like what? If it's not too private."

"Like about her girls. And why she decided to stay in Ashby. And how now she thinks that was a bad decision, and that it was really hard for them, trying to make that adjustment. Now she thinks it was selfish of her to stay and that's why they don't really speak to her much. She says they felt like everybody thought it should have been them who died, not two kids who had nothing to do with Zoe. Not somebody else's kids. I don't know if that's true or not. If people really felt that way. But I guess the girls felt it like a pressure, you know?

"But I'm getting off track. I just meant to say that it went both ways. She believes in me but not herself. I didn't believe in myself, but I believe in Zoe. You know, it really helps to have one person who believes in you, even if it's not you. Even if you can't quite do it yourself yet."

I opened my mouth to say something. Probably that I could imagine what a game changer that would be. Or maybe "lifesaver" would've been a better way to phrase it.

But just then the kitten came out and leapt onto Connor's back and grabbed on with her claws into his shirt. And obviously also into his skin, because he screamed. But he sort of laughed and screamed at the same time.

He reached around carefully and took hold of her and pulled her close to his chest, where she couldn't do much harm.

"We have *got* to cut your nails," he told her.

We didn't talk about serious topics anymore that day.

In fact, we didn't talk about those early times of his going to see Zoe Dinsmore ever again. Not that I can recall.

Then again, what more needed to be said?

If something works, I figure . . . just leave it alone. Let it be a thing that worked. Not everything needs to be picked apart for better understanding. Sometimes it's okay to just say thank you in the quiet of your head and move along.

PART TWO: PRESENT DAY

AFTER FIFTY YEARS OF MOVING ALONG

Chapter Nineteen

All You

I could have said right from the start that I'm retelling this story standing beside the freshly dug, open grave of Connor Barnes. While I'm waiting for my friend's casket to be lowered into the ground. I was tempted to. But I might've given a false impression if I'd done it that way.

It might have sounded like I was saying Connor didn't make it.

Connor made it.

He made it another fifty years, after which he died of stomach cancer at age sixty-four.

We would've loved to have had Connor around another ten or twenty years, but still, he had a good run. And he left the world a lot of value from his time here, not only in the form of the decent life he managed to live, but also in the form of three beautiful daughters and seven grandchildren—five boys and two girls.

I'm standing here talking to one of the grandchildren, and I have been for what seems like a very long time.

His name is Harris, and he's fourteen. He looks a little like Connor did at his age. Lanky and awkward and hopeless to sort out the world he's been given. It doesn't escape my notice that he's the same age

Connor and I were in the story. I hope that makes my ramblings even more meaningful to him.

"So why do we call you Uncle Luke?" he asks me, shielding his eyes against the sun. "If you hate to have anybody call you Luke?"

He doesn't ask why everybody calls me Uncle Luke even though I'm not blood family, and even though I would be a *great*-uncle to him even if I was. But I guess some mysteries are more important than others.

I say, "Yeah, I figured you'd ask me that. But as you get older, a name that makes you sound young loses its sting."

I can tell by the look in his eyes that something I've said has gone over his head for the first time all day. Maybe because it doesn't involve being fourteen. I expect him to ask more about it, but he veers off in an entirely different direction.

"So by the time you were old enough for the draft, the war was over?"

I breathe a huge sigh. Because it's a huge subject. But I'll tell him the truth. I always tell him the truth.

"When I turned eighteen," I say, "the war was still not over."

"So what did you do?"

"I didn't go."

He doesn't say anything. I wonder what he's thinking. I'm watching family wander back to their cars. Slowly, and a few at a time. But we don't wander. Because we're not done.

"Go ahead and call me a draft dodger if you want," I tell Harris. But I know he won't. "There are still a couple of people in town who do, though mostly behind my back. Thing is, there was no dodge about it. I didn't dodge anything. I didn't go to Canada. I didn't bribe or lie to anybody who could get me a better classification in the draft. I didn't even try to register as a conscientious objector. My understanding was that the CO category is for people who have strong religious convictions against any kind of violence. I wasn't going to lie, and it didn't seem right to take one of their deferments.

"I was honest, and I hit it head-on.

"I walked into the sheriff's office and ran into . . . guess who? Right. I knew you could guess because you're good at this stuff. It was old Deputy Warren."

"The guy who broke down Grandma Zoe's door on that day when she almost died?"

He calls her Grandma Zoe not because she was anywhere near the age equivalent of a grandmother to him, but because Connor called her that. Harris never met her, which is a damn shame. She died about a year before he was born.

"The very one," I say. "And if I told you he didn't know what to make of me, let alone what to do with me, that would be an understatement.

"I said, 'I'm not going to register for the draft.' And I held my wrists out so he could put the cuffs on me.

"He stared at them like he'd never seen wrists before.

"'I don't think that's the way it works,' he said.

"'How does it work?'

"He scratched his head for a minute, and then he said, 'I got no idea, son. Nothing like this ever happened around here before.'"

I watch Harris's eyebrows go up. Just a little bit. I keep talking.

"So then he disappeared for a few minutes, leaving me noticeably uncuffed. When he came back, I swear he seemed more embarrassed than angry.

"'Nobody else knows, either,' he said. 'But we figure in time the Selective Service people'll get tired of not hearing from you, and eventually they'll put out a warrant for your arrest. Or something like that. We're talking about the federal government here, son. It's not really our department.'

"I asked him, 'So you're saying I should just go home and wait?'

"'No,' he said, and at this juncture I could hear the irritation rising in his voice. 'No, if you're asking me what I think you ought to do, I think you ought to sign up. You can get a deferment by going to college, at least for a while. That's what all the other boys are doing.'

"I said, 'But they can pull that out from under me anytime.'

"He said, 'A lot of guys get a doctor to write up some excuse.'

"Well, I guess I wasn't a lot of guys. If you know what I mean.

"I said, 'But I'm fine. So that would be a lie. That would be a total insult to the guys who went over there. I'm not going to lie and cheat to live a nice, comfortable life while they fight. I'm going to make a sacrifice that they could make, too, if they wanted. I'm going to go to jail.'

"He scratched his head again, and narrowed his eyes at me. Finally he just said, 'Go home and wait, son. With ideas like that in your head, sounds like jail'll find you soon enough.'"

I know he's about to ask if it did. So I beat him to it.

"I hurried up the process by writing to the Selective Service and telling them I was never going to sign up, and whatever the penalty might be for that, they should just go ahead and get the proceedings going against me.

"I served two years. I didn't have to go to some terrible, dangerous federal prison. I just served my time in the county jail, which I think was fairly irregular as these things go. It was the federal government, like the deputy said. But somehow they referred my case to the local authorities for arrest. Maybe they didn't know what to do with guys like me, either.

"It was a blessing at least to be jailed close to home.

"I got no time off for good behavior, not because I didn't behave well, but because the guards and the warden and the parole board all had some family or friends who'd signed up for the draft just like they were supposed to do.

"The food was incredibly bad, which I swear was the second-worst thing about the place, after the noise and the lack of privacy. But it wasn't supposed to be fun. It was supposed to be the price I paid.

"And damn it, I paid it.

"Roy drove out twice a week and brought me some decent food, and your granddad came out twice on some weeks, three times on others. He promised to take me to the Place for one of those chocolate-dipped chocolate ice cream cones the day I got out. It was the only treat he couldn't figure out how to bring me.

"You have no idea how many of my days in that hole started with a wish for that ice cream shop not to go out of business while I was rotting. I mean, serving my time. Paying my debt to society.

"My parents had divorced by then—I know, what took them so long, right?—but my father flew all the way from North Carolina, where he lived with his new wife, to scream at me and tell me how much I'd disappointed him. How I'd ruined my whole life with this bonehead play.

"And I was a captive audience. Literally.

"But, you know what? It's okay. That's part of the price I paid.

"My mom only visited three or four times in that whole two years, but she was relieved by what I'd done. She never said so straight out, but I knew.

"And Zoe.

"Zoe not only came to visit me now and again, but she wrote me a letter every day. *Every day* for two years. Seven hundred and thirty letters. I actually counted. In jail, you have time on your hands for stuff like that. Some were full of news from town, others were just her thoughts on this and that. Some were longer than others, but I never had to watch a mail call go by with no letter from Zoe. I think she single-handedly kept our little branch post office afloat during that time.

"I still have every one of those letters. Stacked and organized by date and rubber-banded in shoeboxes in my closet."

My head fills with a very clear, very painful image. It's taking me off in a different direction in my head. And I go with it. And I retell it.

"I watched the fall of Saigon from the TV room in the county jail," I say. "I watched those helicopters teetering on rooftops, trying to take off with too many people loading them down. I watched people try to hang on to the bottom of them, desperate to get out of there. I saw how many never made it out.

"*The war is over,* I thought in the back of my head while I watched. But I knew my jail sentence wasn't.

"I remember I wondered how Roy felt, watching that on TV. Or Joe, from the NA meeting. Or Darren Weller. It just seemed like everything they'd gone through added up to nothing—at least, nothing anybody got to keep.

"Next time he visited, I asked Roy what he was feeling when he saw that.

"He said he hadn't been able to bring himself to watch."

I let a beat fall after that statement. In my mind, it warrants a beat.

"What about my grandpa?" Harris asks, his face open with awe. His mother is trying to get his attention from over at the cars, and he's studiously ignoring her. "Was he okay with what you did?"

"Funny thing about that," I say. "We actually only talked about it once. He came to the county jail to pick me up on my release day, your granddad, because Roy had to work. He took me out for that ice cream, just the way he'd promised.

"'Chocolate ice cream with chocolate coating,' he told me while we waited in line. 'That still seems like an awful lot of chocolate.'

"I said, 'You still don't say that like it's a good thing.'

"When we'd gotten our cones, I purposely led us to a table right by the front window. Because the whole point of not going to Canada was to be able to hold my head up and feel like I had nothing to hide.

"We licked our ice cream in silence and just sort of watched the town go by. Some of the locals waved at me, like they were glad to see me back. Others looked away like I was invisible. Except . . . if I'd been invisible, they wouldn't have needed to look away.

"I did better with the mothers than the fathers, and better with the young women than the young men. But that was just a generality. Somebody will always come along and break the mold.

"After a while I said to your granddad, 'I never could bring myself to ask you this. I purposely never asked. But I'm going to ask you right now. Do you think I did the right thing?'

"He said, 'I think you did the right thing *for you*.'

"After that we never spoke about it again. Probably not because we didn't feel we could. Probably because we never needed to."

"Oh," he says. "Good."

He's not saying a lot, but he's deeply invested. I can tell. I'm sure this isn't all new information to him. He must've heard bits and pieces. He probably never heard my side of the thing.

His mother is trying to flag *me* down now. And now *I'm* studiously ignoring her. Because I'm telling this kid the truth. If there's one thing I learned growing up, it's that you have to talk to kids a lot, and you have to tell them the damn truth.

"But you said people still call you a draft dodger," he says.

"Some. Not all. Different people have different opinions. My dad was right about one thing, though. It does follow you around, all through your life, that time in jail. I'm not saying nobody would hire me after that, but the pickings got slimmer. I had to look at that same decision that faced Grandma Zoe after the accident. Should I just get out of this town and go someplace where nobody knew me? But I didn't think that would work well in my situation, because the arrest record follows you wherever you go. Anywhere I lived, when I applied for a job, a simple background check would turn up that conviction. I figured I was better off staying close to home, where people had a fair shot at knowing it was my version of a principled stand. I say 'fair shot' because I knew not everybody was destined to see it that way. You can't change the way a person's going to see a thing. If there's only one thing I've learned in my sixty-four years on the planet, it would be that.

"But some people understood it." I end on that. Or try to, anyway.

"But you were doing what you thought was right," he says.

"Yeah. But some people don't want you to do what you think is right. Some people want you to do what *they* think is right. Anyway, it all shook out okay. I ended up working a pretty menial job at the hardware store. The owner had lost his son in Vietnam. You'd think that would've pitted him against me, but it was just the opposite. He was burned by what I guess he felt was the pointlessness of the whole thing, and wishing his son had taken jail time instead. So he hired me, and he treated me with respect.

"I worked hard, lived over the store, and put away every cent I didn't need to live on. And on the other side of town your uncle Roy was doing the same thing. And we weren't even talking to each other about it. It wasn't even a plan.

"Now the old owner is deceased, and we own that store."

"I knew *that*," he says. "I didn't know all of this, but I know *something*."

"Of course you do."

His mother is waving to me again, and I raise one finger high. Asking her to wait. To let us finish. Surprisingly, she does. I guess she just needed to be acknowledged.

"Here's a thing I don't know," he says. And I wait, and let him figure out how to say it in his own way. "Nobody really told me why Grandpa didn't have to go fight in the war. I asked my mom once, but I never really got a straight answer."

"I can understand that," I say. "It hits on a touchy subject. But you're a smart boy, and you're mature for your age. And you know your great-grandma Pauline was not always very . . . well."

"In the head, you mean?"

"Yeah. That."

He nods. He knows.

"It's like this," I say. "Grandma Zoe had this thing she used to say. 'It's an ill wind that blows no one good.'"

He wrinkles his nose. It almost makes me laugh. "I don't understand that saying at all," he says.

"You know, honestly, it never made a great deal of sense to me, either, but for years I didn't say so. It sounded like it just meant 'bad things have bad effects.' And I thought, *Yeah, so . . . what's your point?* Finally one day I was a little grumpy and tired, so I called her out on it. Turns out it means even most really bad winds are going to blow something good to somebody.

"Which leads me to my point about Connor and his mom. It would be nice to report that everybody's story had at least a fair or satisfying ending, but that's not life, is it? And you're old enough to know it. And I'm not going to lie to you about life, Harris. Your great-grandma Pauline didn't fare well. She had a breakdown when Connor was sixteen. At the time we all thought, well, people come back from breakdowns. But she never did.

"They couldn't afford to put her in any kind of facility, at least not one Connor could bear to think of using. And they couldn't afford any kind of in-home nursing or professional care. So Connor took care of her.

"In our last year of high school, Zoe came over and sat with Pauline every day while Connor went to school. After he graduated, Connor found a college that would let him earn a degree from home—you know, a correspondence course sort of thing.

"He got a nice, cushy job in the county planning department and bought a house for your grandma Dotty before he even asked her to marry him. It's just who he was. He didn't want to live and raise a family in that spooky old house he'd grown up in, which I think was a smart move. So he sold it and got a new one with no bad memories, where they could make a life from scratch. With four bedrooms. One for them. A couple for all the kids he knew they wanted. And one for his mom.

"Your grandma looked after Pauline for years while Connor worked. It wasn't all that hard a job to do. Pauline was never difficult or unpleasant. She just couldn't do much of anything for herself. She died of a blood infection in 1984. But maybe that part you knew."

"Right," he says, "I did. But I still don't get the part about the wind."

"I was getting to that. So that ill wind blew something good to someone. Connor—your grandad—was her sole caretaker when he turned eighteen. And that kept him deferred from the draft. And he didn't have to go."

"Oh," he said. "Yeah. I think I finally get the part about the wind."

I feel a little tug on my jacket sleeve. I'm wearing a suit jacket, even though it's summer, just like it was where I started this story. Even though it's hot. I look down, and it's Connor's youngest granddaughter, Evvie. Tugging at my jacket sleeve.

"Uncle Luke, Uncle Luke," she says.

For some reason, Evvie has a tendency to say important things twice. Most things, actually. I think she's at that age when everything on her mind feels terribly important. The repetition must make her feel that she's properly expressing her urgency.

Life is a very urgent place when you're seven. I seem to recall that, though it's been a long time.

"Yes, Evvie?"

"Why are you just standing here? You're just standing here."

She doesn't say, "My mom told me to come get you." She doesn't need to. I know.

"I guess we should go, then," I say to Evvie, in that voice you use with a child when you're admitting that they're entirely right and you're entirely wrong. That's always a satisfying moment for a kid.

"Grandma wants to know if you're coming to the house after. She wants you to come to the house."

I look up at Dotty in the distance and offer her a sad little smile, but she might be too far away to see.

"Try to keep me away," I say.

"But we don't *want* to keep you away," Evvie says, clearly frustrated with me. "We want you to *come*."

"Okay," I say. "Fair enough. Let's you and me go together."

Evvie and Harris and I walk back to the cars, through the neatly tended gravestones. Evvie and I walk hand in hand.

"What about the kitten?" Harris asks me. "You never told me what happened to the kitten."

"What kitten?" Evvie asks, but her cousin shushes her.

"Oh," I say. "Right. I forgot about the kitten. Well. She didn't stay a kitten for long, of course. Connor named her Sky after the color of her eyes, and she grew into a big cat. Nearly twenty pounds. She lived to be twenty-two years old. No joke. He got her when he was fourteen, and his little girls knew her through most of their childhoods."

"My mother knew her?"

"She absolutely did."

"And *my* mother knew her?" Evvie asks.

"She absolutely did. Everybody cried like a baby when she died. Even me. But I wouldn't say anybody was devastated. Just sad. I mean, she lived so long."

Harris stops walking. Suddenly. We almost leave him behind before we notice.

"That was a sad story," he says.

"It's really not a sad story. Not to me."

"But everybody dies."

"Well, that's not the problem with *my story*," I say. "That's a problem with life. But anyway, it's a story about a lot of people doing a lot better than they expected to. A lot better than anybody thought they would. And I don't mean to be wrapping it up on a bunch of sad notes, but, the trouble is, I'm in a bind here, Harris, because how do you tell a fifty-year-old story without reporting that most of the principals have ended their run on this earth? Well, there's really only two possible answers for this one: You lie. Or you can't do it. And you know me. I'm not one to lie. But I still have to say it's not devastating that people and animals live and then die. Other people may think so, but I don't. It's hard, but those are the rules of the game."

We walk again.

And I think to myself, *If you think having and losing is so bad, try never having. Now* that's *devastating.*

———

By the time we get back to the Barneses' house together—Evvie took me up on my offer to ride with me—Dotty, Connor's widow, is already a little bit in her cups. And Dotty was never much of a drinking woman.

Her family is trying to gently pry the glass out of her hand and talk sense to her, but I don't interfere. I figure if she can't get drunk on the day she buries her only husband, on what day of her life will it be okay?

As I step into the house, she's surrounded by all three of her sons-in-law, all trying—mostly at cross-purposes to one another—to get her to sit down on the couch and relax. But she doesn't. She looks up and sees me, and her gaze just locks on me. It's almost a little scary. She's like a bird of prey, tracking on a scampering mouse in the grass.

I move across the room, but her eyes follow me.

"You," she says.

Just in that moment it doesn't sound like much of a compliment.

I move in her direction, thinking a hug might help.

But she stops me with one hand extended, her index finger pointing at the "you" in question. Her dark hair, which was pinned up in a careful bun at the funeral, is coming down in wisps across her face and shoulders. Just here and there. She looks a little too red in the face.

"You," she says again. "It was always you. Connor told me so."

She has a son-in-law holding her by each arm. The third is behind her. And now they're all four staring at me. Probably everybody in the room is staring at me—though I don't look around to see—wondering what I've done.

In that split second before I answer, I swear you could hear the proverbial pin drop in that living room.

"What did Connor tell you?" I ask Dotty. My voice is soft because I know Connor never said a bad word about me to her. I don't doubt what I know. You don't know a guy for sixty-one years and then start having doubts like that.

"He said we never would've met if it wasn't for you, because he wouldn't have lived that long. He said it was all you. Everything after he was fourteen was all because of you."

"It wasn't all me," I say.

I still don't look around, but I can actually hear people start breathing again. Because now we realize her grief has simply brought out a passion and an intensity in her face and her words that was making even a good thing sound bad.

She's shaking her head hard now. Too hard. She looks as though she might unbalance herself. Then again, those sons-in-law will never let her hit the carpet.

"He said it was you."

"It wasn't. It was Zoe."

"But who introduced him to Zoe?" she asks, her voice far too loud, her arms flailing wildly for some kind of inexact emphasis.

"I'll take credit for introducing him to Zoe," I say. "But I can't take it all. Connor was a kind man. He was generous. He gave me too much credit. The truth is, it wasn't me. The truth is, we took care of each other. Zoe and Connor and Roy and me. We just took care of each other. That's all that was."

She reaches out and pats my cheek, then nearly falls over.

The sons-in-law usher her out of the living room and into her bedroom for a much-needed nap.

—

Harris corners me on the back deck a few minutes later and reminds me I never told him what happened to Rembrandt and Vermeer. It seems like a question with an obvious answer. I mean, it's a fifty-year-old story. So on one level, he knows. But he clearly wants more details. More color, as they say on *Monday Night Football*. So I drop back into my storyteller mode.

"They lived pretty long lives for Dane mixes. Rembrandt lived to be eleven, Vermeer nearly thirteen. I ran with them up until nearly the day they laid their heads down on their beds and chose not to pick them up again. I'm not saying that's always a choice. I'm just saying in their cases I think it was."

"Wait. How do you know?"

"Now . . . that's a question I can't answer. It's not a thing I can wrap words around. You just had to know them. If you knew them, I think you'd understand. Anyway. They both passed quietly at home, in their doghouse next to their cabin in the woods.

"I cried like a baby both times.

"I had my own dogs by then, but that didn't help as much as you might think.

"Grandma Zoe swore she was done with dogs, I think because the losses hit her so hard. But not three weeks after Vermeer left the world, somebody abandoned a litter of puppies at the county pound, and the shelter was in an overflow situation. Word got around that they were going to put the puppies down straightaway, so Zoe drove over there in that same old pickup and took two of them home. She didn't even know what kind they were, but she took them.

"They grew up to be crazy to look at. Some huge mix with wild hair like some kind of wolfhounds, or maybe those big long-haired sheepdogs. Or both. They were nothing like the two we lost, but maybe it's better that way. They barked like crazy, and they grew up to be big, goony clowns, but we loved them. They liked to run with my dogs and me, and that's what really mattered. To me, I mean. To Zoe, they stayed close to the cabin and made her feel safe.

"They were good dogs in their own way.

"Then she had two more sets after that.

"She had a pair of big dogs when your grandad Connor finally talked her into coming out of the woods and into town. He'd spent years trying to get her to take that spare bedroom his mother had left behind, but Zoe wasn't having any of it. But then she got into her late seventies, and the strain of living out there in the middle of nowhere finally wore her down. There's only just so long you can chop your own wood to stay warm and carry your own water from a hand-pump well. Time catches up with everybody. Even Zoe Dinsmore. She lived with your grandma and grandad for a decade, and it was a good decade. I can say that for a fact because I was there. Not living there, but there enough.

"She made peace with one of her daughters before all was said and done, but the other one never came around. Still, both daughters let her see her grandchildren, and that's no small matter. And then she finally left the world at age eighty-nine. Quietly, at home. Just like her dogs. I thought Connor would be devastated. I thought Roy would be devastated. Hell, I figured it would kill *me*. But we were fully grown adults by then. We weren't little boys anymore.

"That's not to say that grown-ups don't feel the pain of loss, or that being grown gets you out of a thing like grieving. All I'm saying is that we had her when we needed her the most—when we were scared and lost and all the grown-ups around us were letting us down."

"That's funny," he says. But not really like it's something you would laugh about.

"How so?"

"It just seems funny how all the grown-ups were always warning you about Grandma Zoe. Like she would hurt you somehow."

"Right. Good point. And meanwhile they were damaging us every day without even knowing it. And it was Zoe who helped us come home to ourselves. Yeah. I guess that is funny. Here's why we were more or less okay when she died. We had no good options when we met her. We didn't have tools or skills to figure out the world, or get by in it. When she died of old age, we had more of that stuff. Because we'd gotten so much of it from her."

"But then you never got married," he said.

It's one of those direct—bordering on rude—statements a grown-up would know better than to make. It's also incorrect. I did get married. Twice. But both times were long before he was born.

"I got married twice," I tell him, "but it never really took. They weren't bad marriages, exactly, and the splits were amicable enough. I still talk to both my exes from time to time. I think we have these ideas about success and failure, and sometimes we fall into the trap of thinking one size fits all. Some guys like Connor were born to be family men. Then there are guys like me who do really well with a couple of good dogs. So that's the way I went. I went with the couple of good dogs."

———

Roy is on about his tenth club soda. An event like this is harder when you don't drink. I should know, because I don't drink around Roy. At all. After all these years, I'm sure he wouldn't care if I did. But *I* care.

It's just one of those things you do for your brother, out of respect.

Zoe and my brother Roy always had the same clean date in the program, which is a very weird thing for a guy to share with his sponsor. But they both started their time that night Zoe walked back into the meeting and got Roy to share for the first time, and they never messed it up and had to start over from scratch.

Zoe had a little more than thirty-five years clean and sober when she died.

That means my brother Roy has fifty years and counting.

He and I are talking partly about Connor and partly about Zoe Dinsmore. We have been for nearly an hour. Someone who didn't know me so well might think I wasn't taking Connor's death all that hard. But Roy knows me. He knows it just hasn't hit me yet. When Zoe died, it took me two weeks to get that she was really gone.

The kids are all in bed, even the teenager, and I'm thinking it might be close to that moment when we can make a gracious exit. But we haven't done it yet.

"You think her old place is still standing out in the woods?" he asks me.

I'm more than a little bit surprised by the question.

"Yeah, of course it is. I go by it every day on my run."

"Why do you take the same path every day?"

Roy is not a guy who would take the same path every day.

"I don't know," I say. "I just do. I thought you knew."

"No, I knew you run every day. But I'm not out there following you, you know. I figured you mixed it up."

"Be right back," I say.

I get up and walk across the room to Dorothy, Connor's oldest. She knows why. She hugs me and kisses me on the cheek and thanks me for coming. Like that was ever in question. Like that could ever in a million years have been in question.

Then I shoot Roy a signal that we're leaving, and he meets me at the door.

"Come on," I say. "I'll take you home. We'll go the long way."

———

Being a hardware man means always having a good, strong flashlight in your glove compartment.

I take us out via the River Road, because that's the shortest walk.

For what it's worth, Roy walks fine. He still has a limp after all these years, but you'd almost have to be focusing on it to notice.

He uses a sort of prosthetic that goes inside his shoe, so he can balance well when he walks. After fifty years you can imagine he's had a lot of practice with it. But he still takes it off as soon as he's not in public, so I think it's always bothered him a little. Maybe more than he lets on. Once he told me a few details about it, and it has something to do with the nerve endings at the point of that amputation. But he doesn't like to talk about that, because it makes him feel like a complainer.

He still keeps more of his insides to himself than I might've hoped for, but things like that are never a zero-sum game. You get progress, you be grateful for it. In the realm of wounded humans, you're never going to have it all.

Also, I should note that in my opinion, we're all wounded humans. The rest is just a matter of degree.

He never married. He keeps to his own company and seems to get by okay, considering that *okay* is also a relative term.

He drives fine, too, though he needs an automatic transmission because he drives with his left foot. It makes him nervous to have something as vital as a brake pedal operated by a part of his shoe that doesn't even have a foot in it. That he can't even feel.

The only reason I drove him to the funeral is because his truck wouldn't start.

"We're seriously going out there in the dark?" he asks as I park on the shoulder of the road.

"Sure, why not?"

"But why are we doing this again?"

"Because you didn't even know if it was still standing. And because it is. And because it brings back so many memories, you won't be able to believe it. It just brings her back so crystal clear in your mind, you feel like she might be standing right behind you. Like you might turn around and slam right into her."

He nods a couple of times. I can see it in the dash lights as I turn off the ignition.

"Okay," he says. "I'd say I'm up for that."

———

"What happened to the floor?" Roy asks me.

"Drifters," I say. "It's been broken into a couple of times."

We're sitting with our backs up against the wall where the head of Zoe's bed used to be. Roy started a fire in the old potbellied stove with some ancient kindling that got left behind on the hearth. It's very dry, that kindling. It's possibly had as much as twenty-five years' worth of drying time. It's burning hot, but it won't burn long, and that's just as well. We don't plan to sit here all night.

"What did they want to go and mess up the floor for, though?" he asks. He sounds like a kid who thinks something isn't fair.

"I have no idea."

He's pulling off his right shoe, which is not a surprise. Like I said, he always does when the opportunity presents itself. His sock has been shortened, a process he performs himself with scissors, a darning egg, and yarn, so all that extra sock doesn't bunch up and irritate him.

"Who owns this now?"

"Grandkids," I say.

"They're not doing anything with it, though."

"Not at the moment, no. But I figure one of these days one of them'll need the money they could get for the land. That's another reason I figured we should come out here sooner rather than later."

"Here's a question," Roy says. "How come so many people we know are dying?"

I laugh out loud. I can't help it.

"What's funny?" he asks.

"You are. It's because we're *old*, Roy."

"Speak for yourself," he says. "I'm not that old."

"You're going to turn seventy next year."

"Oh," he says. "Yeah. Wow. I guess that *is* pretty old. When did we get to be so old?"

"I don't know," I say. "It's crazy. We always used to be so young."

———

For a while we talk about Mom, and I'm not sure why.

"I told you about the last time I got to see her," he says. "The last time I got to talk to her. You never did. You kept those cards close to your vest."

Our mom died in 1998. She was living in a nursing home by then, and her mind had mostly gone. Every now and then it would come back in a flash, and she'd know who I was. But before I could mount a response to that momentous occasion, she'd be gone again.

When the nursing home called to say a last visit had better happen soon if we wanted one, Roy and I had to go see her separately because of our work schedules.

Honestly, I wasn't trying to play those cards close to my vest. I figured I'd told him.

"Well . . . ," I begin. Trying to bring back details as I go. "I sat beside her bed and watched her fade in and out, and at first I didn't say anything, because I thought she was too far gone to hear me. Then I figured at least her spirit was still there.

"So I said, 'Hey, Mom. It's me, Lucas. I came to say goodbye.'

"She turned her head toward me and looked me dead in the eye, and she said, clear as a bell, 'I know I wasn't a good mother and I'm sorry.'"

"Holy crap," he says. "How do you answer a statement like that?"

"I know, right?"

Now, I had a lot of anger toward my mom. I won't lie about that. She was *not* a good mother, and in most other moments of my life I would have agreed with her. Just straight out. But I think a parent needs something different on her deathbed. In the absence of actual abuse, I think in that final moment if you can't see it's not about you, then you're just not living the right kind of life. I could get into therapy and tell my counselor how unhelpful she was for the rest of my days, but this was my last chance ever to say something to my mom.

I tell Roy, "I fell back on something Zoe Dinsmore said to me, and in defense of *you*, by the way. I quoted it word for word, as best my memory allowed. Except I only repeated the first half of the thing. 'We're all just doing our best.' I left out the second part. 'Even if it doesn't look so good from the outside.' Because why plant the negative part of the thought in her head at a time like that?"

"You think she heard you?"

"I have no idea if she heard it. I have no idea if she took any of it in. But I know they were the right words at the right time. And besides, I heard it."

—

"Remember that thing with Zoe at your track meet?" he asks me.

The fire is beginning to die down, but we're making no move toward leaving.

"Which one? She was at practically every meet."

So was Roy, but I don't say that out loud, because he was there, so he knows.

"The one where that kid's father said something . . . *unpleasant* to me?"

Roy didn't get to keep his war hero status. Word got around. But it was okay, he told me years later. Much the same as jail and that dressing-down from Dad was okay for me. It's the price we paid. It's the price we chose.

"Remember what Zoe did?" he asks when I don't answer.

"I was out on the track, but I remember hearing about it. But I don't remember what she was supposed to have said."

"She didn't say anything. That was the beauty of the whole deal. She got between him and me and just stood there facing him with her arms crossed over her chest. And she never said a word. And he said every word under the sun. He tried reasoning with her. Then he made fun of her. Then he tried getting mad, or at least pretending he was mad. Then he started telling her she was crazy, because she never said a word. She barely even blinked. Then finally he got freaked out by the whole thing and just . . . you know . . . retreated. It was amazing."

"She was a scary woman," I say.

And it's funny the way I say it, because it's in this wistful voice, like I miss her and that was the best compliment I've got in the box. Well, I do miss her. Every day. But I'm sure I could think of better ways to express it than that.

"Boy, you can say that twice," Roy says. "That lady was a force of nature. Why do you think I stayed clean all those years? I would've been too scared to go and tell her I messed up."

"But she's been gone fifteen years, and you're still clean."

"Knowing Zoe, she'd haunt me."

"I get it," I say. Then I add something that's sort of tickling at the edges of my thoughts. "If she was so terrifying, which she totally was, and we were such cowards, which we totally were, how did we manage to love her so much?"

"Oh, that's easy. She was on our side." While I'm pondering the truth of that, he says, "You won't have a best friend anymore."

I notice that the last of the embers are winking out. It's dark in here now. My flashlight is turned off. And I'm not answering.

"You've had a best friend since you were three," he adds. "Now what?"

"I have the dogs," I say. "And you."

"I'm not sure if I'm best friend material."

"You'll do," I say, a little sarcastically.

Then I bump his knee in a signal that it's probably time to get up and go home.

He puts his right shoe back on and struggles to his feet. I reach out a hand to help him, but he doesn't seem to notice it in the dark. Just as well. He doesn't need it. He's been getting to his feet on his own since before I was born. I'm not sure what I thought I was doing with that.

He says, "Ask around town, and most people'll tell you I'm not best friend material."

"Yeah, but some of them told me the same thing about Connor."

"Oh," he says. And in that moment he pauses in his movement toward the door. "That's right, isn't it? And they sure were wrong about him."

"It's really important," I say, "when you're thinking bad thoughts about yourself, to remember that they might turn out to be wrong."

———

We're standing outside, taking one last look. The stars are just wild. There are millions of them, really sharp and clear between the trees. I've never stood beside the cabin at night before. Not once in all these years.

I think, *No wonder she loved it out here so much.*

And then after the fact, I realize I said it out loud.

"Yeah," he says. He's looking up, too. "People think she did it to punish herself, but I know she really loved it out here. It may have started as penance, but this became her place. You were right when you said you feel like you'll bump into her when you turn around. It feels almost like she's still here."

I'm looking half at the stars and half at the chimney, imagining smoke coming out of it the way it used to in the winter. Or even on a few cool summer evenings. And, yes, I'm positive I'm imagining it. We made sure our fire was out so we didn't burn down the cabin and the whole forest with it.

I turn on the flashlight and shine it all around again for one last look. Because, even though I guess I could be wrong, I get the feeling that it's my last look.

The sweep of the light touches on something. A flash of color. I keep the light trained in that direction. On either side of Zoe's outhouse there's a riot of untended flowers growing. Colored blooms on long stalks. Some are yellow. Others are purple or red.

Roy comes up behind me. I can hear his footsteps in the dry leaves.

"Whoa," he says. "I thought those would die without her, but they've really taken off since she was gone. There used to be just a little tended patch of them hidden behind the outhouse."

"Which explains why I never saw them."

"But you knew, right? You knew she grew flowers and left them on the two graves. Right?"

"I did and I didn't," I say.

And he knows me too well to ask for a clarification of that.

I turn off the flashlight. We hang in this place for a time, our eyes adjusting to the darkness again. I can feel how neither one of us really wants to leave.

"You know," Roy says. And then pauses. "That wasn't true what you said to Dotty today."

"What did I say to Dotty that wasn't true?"

"You did more than just introduce Connor to Zoe. You saved Zoe's life. It's only because of you that she even survived long enough for you to introduce him."

"Oh," I say. "Right. I guess I wasn't considering that part of the thing."

"If you hadn't developed that weird habit of running with some-body else's dogs, she would have died in her cabin that day, and there would have been nobody to pull our butts out of the fire. We probably would've lost Connor. And I'm not sure if I would've gotten clean. Or how I would've turned out if I hadn't."

I look away from the stars and the chimney. The wild stalks of flow-ers. Then, with no real outward signal to each other that we're about to do it, we make our way back toward the road together.

I don't turn on the flashlight again. Our eyes are adjusted to the lack of light, and besides, if there's anybody who knows how to navigate a dark night, it's me and my brother.

"I wouldn't have been running with somebody else's dogs if Mom would've gotten me one of my own," I say as we reach the River Road together.

"Then it's a damn good thing she wouldn't get you one of your own."

And in this one perfect but probably fleeting moment . . . nothing in my life has ever been a mistake.

STAY BOOK CLUB QUESTIONS

1. In this book the author highlights how a single choice can alter the path of one's life. How might Lucas's life have been different had he not chosen to take a shortcut through the woods and encountered two strange dogs?

2. In the face of life-threatening circumstances in Vietnam, Roy makes a choice that ensures he will be sent home. How does this action, coupled with keeping the truth a secret, affect his life going forward?

3. As a boy growing up, starting at a young age, Lucas felt responsible for everyone and everything. In what ways did his family dynamics play into this type of behavior?

4. In contrast, his best friend, Connor, chose a completely different way to cope, leading nearly to a tragic end. What was missing in both boys' homelife? How did meeting Zoe help fill that void for both of them?

5. For many years, Zoe has carried the guilt of being responsible for the death of two young children. Do you think one can ever make amends for something so heartbreaking? Ultimately, how did this tragedy shape her to become the person Lucas and Connor come to rely on?

6. Lucas interprets the dogs' facial expressions about Zoe to mean: "Well, we all know how she is, don't we? We know

how she can be, but we love her all the same." He goes on to observe "that's what you really do get from dogs." What do you think the author was trying to convey in this passage?

7. During the second part of the book, it is revealed that Lucas felt so strongly about his conviction not to fight in the Vietnam War, he chose instead to go to prison. This was a brave choice during those turbulent times. Was his decision worth the consequences?

8. At the end of Lucas's retelling of his life, Harris remarks that everyone dies in Lucas's story. Lucas replies, "But I still have to say it's not devastating that people and animals live and then die . . . It's hard, but those are the rules of the game." And then he thinks, *If you think having and losing is so bad, try never having. Now* that's *devastating.* Do you agree or disagree with Lucas's philosophy on life?

ABOUT THE AUTHOR

Catherine Ryan Hyde is the author of more than thirty published and forthcoming books. An avid hiker, traveler, equestrian, and amateur photographer, she has released her first book of photos, *365 Days of Gratitude: Photos from a Beautiful World*.

Her novel *Pay It Forward* was adapted into a major motion picture, chosen by the American Library Association (ALA) for its Best Book for Young Adults list, and translated into more than twenty-three languages for distribution in over thirty countries. Both *Becoming Chloe* and *Jumpstart the World* were included on the ALA's Rainbow List, and *Jumpstart the World* was a finalist for two Lambda Literary Awards. *Where We Belong* won two Rainbow Awards in 2013, and *The Language of Hoofbeats* won a Rainbow Award in 2015.

More than fifty of her short stories have been published in the *Antioch Review*, *Michigan Quarterly Review*, *Virginia Quarterly Review*, *Ploughshares*, *Glimmer Train*, and many other journals, and in the anthologies *Santa Barbara Stories* and *California Shorts* and the bestselling anthology *Dog Is My Co-Pilot*. Her stories have been honored in the Raymond Carver Short Story Contest and the Tobias Wolff Award and nominated for the O. Henry Award and the Pushcart Prize. Three have been cited in *The Best American Short Stories*.

She is founder and former president (2000–2009) of the Pay It Forward Foundation and still serves on its board of directors. As a professional public speaker, she has addressed the National Conference on Education, twice spoken at Cornell University, met with AmeriCorps members at the White House, and shared a dais with Bill Clinton.

For more information, please visit the author at www.catherineryan-hyde.com.